Acclaim for *Mental State*

"A well-written, fast-paced, rollercoaster of a ride you won't put down until the last paragraph."

—Jack Getze, author of the
award-winning Austin Carr Mystery Series

"Sinister, engrossing and devilishly finessed."

—Les Edgerton, author of *Adrenaline Junkie*

"The Professor's murder mystery delivers the rough and tumble goods, and it will leave readers wanting more."

—Kurt Schlichter, lawyer and bestselling author

"A pure page-turner. A must-read if you love the country, the Supreme Court, or just a book that will keep you up at night."

—Ben Shapiro, public intellectual,
talk-show host, and bestselling author

"Try as I might, I could not put *Mental State* down. It's terrific. At times hilarious, always interesting, and in parts truly disturbing. I loved it."

—Michael Seidman, Professor of Law
at Georgetown University Law Center

"Henderson's debut novel had me white-knuckling it from chapter to chapter in this heady, emotional, suspenseful and expertly-crafted page-turner."

—Mark Feuerstein, film and television actor

MENTAL

STATE

M. TODD HENDERSON

MENTAL

STATE

Down & Out Books
3959 Van Dyke Rd, Ste. 265
Lutz, FL 33558
www.DownAndOutBooks.com

The characters and events in this book are fictitious. Any similarity to real persons, living or dead, is coincidental and not intended by the author.

Edited by Elaine Ash and Chris Rhatigan
Cover design by Chuck Regan

ISBN: 1-948235-33-1
ISBN-13: 978-1-948235-33-4

For TFO

Actus non facit reum nisi mens sit rea.
(An act does make the person guilty
unless the mind be guilty.)
—Edward Coke,
The Institutes of the Laws of England (1628)

*"Yes, for our task is to stamp this provisional,
perishing earth into ourselves so deeply,
so painfully and passionately,
that its being may rise again, 'invisibly,' in us."*
—Rainer Maria Rilke

CHAPTER 1

April 2015
Pittsburgh, Pennsylvania

The phone on his government-issued desk shimmied and shrieked, red light flashing. Royce kept his feet up on the desk, ignoring it, and turned back to an x-ray he was holding up against the light. The bullet sat there in the lung's right lobe, taunting him. After two decades of doing this, the last few years on a narcotics squad, he didn't need a ballistics report to tell him it was clearly a .38. But who put it there?

Blink, blink, blink. The phone insisted, throwing flares over his dingy steel desk. When it went solid red, he knew the secretary had answered.

He peered through the blinds that gave some privacy from the agents scurrying along the corridors of the FBI's Pittsburgh Field Office. Ms. Rachelle had the phone lodged between her head and shoulder, holding newly polished nails out at an angle—Steelers colors, of course—while she waited for him to pick up.

The red light died when he stabbed it with a finger.

"Special Agent Johnson."

"This is Officer Dziewulski of the Rockefeller University Police Department. I'm afraid there's been an incident involving your brother."

Royce jerked his feet off the desk. No good conversation

1

started with the word "incident."

"What did Alex do now?"

There was a pause, and through the muffled phone line a door opened and closed. "We're working on it. Chicago PD is sending detectives."

On a far wall of the office, a picture caught his eye. Officer Dziewulski's voice droned into white noise for a moment. He and Alex were on the Salmon River in Idaho together, running a two-man kayak down class-five rapids. Royce could taste the beer on his lips and hear the icy water racing past them in an endless rush to the sea.

The university cop's voice intruded again. "Forensics just arrived..."

Forensics? Royce felt his stomach go into free fall.

"I'm really sorry, sir. I can send you information to claim the body. There'll be a post mortem. When a firearm is involved, you know..."

"Wait a minute." Royce's tone was steady but his hands had developed a tremor. "Which Alex Johnson? There must be more than one. This one teaches—"

"It's him, sir. It's your brother. The body is on route to the morgue."

An image of Alex, with his pale skin against the cold metal of the embalmer's table, overwhelmed his ability to speak. He'd been in that room. It was always someone's brother, someone's father, someone's son. Now it was his.

"Can you hear me okay, Agent Johnson?"

"I can hear you. Tell me what happened."

"I'm really not supposed to go into—"

"Please." The word gasped out.

Dziewulski mulled it over for a moment.

"A neighbor called us a little before eleven this morning. Heard a strange noise at your brother's residence. The door was unlocked, we went inside, there he was. Single gunshot...to the temple."

"Suicide?" He felt his voice break on the last syllable.

"Seems like it."

"He got divorced last year. Maybe six months ago." Conversations with Alex were like Facebook posts of family, sports, and kids—little happy glimpses and moments, but incomplete. His brother had tenure. *Wasn't that a pretty stress-free life, damn it?*

He choked out another question to Dziewulski. "Weapon?"

"Glock. Nine mil. By the body."

"Was it his?"

"Don't know yet. Serial number wasn't clear, maybe filed off; it'll take a little longer."

The conversation stalled. Royce couldn't muster a word.

"We talked to the dean over at the law school." Dziewulski leafed through a notepad. "She said...uh...Professor Johnson didn't seem himself recently. She forwarded an email exchange from a mutual friend in the psychiatry department."

Royce snapped back from brother to agent.

"How did you get all this? I thought Homicide wasn't even there. The crime scene hasn't even—"

"She reached out to us. The dean, that is. I guess she heard from, well, I'm not sure how word spread across campus so quickly."

He wrote "Dean" on his desk blotter, and circled it, followed by a big question mark. "Any note?"

"None yet. We're still looking. He has a lot of papers in his home office. A lot. We usually find notes close to the body. So maybe there isn't one. I probably shouldn't be, er, guessing either..."

Dziewulski droned into white noise again as the investigator's rush came on—skin tingling, mind racing, mouth dry. Royce sat up in the chair and breathed deeply. Picked up his badge and rubbed it like a genie's lamp.

No way his brother owned that handgun. Claire would never have allowed a gun in the house with a bunch of little kids running around. For all Alex's conservative politics, he wasn't a gun guy—especially with a black-market Glock. Plus, if he'd planned his own death, he would have written good-bye. The farewell note would have taken up forty pages in the *Harvard Law Review*.

It wasn't suicide.

"I should probably go now," Officer Dziewulski's insectile voice chirped through the receiver. But Royce's end of the connection was already dead.

CHAPTER 2

The Pittsburgh Field Office of the FBI occupied three floors of the six-story Carnegie Building. Royce sprinted out the front door toward a cab idling at the curb. It had taken less than an hour to get bereavement leave from his squad SSA and unload his active cases on the squad deputy.

He sprang into the back of the cab flashing his badge. "Airport."

Two whiskies and twenty thousand feet later, he was hurdling toward the crime scene on a United 737. He couldn't stop seeing Alex lying lifeless in his living room. *Who would want to kill a law professor?*

On reflex, he threw his hand up and downed the rest of his second whiskey. Reaching for the call light, he signaled for another.

In a murder case, the ex-wife is always a suspect, but Claire struck him as incapable of hurting anyone. He'd actually seen her scoop up spiders and set them free on the front porch of the home she shared with Alex before their divorce. The home where they were currently bagging his brother.

Was a pediatrician even capable of murder? She was as big-hearted a person as he knew. But breaking up can make people crazy, and Royce had seen her fly off the handle a few times. Not far enough off the handle to hire someone to kill her ex-husband. But on the other hand, under the right circumstances, people are capable of anything. Alex could be a bit of a dick, especially when he felt wronged.

He wrote Claire's name down, first with Johnson, then crossed it out. He started to form a letter, but realized he had no idea what her maiden name was. He didn't really know his brother anymore. He knew the little boy version, the teen version, the college version, and a bit of the law school version, but that was it. Once his kid brother became a man, he was a blank screen. He didn't even know him well enough to guess who would want him dead.

A vision of himself at fourteen years old sprang to mind. Alex was ten, dancing around the bedroom in a broad half circle, white tube socks pulled up over his hands to above his elbows. Alex lunged forward, head down, with his hands covering his face, and then flailing upward.

Royce, also wearing white socks over his hands, and with at least six inches and fifty pounds on Alex, bobbed backward and let loose a flurry of blows to the side of his brother's head. No doubt, he was the better slap-boxer, but Alex kept on challenging him. Why had the kid endured the beatings? Now, somewhere over Ohio, it came to him: Alex wanted to be with him, no matter what. If it had to be slap-boxing, then so be it. Alex used to trail after him, shouting facts from his *Guinness Book of World Records* to get attention. *"Did you know that the fattest man in the world weighed over a thousand pounds? Robert Earl Hughes was his name. He's dead now."*

Royce came back from the past, chuckling softly. Then the image of Alex now, gray and stiff and lifeless in a drawer at the morgue, rushed back. Reaching for the call light, he signaled again to the flight attendant, *make it a double*. He'd have to wait. The hospitality cart was positioned abreast of the hallway. Behind it, a pilot emerged to use the restroom. The flimsy cart was supposed to protect the cockpit from a bum-rushing terrorist. Royce shook his head. He knew better.

His thoughts drifted back to the day his job changed forever.

On that clear September day in New York, fifteen years ago, he was across the street from the World Trade Center interviewing a CI when the first plane hit. The rest of the day was a blur of helping direct traffic, screams and smells of burning flesh and jet fuel, aiding the wounded and terrified, running from the falling debris.

The trauma of seeing jumpers explode just a few feet away came at night. Every night. It didn't help that fighting terrorism also became part of his waking life. "Every investigation is now a national security investigation," the assistant special agent in charge told his squad on September twelve. Royce liked his job less from that moment forward. He'd signed up to get John Dillinger, not Osama Bin Laden.

Now his job had changed again. Now it was personal.

Jack Daniels in hand, he turned back to Alex. Did he have enemies, rivals, spurned lovers, people he betrayed or disappointed? Certainly all of the above. But ones that would be moved to violence? He honestly didn't know.

So, he wrote down some general categories: "Student," "Work colleague," "Lover," "Creditor." Next to "Student," he added, "Tough grader? Recent run-ins with students?" He remembered half-sleeping through a recent *Dateline* episode that chronicled a student who had been caught cheating. The young man hired an assassin to kill the only person who knew the truth—the law school secretary. Royce made a mental note to pay a visit to the law school where Alex worked. *Used to work.* "Damn," he said it loud enough to catch the attention of the woman reading *People* magazine in the seat next to him.

As for other possibilities, he knew what Alex *could* have done—the FBI exposed him to the worst in everyone. Squeaky-clean do-gooders with drug problems, vengeful mistresses, guys who'd done business with the underworld. Maybe Alex borrowed money from a local thug and got behind on the juice. But that didn't make sense. Dead guys can't pay debts.

And why would the Outfit cloud the message to make it look like suicide?

The stewardess—he never got used to calling them flight attendants—came by again. The Jack Daniels burned in his throat along with the knowledge that however it happened, everyone involved would want Alex's death to be suicide. Especially the university. This could turn into the kind of viral story that would significantly impact a law school's *U.S. News* ranking. Imagine what the popular website Above the Law would run if Professor Alex Johnson were killed in his home a few miles from work because his Socratic style humiliated someone in class? No wonder the dean was involved.

Out the window, ten thousand feet below, Chicago looked like a circuit board. Thousands of orangish streetlights lapped up on the western edge of Lake Michigan. Mayor Daley, the Elder, designed the bright lights with a peculiar orange glow to signal the arrival to the Great City, gateway to the West. Royce cringed.

The Chicago PD would want to wrap this case up and put a bow on it as soon as possible. Officer Dziewulski bungled his only job, and probably couldn't be relied on to do more than put up yellow tape. The city cops would be slightly more competent but less pure of motive. Average cops almost always took the path of least resistance. In this case, that path was clear: suicide.

Royce leaned his head back and thought of Alex slap-boxing in the bedroom. Rafting on the river. Cold on an embalmer's table. He squeezed his eyes shut tight against tears. When they opened, the 737 had dipped below five thousand feet and the buildings of Rosemont were looming.

Maybe it was time to call Claire. Maybe if she sobbed or had hysterics over the phone it would help with his own mental state. He'd have to hold it together for both of them. Being the rock would help him forget.

The stewardess signaled that he wasn't allowed to use his

phone, so Royce pulled his badge and flashed it.

Three rings later, Claire answered.

"Royce? Have you heard?"

"I have, Claire. I'm so sor—"

"Are you going to be taking care of the arrangements?"

Her cool demeanor took him by surprise. He heard talking and machines beeping in the background.

"Are you at work?" he asked incredulously. In the Johnson family, this was called "stupid stubborn." But Claire would have called it dedication or, maybe, coping.

"Kids getting chemotherapy don't care that my ex-husband was a selfish asshole."

He heard her muzzle the phone and bark instructions at an intern.

"I'm at O'Hare. I can be at the hospital in an hour, hour and a half."

"It is not appropriate for you to come to my work, Royce." She said it without contractions to make the message as pointed as possible.

The plane touched down with a jolt.

CHAPTER 3

Royce rounded the corner on the fourth floor of the Children's Hospital in his narcotics-squad uniform—a Penn State sweat-shirt and a black Pirates cap. He was aware the look was more fugitive than cop, or mourning ex-brother-in-law. Couldn't be helped though.

Claire was standing at the nurses station talking to another doctor and rubbing her eyes the way people do when things aren't going well. Making eye contact, he raised a hand up to his shoulders, fingers spread, as if to say a gentle "hello." Claire nodded toward a plastic seat in the waiting area where some kids were coloring on a low table. *Finding Nemo* played on a flat-panel television, hung on the wall like a picture. Royce sat awkwardly and saw that one of the children, a girl about seven years old, was bald. A pink ribbon clung to a few stands of her hair. She smiled at him, and he swallowed hard, managing a half smile and a nod. The children made his pain easier to handle. They gave him perspective.

On the other hand, he heard how Claire always played cancer as a trump card in her fights with Alex, and now he understood why his brother resented her so.

Half an hour later when Claire tapped him on the shoulder, he jumped.

"Follow me," she said coldly.

Picking up his bag, he trailed after Claire, who had already used her ID to open a set of security doors leading back to the

10

ward. The door was closing behind her, but he hustled and got his hand on it before it shut. Down the hall, the back of her leg vanished into a procedure room. She had the calves of a woman with a three-times-a-week personal trainer and a budget for fancy things. He slid in as the door shut behind them.

"What do you want? I told you not to come here." She stared at her pager while she talked.

"Why are you being like this?" He was genuinely puzzled.

"I'm at work. What do you want?" Her curtness made his blood tingle.

She looked up from her pager and met his eyes. He stared for a long minute, and she stared back. He didn't know her well enough to interpret this behavior. Was she always this cold or just in shock? Was this a game? The staring contest could have gone on for a while—neither of them liked losing, at anything.

Finally, he'd had enough. "You were married nearly twenty years. Four kids. You loved him once."

"I moved out a long time ago. My kids will carry this the rest of their lives. They're the ones I care about. Fuck him!"

"Claire—"

"If you need my help with the funeral or whatever, I'll obviously try to find some time." She could sense his shock at her impatience and vulgarity.

"Jesus, Claire. The investigation just got started. Nothing's for sure."

Her pager beeped. "Are we done here?"

"No." His tone was straight from Quantico, a voice to seize control of a situation. "No, we are not. Sit down."

Claire didn't appreciate anyone telling her what to do. She stood firm.

He reached out and grabbed her arm, leading her to examination table. He pulled a swivel chair away from the desk in the room and took a seat.

"Alex was murdered."

"What?" Claire's arms fell to her sides, and for the first time in this conversation she wasn't looking at her pager or phone. "The police said suicide. A gun was next to his head. All the telltale signs, they told me." She used her fingers to make air quotes around "telltale."

"I know what *they* think."

"I even talked to his dean, and she said Alex was acting strangely in the past few weeks." She sounded panicked.

Royce was surprised. Alex's boss was on Claire's list of things to do when she first heard her ex-husband was dead? Or had the dean called her?

"*I* don't think it's suicide, Claire. I'm here to find out what really happened."

"The FBI is involved?" Claire whispered, even though they were alone.

"No. This is between you and me. I'm not sure how I'm going to swing this work wise, but I owe it to my baby brother. There's a killer out there, I'm sure of it."

"Do you really think the Chicago Police, the University Police, the dean, everyone is lying?"

"I didn't say that. Or suggest it. I just think they don't want to know any different."

He stood up and walked toward the window. Hardball wasn't working. He had to find a way past the armor, so he slumped his shoulders in defeat.

"Look, maybe I'm wrong. I just need to fill in some missing pieces of this puzzle. I need it to add up for me. Does that make sense?"

Claire slid off the exam table, walked over, and patted him on the shoulder. "Are you sure you aren't just, well, you know, playing the hero? He's gone, Roy. Maybe we don't need a hero. Maybe we all need to just say goodbye."

If a nurse walked in at that instant, they might have thought it was a genuine moment of sharing and empathy, but

12

the actors were too practiced for this to be the right conclusion. Royce knew how to play a witness or suspect, and Claire how to feign compassion. It was cop and doctor 101.

"I appreciate how you feel but I think you're wasting your time. And I'm worried you're going to be making a lot of pain for a lot of people." She walked toward the door and turned the handle. "Give my love to Jenny and the girls."

She needed to believe the easy story everyone was selling—that her husband was a prick and he let his demons get the best of him—and get back to her patients and her life. A real killer would play it differently, pretend to be helpful. A real killer would hide this much hostility.

"I need your help." This time he didn't hide his desperation.

She snapped back toward him, still holding the door handle.

"Look, in room four-oh-six I've got a six-year-old girl surrounded by her family. She has acute, nonheritable retinoblastoma. Do you know what that means?"

"No." He gulped.

"It means she's going to die, and I've got to go in and tell them all that. Do you know what that feels like? Do you know how much energy that takes? I don't have time for a wild goose chase. Alex killed himself. It's too bad, but I've got to go." She stepped out into the hallway.

He stiff-armed the door so it wouldn't swing closed. "Has Alex been out of the country lately? Has he been to the Middle East? I need to know right now."

Claire froze. She muttered flatly, "He was in Lahore in June." She jerked herself away, but not before a tear sparkled in her eye.

CHAPTER 4

March 2014
Chicago, Illinois

At a marble side table in an expansive office on the sixth floor of the Hutchins Law Library, Professor Alex Johnson held his head in his hands. Stacks of exams were to his right and left, suggesting he was about half way through. Grades were due tomorrow. It was the worst part of the best job in the world. Taking a sip of stale coffee, he groaned. It was at about this point every term that he dreamed of doing a "stairway special"—throwing the exams down the stairwell and giving A's to the ones that went the furthest, B's to the next furthest pile, and so forth. When he was a law student, his professors joked that this was how they'd graded exams. Now, Alex sort of believed them.

The sound of glass shattering heralded an incoming email. During exam-grading season, he set his email alarm to an annoying sound, so he had as many distractions as possible. He got up and headed over to the standing desk that held his laptop.

Opening his mail, he saw a message from a professor at the University of South Asia, in Lahore, Pakistan. Alex received lots of invitations to speak at conferences, to present academic papers to various law faculties, and to teach mini-courses at various law schools in Europe and Asia. He agreed to go to more than he should have. He loved getting away and feeling important, and he always felt more important when speaking abroad. A second-rate professor at an American law school was treated as a rock star at the best law school in any other part of the world.

Plus, Alex, despite his Anglo name and appearance, was half Lebanese and deeply intrigued by the Muslim world. He'd spent countless hours bouncing on his great grandmother's knee as she sang to him in Arabic and let him sip from her arak. Every time he went to the Middle East, he remembered the smells and sounds of his great grandmother's house in East Palestine, Ohio, and felt at home.

He didn't recognize the professor or the law school, and the topic of the conference seemed a bit odd. But he'd never been to Pakistan. Thinking about the trip would get him through the next few weeks of tedium at school and increasing fights with his wife.

He didn't bother to check his schedule, consult his wife, or think about the potential hazards of traveling to Pakistan before typing back:

I'd be delighted to attend your conference on "Rethinking Banking Regulation: What South Asian Regulators Can Learn from American Failures." Please send me details regarding my presentation panel and logistics.

Yours sincerely, Prof. A. Johnson

Returning to the stack of exams on the marble table, he picked up an anonymous answer—from Student 1189—and turned to the first page. The first thirty questions were multiple-choice. Student 1189 got three correct. The average student in the first half of the exams got sixteen. Alex recorded a three in his Excel file of student scores but immediately went back to double check his work. Going through the answers again and confirming the score, he almost doubted the answer key and the first fifty or so exams he graded. At elite law schools, there was often quite a variance between the performance of the best and the worst students—standardized tests and grades in college were roughly predictive of law school performance, but the difference between a four-point-oh from Arizona State and a four-point-oh from Harvard could be enormous, even if both students scored the same on the LSAT. There were also people who got in for reasons having nothing to do with merit—alumni kids, rich kids, minority kids. But Alex had never seen a performance this bad. He wondered whether the student might have fallen ill or had a panic attack.

He moved to question two, an essay question in the more traditional law school style. The question was a detailed, three-page hypothetical involving multiple issuances and sales of stocks and bonds during the formation of a business enterprise. Professors called these "issue spotters," because they deliberately buried many, sometimes dozens, of tough legal questions. The elaborate facts, often zany and convoluted, were constructed to distract and mislead. A prized skill of a good lawyer is seeing through the messy stories and getting to the nub. To see the issues, then wrestle them to submission.

In this question, Professor Johnson's answer key identified six major issues for students to find and analyze, as well as four difficult bonus issues that top students were expected to find. Student 1189 spotted only two, both easier ones, and offered what Alex viewed as unacceptably weak legal analysis.

Up to this point, Alex was curious. Now, he was sad and a little bit afraid. Sad because Student 1189 shouldn't be paying fifty thousand dollars a year for law school, or at least this law school, and because in a few weeks he or she would be hurting, big time. Alex was afraid not just for the student, but also for himself: extreme events, like failing a student, could create risks, headaches, and work even for tenured professors. As he approached question three, Alex was cheering for a home run—perhaps Student 1189 allocated his or her time badly, and the score on the final question would make up for the other two. "Yes, that must be it," Alex said aloud to the empty room. He hoped.

Question three was a policy question, meaning an open-ended statement about legal doctrine that gave students an opportunity to demonstrate their ability to do high-level brain work, and argue for big-picture changes in policy. The average student over the years wrote about ten double-spaced pages of analysis for policy questions like this. Student 1189's answer for question three was blank. Nothing.

Alex doubled checked the email file and confirmed with the registrar that he had all the pages that were turned in. The file was complete and not corrupted. Student 1189 ran out of time or maybe didn't remember or ever understand the Modigliani-Miller theorem or modern portfolio theory. Maybe he never even came to class. Alex was supposed to take attendance to ensure students complied with the American Bar Association rules, but he hated all cartels, especially the ABA, so he chose to flout that rule.

He often did things like that. Alex was the guy who confronted line jumpers at the movie theater, even when he was early and would easily make the previews. He was the guy who kept a dangerously close distance to the car in front during merges so as to prevent cars from going around the line and sneaking in at the last minute. He was the guy who wouldn't get gas at Citgo, even if about to run out, because the Venezuelan government owned it.

Alex leaned back in his chair and sighed. He'd never given an F in ten years of teaching and didn't want to start with Student 1189. Alex lamented grade inflation—when he was a student, a B minus was the average grade, and today, it was an A minus. He was always pushing for more honest grading, but an F had serious consequences. The class wouldn't count. If the student were a 3L, he or she might not graduate. It would be a black mark on any transcript and a red flag to potential employers. Ten years ago this might not have mattered, but with the legal market in a severe downturn, an F might mean Student 1189 would be headed for a job as a barista, not a barrister.

But this was F-level performance. Alex wrote "F" in a red Sharpie on the top of the first page and made a mental note to talk to the dean of students in the morning. If he was going to give Student 1189 an F, this was going to a life-changing event and that wasn't something to be taken lightly. But maybe it was the right thing to do—to let the student know what was expected of a lawyer, especially a Rockefeller lawyer.

Alex often told his students about the former CEO of General Electric who said that firing the bottom ten percent of workers each year was actually a favor to them, because it allowed them a chance to find work that was a better fit. But Alex was a professor precisely because he didn't have the stomach for the business world. Admiring was one thing, doing quite another. He scratched out the "F" and put a "D" there instead.

With Student 1189's fate swirling in his head, Alex tossed a sheaf of exams into a folio, trekked to his car, and headed the mile down Cottage Grove Avenue to his home in the Kenwood neighborhood of Chicago. To get there, he had to pass through Bronzeville, once known as the Black Metropolis—a hub of African-American cultural renaissance after the Great Migration brought about six million descendants of slaves from the South to Chicago and other northern cities in search of a better life. Like Harlem in New York City, Bronzeville attracted many legendary intellectuals, performers, and entrepreneurs. Ida B. Wells lived there. So did Louis Armstrong, whose house on 44th Street was just a few streets from Alex's office. Muhammad Ali, Louis Farrakhan, and Jesse Jackson all lived nearby too, although they were on the border between Bronzeville and Kenwood, the lush and more integrated neighborhood directly to the south.

Wealthy African Americans fled Bronzeville when its vibrant society collapsed in the 1970s after the riots of the civil rights era and white flight took a lot of wealth and human capital to the suburbs. The Bronzeville where Alex worked was no longer attracting talent but repelling it. Rockefeller was still a magnet, but even it faced problems competing for the best students. Rockefeller's campus occupied a sixteen-block parcel surrounded by poverty on three sides and by twenty percent of the world's fresh water on the other. Burned out buildings and vacant lots, liquor stores and derelicts loitering out front made the short drive home the worst part of Alex's day—not because he didn't care about the people who lived where he worked, but because he did. The solutions routinely offered to help them were, in Alex's opinion, making things worse. With NPR's *All Things Considered* playing in the background, Alex scanned the horizon and shook his head that this was possible in America.

His mind wandered back to Student 1189. Grading was anonymous to remove any potential biases of professors and to encourage students to compete on substance instead of brown nosing. Of course, Alex had the power to find out who the student was in advance of issuing the final grade; he did this every quarter when he adjusted his raw scores to account for class participation. But he didn't ask for the names from the registrar until the grades were nearly finalized. And, he wasn't yet sure he wanted to know who this was. Better to be safe than sorry in this high-stakes game, he thought. His rendezvous with Student 1189 would have to wait a few more days.

CHAPTER 5

April 2015
Chicago, Illinois

Leaving the Children's Hospital, Royce stumbled wretchedly down the street. How had his brother's life shipwrecked without him knowing? Claire was so deeply hostile; seemingly as cold as any sociopath. Was she keeping her strength up with rage? Maybe behind the façade was a woman who couldn't afford the luxury of falling apart.

He tugged the Pirates cap down over his eyes, and as he did he passed a hand over his cheek and found it was wet. Jenny and the girls back home were unaware the world had imploded. But he was in no shape to break the news to them, and it was probable they still didn't know. University Police had notified both him and Claire, the next-of-kin, but the story hadn't broken yet. Claire had given no indication that she'd reach out to her former sister-in-law. There was time.

Immersing Jenny in this right now wasn't going to solve the case or mitigate damage. This evening was time to deal with it. So he fiddled with his phone and sent a standing order of flowers to a shop back home that kept his credit card information. They would deliver a bouquet of snapdragons to Jenny with a blank card attached. It was their code that he had to disappear without notice on a case. Jenny would stay blissfully ignorant for another few hours, and she'd be okay

20

with his absence. It came with marriage to a special agent. Or, at least with this one.

He continued along the street outside the hospital, heart still pounding. At the end of the block, the light turned red, leaving him staring into traffic. Across the street was—lucky coincidence—a bar with two things he needed: whiskey and Wi-Fi.

He needed to depersonalize this, make it about the bad guys, not family wreckage. So he forced his thoughts onto Pakistan. Lahore was the game changer, the piece of the puzzle that turned his hunch into a lead.

He wasn't usually a rule breaker, boundary pusher, or line crosser. Not in his personal or professional life. But here he was on the threshold of an unauthorized and arguably illegal investigation. He'd never had a case that made him desperate to break any rule to get his man. Until now. For the first time, Royce knew what Bruce Banner felt like—the beast inside was stirring.

Inside the bar, he took a seat on a rickety plastic-covered stool, flagged the bartender, and ordered two Whistle Pigs. He put his hat on the stool next to him, as if he were saving it for Alex, and slid one of them over.

When he opened the folder titled NSL, Royce could feel in his bones that the regular guy in him was not leading this investigation.

The first document in the NSL folder was a template for writing a national security letter. NSLs were basically secret subpoenas that, under the authority of the president, allowed the FBI to demand private companies, like airlines and telecommunications firms, turn over administrative records regarding the subject of a national security investigation. The great thing about an NSL was that judicial approval was not needed before issuing one, and the potential for judicial review after the fact was fairly remote. It was a way for him to conduct a covert investigation entirely outside of normal jurisdiction and without many questions from his chain of command. He just needed to get one authorized. It would have to go through Ms. Rachelle for processing, but it wouldn't have to go through the supervisory special agent for a few days.

Royce had little experience with NSLs. They'd been used since the late 1970s, but it wasn't until the Patriot Act of 2001, passed in the wake of 9/11, that the use of NSLs took off. FBI agents now wrote thousands of NSLs every year. Royce had only used them a few times, since he spent most of his time chasing drug dealers and corrupt local cops, not Al-Qaeda, much to his boss' chagrin.

For the first time in two decades with the FBI, Royce was about to lie. He was sure Alex's trip to Lahore last year was for a boring and utterly benign academic conference on financial regulation. He knew his brother wasn't a dupe for terrorists or, even worse, a terrorist himself. But travel to Pakistan coupled with a suspicious murder was sufficient justification to demand Verizon, Comcast, United Airlines, and Bank of America turn over "non-content" information to the FBI. Within a day, he would have a list of numbers that Alex called and numbers calling him for the past year. Although NSLs would not provide the content of calls, just knowing who Alex called, what websites he visited, what trips he took, and what money was moving in and out of his accounts would be helpful. The NSL was also a great smokescreen and a reason for him to be in Chicago, hunting Alex's killer.

Royce was half way into his whiskey when he felt a tap on his shoulder. "Hey, what are you writing, man?" the words were slurred and stank of Old Style.

Royce slammed his laptop closed and turned aggressively toward a chubby salesman who grinned at him stupidly.

"Whoa! Relax. I'm not into your stuff. Jus' making conversation."

Royce looked at the floor next to the bar stool to check

out the salesman's briefcase. Tumi. Royce shook his head.

"My brother just died," Royce scolded him.

"Jesus, are you serious? I'm sorry, man." The salesman ducked his head and looked in the other direction. Royce felt ashamed, but he was in no mood. He stuffed the computer back in his bag, dropped forty dollars on the counter, and looked at the Whistle Pig he'd ordered for no one sitting there on the bar. He slid it across to the salesman, and headed outside, fumbling for the phone.

Ms. Rachelle picked up on the fourth ring.

"It's me."

Her brusque tone melted into the receiver. "I heard the news, so sorry—"

"I need an NSL processed."

"But you're on bereav—"

"True, true, but you know me. I'll go stir-crazy if I don't do something—I mean—have something to do."

A tsk, tsk of sympathy, then a note of suspicion. "Where are you?"

"In Chicago. Taking care of family business." He wasn't lying. Much.

"Oh, you poor thing."

"Just do me a favor, Rachelle? Send my NSL to be processed, but don't spread it around."

"Well I suppose—"

"I don't want anybody to think I'm hard hearted. I just need to get my mind off..."

"Oh yes, yes," she exhaled. He could picture her forehead wrinkling with concern.

CHAPTER 6

October 2014
Lahore, Pakistan

Alex flew twenty hours to Lahore, where a thin, very dark-skinned man in a suit two sizes too big and a mustache that looked like Alex's badger-hair shaving brush was waiting for him with a sign that misspelled his name. He'd flown for what seemed like days and arrived in the sweltering heat of two-in-the-morning Pakistan. The next day was a blur. At a hotel near the airport that was supposed to be upscale but seemed like a run-down Red Roof Inn, he had a terrible sleep on a mattress that would have made Civil War soldiers complain, then a breakfast of mystery gruel with fruits he'd never seen, before heading off to day one of the conference.

The University of South Asia turned out to be a real place, with professors and students milling about in the heat of under-air-conditioned hallways and lecture halls. The buildings did not evoke Oxford or Hogwarts. The Institute of Management Studies, where the conference was held, looked like a low-budget apartment complex one would find in Memphis or Little Rock. Only scattered air-conditioning units with spinning fans groaning to keep up with the oppressive heat broke the stark brick walls of the exterior. They were no more successful in their work than in their architectural beauty. Everything seemed to drip sweat. Palm trees dotting the courtyards and bougainvillea climbing some of the walls gave it a tropical feel, but in a kind of pathetic way. It reminded him of what run-down Cuban sugar cane plantations must look like now that Soviet subsidies are dried up.

The conference was sparsely attended, even by relatively low expectations. About a dozen or so people were scattered about in the audience, and four people sat on the dais when Alex walked into the room five minutes early. Introductions were short and involved excessive praise for Alex. He was here in part to be sucked up to, and even false praise felt good sometimes, but this was over the top.

These trips never gave much time for reflection—the jet lag and unfamiliarity of space heightened the senses, making the colors and smells and foods all the stranger and disquieting. Normally, Alex considered this a feature not a bug of his vagabond lecture circuit, but there was something out of whack about this one, he was sure. He just couldn't bring his brain around to focus on it. It was too busy trying to process the scene.

Alex took his place on stage and was the first to speak. He gave a lecture on the financial crisis that he'd given many times before. He talked about the causes of the crisis and a criticism of the legislation passed in its wake. Alex had especially hostile comments about the president's plan to institute a national pension scheme that would replace all private 401(k) and IRA accounts, banning average Americans from owning non-government-managed retirement plans. Only those with a net worth of more than five million dollars and who passed a financial literacy test would be allowed to invest in private accounts. The Supreme Court was likely going to review the law in the near future, as cases challenging it were working their way up through the lower courts. Alex made a sustained argument against its constitutionality and wisdom. It was how American law academics talked—high level, critical, and, he thought, interesting.

The panelists who followed spoke English, but Alex didn't understand much of what they said. Sitting there trying to keep from nodding off, Alex spent most of the time attempting to figure out whether he couldn't understand them because of their thick accents or because the arguments were just this side of gibberish. He had a low opinion of foreign law professors, not only because he believed passionately in American exceptionalism. His colleagues at Rockefeller and other top American schools struck him as insightful, while friends at German, Italian, Japanese, and Chinese universities were, despite being interesting people, trapped in an academic culture that favored arcane interpretation of legal doctrine and rules, rather than creative thinking. The Pakistani panelists weren't even up to these low standards he'd come to expect from foreign law professors—they reminded him more of Student 1189 than his colleagues.

The lunch break came a bit before noon, and it felt like a death row reprieve from the governor. He stepped outside into a steam room. His glasses fogged up. Coupled with the lack of sleep it was dizzying. In the courtyard, a few students were aimlessly launching balls at a dilapidated basketball hoop. Three burqa-clad women stood like statues watching, looking like a Pakistani version of the Dallas Cowboys cheerleaders. Alex smiled at the thought, then felt bad about it. Decades inside the liberal bubble of academia had nearly purged him of his old sense of humor, dealing as it did in cultural stereotypes and put downs. After all this time, Alex wasn't sure whether this was a good thing or not. He was a lawyer, which meant he could see both sides of the argument.

After wiping his glasses off, Alex saw two men standing a few feet away looking at him. This wasn't unexpected. He was used to being stared at in foreign countries—at over six and a half feet tall and with skin the shade of a glass of milk, he didn't fit in many places outside of Scandinavia. He was a curiosity in photo albums across Japan, based on the number

26

of times he'd posed with groups of bemused locals on his many trips across the country.

Alex ignored them. Standing out in Tokyo was one thing; Americans—he was obviously an American—weren't exactly popular in this part of the world. He glanced down at a map of the university, trying to figure out where the lunch buffet was. But he looked up when he felt the stare lingering. Their posture and intense glare were startling.

"Professor Alex Johnson?" the smaller of the two men asked.

"Yes," Alex said with an appropriate amount of caution. The larger of the two men introduced himself.

"I'm Ibrahim Khan, Dean of the Institute, and this is my colleague, Sameer Rajput, Dean of the School of Law. We are delighted you are here."

Alex saw in their eyes that this was not the first time they'd seen a fish out of this particular water. "Sorry. I'm just a bit sleep deprived." He felt the relief wash over him. It revealed guilt at jumping to conclusions.

"We'd be delighted to take you to lunch with our gracious benefactor who made the conference possible," the law dean said.

"Aren't we...isn't there a lunch for the conference?" Alex wasn't trying to be difficult; he was just confused.

"Yes, yes, of course, of course," Khan nodded vigorously. "We have a special event planned for you." He smiled a toothy grin. "You've come too long a way to eat cafeteria food. Plus, I think you will enjoy meeting Mr. Chowdhury. He is a very important person in Pakistan."

"Okay," Alex said without much thought—these were men of authority and the special treatment pushed his ego button. He'd never heard of Chowdhury, but the idea of escaping the dreary campus and upgrading on the food front was appealing. He followed the men, who didn't seem to have been awaiting his response, and climbed into a waiting Al-Haj Sirius S80. Alex squeezed his giant frame into the front seat of the Chinese-built SUV and directed the air conditioning toward his face. The SUV raced off the campus grounds and headed north out of the city.

About thirty minutes later they pulled into a walled compound that abutted the River Ravi on the west side and the Shahdara Reserve Forest on the east side. The scene was beautiful, but the buildings had the crumbly, third-world feel of the Bin Laden compound. Ten-foot-tall iron gates opened and they drove through on a gravel driveway. Alex shivered. This was a first for any conference he'd attended.

Inside the compound, dozens of men milled about. Everyone wore a jacket that was some variation of the Members Only jacket Alex remembered were popular when he was a kid. They were not only anachronistic, but an odd choice given the heat. Alex sensed they were covering more than bodies; he suspected many were shielding submachine guns from plain sight. The thought of being surrounded by armed men made his stomach turn. He was afraid for the first time in a very long time, and strangely exhilarated.

The SUV pulled in front of a grand entrance where a large man with a snow-white smile and skin the color of a lion's mane greeted them.

"Assalaam-o-Alaikum!" the man shouted as Alex folded himself out of the SUV.

The man introduced himself as Mohammed Chowdhury, and he embraced Alex with arms like a pair of pythons. The familiarity shocked Alex, but he was too unsure of the situation to mount a protest. *When in Lahore*, he thought to himself.

Chowdhury led the way into a large inner courtyard lined with fruit trees and buzzing with staff of various kinds. They were seated on the floor on plush mats and served tea and an assortment of cakes and finger foods. Bowls of every shape and size covered the table, filled with dips and sauces and yogurts. Alex was famished, so he tried everything put in front of him, recognizing some of the treats from his grandmother's cooking.

Chowdhury spoke with a stiff but welcoming manner. He read from a small blue notecard.

"We are delighted you are here, Professor. My associates and I are eager to hear your views on the reforms to the financial system that will make us all better able to prosper."

Looking around at the assembled group, Alex thought the financial system was as relevant to their lives as the moon landing. And he had not expected to be "on" during lunch.

Chowdhury sat back on his elbows and looked invitingly at Alex. By this time, a small crowd had gathered around, and there were about twenty men sitting on their heels like catchers at a baseball game. The crowd was bigger than at the conference, and Alex never missed a chance to talk when handed a microphone, so he stood and addressed the audience as if they were bank regulators or academics back home. He went on without notes for about forty-five minutes, then asked for questions, but seeing none, thanked his host in generous terms and sat down.

"I hope that was what you were looking for," he tilted toward Chowdhury and whispered in his ear as the crowd clapped politely. Even someone as confident as Alex felt like an imposter on occasion, and fishing for compliments was a symptom of that particular disease.

Chowdhury rose to his feet, spoke in a language Alex did not know, and the crowd dispersed. Within moments, they were alone in the courtyard. It was spooky how quickly everyone vanished. His host took him by the arm, and they strolled the perimeter together, walking in the welcome shade of persimmon and pomegranate trees.

"I am a great admirer of yours, Professor Johnson," he started. "I have read your work, and know you to be a fine thinker, a prolific scholar, and a friend of Islam." The first two points were platitudes, but Alex never minded having his ego stroked; the final comment made the flesh on his arms tingle.

Chowdhury went on: "I know your mother is Lebanese, and that you were raised in a home that understood and appreciated Muslim traditions and values. We in Pakistan need friends of influence and intelligence in the American elite who have these traits. I hope our chat will be the first of many, and, to paraphrase my favorite American movie, that this is the beginning of a great friendship between us."

Alex nodded, more than a little uncomfortable. He and Chowdhury paced around the perimeter with the sun dropping lower beyond the river in the distance. Their conversation turned to the rules of cricket and the names of the trees that lined the courtyard. Alex told of his family and his interest in the subcontinent; Chowdhury lamented the clash of civilizations but sounded optimistic about the future of his country and the region. Alex loved ideas and anyone that loved them. After thirty minutes, he was in love.

They finally returned to where deans Khan and Rajput were waiting. It seemed they were standing in the same spots with the same expressions on their faces as when they dropped him off three or four hours ago. The scene added to *The Truman Show* quality of the whole trip so far: as if the conference was staged just for him and that when he left the room, nothing went on until he returned.

Alex missed the rest of the conference that day, so he dined alone in the hotel restaurant that night. He skipped the next day of the conference, deciding instead to see the highlights of Lahore. He toured the Badshahi and Wazir Khan mosques, Fort Shahi Qila, the Shalamar Gardens, and the Bagh-e-Jinnah. Alex ate from food stalls and wandered aimlessly through alleyways and markets that seemed to stretch endlessly in every direction. Chowdhury was right that Alex, despite his Anglo name and appearance, was partially of and deeply intrigued by this part of the world. A day in Lahore cemented it. It was the perfect day, and the thing Alex liked best about the freedom of his job.

It almost made him forget the odd meeting he'd had with Chowdhury. But something about it nagged at him. He couldn't help but wonder whether all was what it seemed on this trip. Who exactly was Chowdhury and what connection did he have with the conference? How did he know Alex's mom was Lebanese and why did he think Alex had sympathetic views about Islam?

Alex boarded a flight the next day, and as the plane home chased the setting sun, he couldn't shake the feeling that the trip was wrong. He couldn't sleep or follow the plot of the latest thriller he'd picked up at a bookstore in Heathrow on the way over. Something was off, but he didn't know what.

When he saw on the seatback screen that the Boeing 777 had reentered American airspace in northern Maine, he felt somewhat safe again. He finally fell asleep. By the time they landed in Chicago, he had a message from the dean at his school. She needed to see him first thing Monday morning. It was urgent.

CHAPTER 7

One month later
Arlington, Virginia

Four men in nearly identical pinstriped suits got out of a silver Chrysler 300 and walked in unison into a nondescript glass office tower in Arlington, Virginia. They ranged in age from about forty to sixty; all lawyers at the very top of their profession. The four walked in seemingly practiced unison past the security desk without showing a badge or even making eye contact with the armed guards manning it. They went straight for the elevators, took one to the twelfth floor, buzzed into suite 1201, and without signing in or acknowledging anyone, walked past rows of worker bees in cubicles to a conference room in the southeastern corner of the building. Standing guard was a square-jawed ex-Marine in khaki pants and a blue blazer with a bronze star lapel pin in the buttonhole. He touched his ear and whispered into his collar as the men filed past him into the room. Each took a seat, opened a briefcase, pulled out a three-ring binder, and put it on the oak table in front of them. "Top Secret" was written on the cover of each binder. Fifteen minutes later, the president's chief of staff walked into the room and took a seat at the head of the table.

"Update?"

The most senior lawyer at the table, Bob Gerhardt, Sr., a big-shouldered man with graying temples and a heavily lined face, opened his binder, and started to speak, "If you'll turn to the first page…"

"I don't want you to walk me through this, Bob," the chief of staff said, addressing him as one might a child. "I want the summary of the summary. I've got ten fires to put out today." He had more to say, but picked up his buzzing phone, listened intensely for a few minutes, then said, "Yes." He hung up as abruptly as he'd answered. Then he looked back at the lawyers, spinning a Mont Blanc pen in his hand expertly enough to hypnotize.

Another lawyer, Jay Rudolph, an energetic triathlete with a shaved head and rumored to have a tattoo of a tiger on his right butt cheek, spoke up, "The Pakistan conference was a success." He slid a manila envelope across the table toward the president's man. On the cover was written "Operation Aspida." The chief of staff picked it up, and in one motion opened it and pulled out the pictures inside. He flipped through grainy shots taken from a drone of two men walking arm-in-arm in a courtyard on the outskirts of Lahore, Pakistan.

"Is this Johnson on the left?"

"It is, sir. Chowdhury on the right."

"Good. Well done." He examined the picture with a magnifying glass.

"If you look on, there are some higher-resolution shots our man on the ground took with a camera hidden in his lapel. We also have affidavits in there from several witnesses claiming they saw Professor Johnson enter Chowdhury's compound, address his followers, and leave several hours later after long conversations with him. We think the combination of these makes a compelling case."

"I think these will do. Excellent work. Have you sent the pictures to the CIA?"

"That was not my understanding of the op, sir." It was Gerhardt's turn to speak again. "I understood that we were to get Chowdhury and Johnson together, and to document the meeting sufficiently that it could be used if necessary to discredit the professor. You know, in case he decides to—"

"Okay," the chief of staff held up his hand. "I'll take this to the president. Anything else?"

"I think we should discuss contingencies." It was another member of the team speaking up, out of place.

"Contingencies?" The chief of staff seemed irritated.

Gerhardt always had his teammates' back. He spoke quickly before this one found himself adrift at sea.

"Yes, sir," addressing the chief of staff. "This was a good plan, and it might be a valuable tool in the event the professor decides to oppose the appointment of…you know…But one meeting with an Al-Qaeda bag man is not a sure thing. If he sings a song we don't like, I think you might need more. I know how important this is to the president. I just want to make sure we've done everything we can."

"What do you have in mind?" The chief of staff's interest was piqued, but he sounded skeptical. He stopped spinning his pen and put the cap on and off nervously. One of Gerhardt's team, a lawyer named Sean Flanagan, studiously made notes in his binder.

There was a moment of silence, not because no one around the table was short of ideas, but because everyone was afraid to say out loud what they were thinking. Jay Rudolph took the chance. "If he decides to oppose this appointment publicly, is it likely we will know in advance?"

Rudolph got the nod he was expecting from Gerhardt. He turned to the president's man and continued. "So, if he does, we get out ahead of this before he goes public and frame the guy for something. You know, give him a reason to, uh, change his mind. And, if he won't, we can…"

The chief of staff stood up abruptly, causing his chair to lunge backward and fall over. "I'm going to pretend I didn't hear that last comment and adjourn the meeting two minutes ago. I appreciate the work on the conference—I know a lot went into the op, and it seems like a great success. The president thanks you for your service to the country. I'll be in touch." He turned to the exit, walked out, and slammed the door behind him.

The lawyers waited a minute in silence, then they all started to talk at once. Gerhardt rose and walked over to Flanagan, putting his big hands on the man's shoulders.

"You guys make a game plan. Jay, go visit the place where his Lebanese family is from in Ohio. East, eh, whatever. Does he have relatives linked with any group tied to terrorists? Where are the Muslim skeletons in this guy's closet? If there aren't any, we need to be creative about making some." He squeezed Flanagan's shoulder.

"Finny, you've been quiet today. What's on your mind?"

"The president, sir." Finny believed in hierarchies, and he felt Gerhardt's years of service justified the honorific. "I'm worried that she's putting too much on this guy's shoulders. I mean, there are plenty of qualified people for the job. Yes, the president's Fair America plan is probably headed to the Supreme Court, and yes, the balance of power on the court turns on this appointment, but aren't there other reliable votes? Aren't there other people she can trust? Why this guy? I don't understand why we've got to be running ops like this to protect this guy. Why does it have to be Judge Pham? Or is this something that happens for every nominee to the court?" Finny was not one to question his superiors lightly. When he finished, he slumped in his chair.

"Your concern for the president is duly noted, Mr. Flanagan." Adding the "mister," Gerhardt was just putting him in his place, as he did to enlisted men thousands of times during his career in the Navy. "Your job is not to question our clients' motives or their cost-benefit calculation. That is my job, not yours. Understood?"

"Yes, sir." He let it sink in. "To be clear, I waited until it was just our team to speak up—I would never second-guess the president outside of our squad. I was telling you so that you might think about how to broach this with the president, assuming you think that is the right course." Finny felt the need to defend himself and dig himself back to level ground. He forgot the first rule of holes.

Gerhardt smiled broadly and patted him on the shoulder. It put Finny at ease, and he exhaled for the first time since he opened his mouth. But Gerhardt was not relaxed. He saw something he'd never seen before—a crack in the façade of Frogman Flanagan.

The meeting ended. The lawyers all packed up their bags in unison, like synchronized swimmers in Gucci loafers. They walked back to their car and headed across the Key Bridge to their offices on K Street just a mile up from the White House, where the president was, at that very moment, meeting with the man who was the asset being protected by Operation Aspida—the man the president was about to nominate to be the next chief justice of the United States.

Six hours later, Sean Flanagan walked through the heavy wooden doors of Saint James Catholic Church, a nondescript parish that just happened to be on the way to his house in suburban Virginia. The cross and the smell of incense and the dank feel created by the thick stone walls of the church gave weight to what he was about to do. He headed down the center aisle toward Father Case's office. At this hour, the priest was sure to be next door in the rectory, putting finishing touches on a sermon only a few ears would hear.

Finny rapped softly on the priest's door, then gently tried the handle. As expected, it was safely locked. Taking a sealed envelope from his breast pocket, he bent and slipped it underneath the massive mahogany door.

CHAPTER 8

April 2015
Chicago, Illinois

Royce walked a while in the cool Chicago evening, watching every face. After wandering the streets for an hour, he found a Courtyard Marriott. At two hundred forty dollars a night, this was no bargain, and he was paying his own freight on this investigation. *Better be quick*, he thought as he signed for the deposit.

Inside the room, he dropped his bags, collapsed on the bed, and grabbed the remote control for the large, flat-panel television that hung on the wall. Flipping it on, he looked for a game of some kind that would distract for a few hours. Royce stopped abruptly on CNN, when he saw his brother staring back.

Several bullet points were to the right of his brother's smiling face. Age: 45; Professor, Rockefeller University Law School; Author, *The Future of Liberty*.

The screen split to the anchor and the man recently nominated to be chief justice of the United States.

"Thank you for being with us, Judge Pham," the anchor said obsequiously. "Congratulations on your nomination. I understand you are joining us because you were friends with the late professor."

"I'm sorry to be here under these circumstances, but thank

you for having me."

"What is your connection with Professor Alex Johnson, who, the police tell us, killed himself this morning in his Chicago home?"

"We were neighbors when I was in grammar school in Pittsburgh. I'm a few years older than Alex, but our families were great friends. We were friends most of my childhood."

"I'm told he was going to testify at your confirmation hearings. Do you know if he supported you?"

"I was anxious to hear, frankly." The judge smiled nervously.

"Anxious because he knew you well and you disagreed about law and the proper role of the Supreme Court, right?

"That's right, Susan. Alex and I have different views about the world...I'm sorry, I said that in the present tense. It is still hard for me to imagine he's gone. I think Alex was wrong about a lot of things, but I don't want to focus on that. His was a life that should be celebrated."

"How were his views different than yours?"

"Well, Susan, I believe government exists to help out the downtrodden. I think it is the instrument that allows everyone to have a fair chance in the world, no matter where they came from or who their parents were. Genetics and environment can deal some cruel hands, and government is the great equalizer of that randomness. Government is a force for good in the world. Alex thinks...I'm sorry, thought...that government is the problem, that we have too much of it. I look out at the good things in our country that government has done, and I think there are still more that it can do."

"I know the White House was worried that such a prominent professor who has known you well for so long might come out against your nomination."

"Look, Susan, I don't want to overplay this. My job as a judge is to follow the law, to interpret the law, not to write new laws or just make stuff up. So this disagreement with

Alex, my old friend, is—"

"But," she cut him off, "you disagreed about judges too, right?"

"Yes, we do, er, I guess he did disagree with me. I think the Supreme Court has been and is a great force of change for our society. It has not only created many of the rights we hold so dear, but it has also let the democratic branches make commitments to the people that are vital to our society. The court is political too, I'll admit, and for that reason, it needs to be composed of people who have great empathy for the plight of everyday Americans. Alex believed the Constitution was limited to the literal words on that ancient parchment. He would never have wanted someone as progressive as me on the court, despite our friendship."

Susan smiled a toothy grin. "Judge Pham, I have something to share with you. We obtained a copy of Professor Johnson's prepared remarks for his testimony, and he was going to support your nomination to be chief justice of the United States." She giggled slightly and nodded at him.

"Is that right?" Judge Duc Pham seemed genuinely surprised, but Royce thought this was more a testament to his acting skills than the facts. In fact, Pham wasn't. The appearance was staged entirely—the White House had closely choreographed the scene, right down to the color of the polka dots on the judge's tie. Dozens of public relations experts were engaged full time in managing any potential blow back on the nomination.

The CNN anchor played along: "Indeed he was, Your Honor. We will be posting the testimony on our website later tonight, but the gist of the testimony is that although the two of you disagreed about a lot, he believed that the president should appoint qualified individuals of her choosing and that you are extremely qualified. He speaks of your character, judgment, and common sense. As you can see on the screen, he used the words 'a fabulous choice' and 'a jurist we can all be proud of as Americans.'"

"Thank you, Susan. I'm honored to hear this from my friend, even if it is from the grave. I want to thank Alex's family for releasing the testimony. It turns out his last act was to be a patriot."

Royce flipped off the television as it went to commercial.

"What the fuck was that?" he shouted at the black screen.

He went directly to the minibar and emptied three mini-bottles into a plastic coffee cup, downing it in one gulp.

If Alex really wrote those words, how did CNN get hold of them so quickly? But he realized the question was meaningless. There were now more people who wanted Alex's death to be declared a suicide, including two of the most powerful people in the world. If it were a suicide, the story would just be a tragic footnote to the future chief justice's nomination. One that had just been spun with a Hollywood ending. But an FBI investigation into the murder of a political opponent, even one who was supporting him, that would make things much dicier. It might generate conspiracy theories that could sway an undecided senator. Or give political cover to those who might want to vote against the nomination. Royce was glad to see his old friend about to become chief justice and relieved that Alex didn't let his politics stand in the way. But this just made his unauthorized investigation a whole lot more difficult. And for no reason.

His cell phone rang, and he knew without looking that it would be Jenny.

CHAPTER 9

December 2014
Chicago, Illinois

The dean of the Rockefeller University Law School was upset
with Alex, so she called him to her office. Only his tenure and
relative fame as the school's lone conservative voice made the
trip relatively stress free. No way they could rid themselves of
him, no matter what he might be accused of doing.

Sylvia Ostergaard was the first female dean in the history
of the prestigious school. She was sitting at her desk reading
email from alumni when the door to her office flung open.
With the confidence of someone who couldn't be fired, Alex
Johnson walked in. Before she could acknowledge his presence,
he took a seat at her desk, reaching for the bowl of black licorice she kept on its corner.

"What's up, Sylvia?" he said, stuffing a handful of candy
into this mouth.

"We need to talk about Marcus." Reaching into a drawer
she pulled out a Redweld folder, which she set on her desk.
"STUDENT 1189" was written in bold letters on its flap. She
put on a pair of reading glasses and pulled out a stack of papers bound with a large black binder clip.

Alex stopped chewing. Nothing good was about to happen.

"I assume you are talking about his grade in Securities
Regulation?"

"I am." She paused. "I think—"

Alex cut her off. He wasn't sure what her objection was, but before being caught in a trap, he decided to play both sides. "I took care of this, Sylvia. Look, this was F work. I mean, he didn't answer a third of the questions, and the answers he did give were not acceptable. But I proposed a D in order to, well, to ensure that the institution was protected."

"Well, I don't think that is what you've done here. I am going to tell the registrar that the grade be changed to an F. This is Rockefeller, Alex, not Podunk U. We don't pass those who don't deserve it. Can you say in good faith that this person should be walking around representing clients with our school's name behind him?"

Alex was taken aback. He was the conservative in the room, but here he was outflanking his liberal dean on the left. In theory, Alex opposed judging people by the color of their skin, but he was not blind to the effects of past discrimination and couldn't imagine a law school without any black faces. Theory was one thing, living in the real world quite another. That the Supreme Court's cases approved of affirmative action on what he thought were bogus grounds—having black students in the classroom improved outcomes for all students—was irritating. But he was more or less okay with the status quo.

"I agree with you about that, Sylvia. You know I take our standards seriously. I went here for goodness sake. I care about the value of the degree. But, failing a black student? Me, failing a black student? Aren't you worried about that?"

"This isn't about you, Alex."

"Oh, I know, I get that. I'm just saying, I think this could be a bad PR move for the school. 'Conservative professor flunks out local kid from the projects' isn't exactly the story you want to see on the news."

"I don't want to see, or you don't want to see, Alex?" Her tone was exasperated.

"I'm not being selfish here. Come on. I don't get it. Why are you so set on failing this kid?"

"Because he doesn't belong here. He shouldn't graduate. He didn't earn it."

"You want to talk about earning things, Sylvia? Let's talk about earning things. Did Marcus earn his spot in this school or was it given to him in the first place because of...?"

"What's your point, Alex?"

It was a knee-jerk reaction typical for Alex. It was Fox News talking points. And it was one that worked against his cause in this particular case. He regrouped.

"But it's beside the point," he went on. "We can't fail this kid. The experience of black students here is not that of their white peers. Black students have told me that whenever they open their mouths, they feel like they are representing their race. When the average white kid from Iowa does badly, no one draws conclusions about white kids from Iowa. But if Marcus gets an F, the implications go far beyond him. I don't like tribalism any more than you do, but it is kind of baked into the whole situation."

"Fail him, Alex. That is the end of it." She was cool. "I'm not overriding your judgment on this. I'm merely applying the scores you gave on each question to the curve you provided. It is purely mechanical. I won't let you make value judgments laced with your own ethical views or what you think the school's ethical views are or should be. Your job is to grade the answers, mine is to decide what kind of school we are. Understood?" During the entire speech, she didn't break eye contact with him.

She rose and put out her hand. Alex knew it was a sign to leave. He wanted to fight, but he'd lost track of what exactly he was fighting for. He had no brief for Marcus Jones. Alex remembered him for a handsome smile and because he sat in the front row and took copious notes on a dingy old laptop. Alex had called on him several times, and he seemed eager and interested, as keen as the average student in the class. Marcus had come to office hours a few times and asked reasonable questions that suggested he was doing the reading and comprehending the lectures on the gun-jumping rules and the elements of securities fraud suits. If asked to predict Marcus's grade before grading exams, Alex would have said a solid B, even an A-, not an F. But he earned an F, and now the dean had given him permission to do what he'd wanted to do anyway.

But as he walked back to the elevator, Alex sulked. He lost the argument, even though he thought the outcome was the right one. And he got caught up in it too. His boss was upset with him, and he demonstrated values at odds with those she was now telling him were in vogue at his school. He also thought less of Sylvia now, and he hated when colleagues disappointed. She was manipulating this situation, although Alex wasn't sure why or to what end. He'd always known Sylvia was a climber and a tool, but to see it so clearly upset him. She'd built her mind around her ambition, and that was the most dangerous thing Alex could imagine.

The worst part was that he was now going to bear the brunt of the aftermath of telling Marcus he'd failed. Waiting for the elevator, he played out how he'd break the news and tried to guess how Marcus would react. What would Alex say when he was asked to regrade the exam? What if the student confronted him in person? Students these days had easy access to their professors, and Marcus had this more than most. He had been to Alex's house twice—once for a reception Alex hosted for a conference in which Marcus was a student volunteer, and once for a book club that Alex had for students interested in the recent financial crisis. He'd also accompanied Alex and several other students on a clay-pigeon shooting trip Alex donated to raise money for student scholarships. Marcus had been in his car, met his kids and wife, and could find Alex at pretty much any time of day. This frightened Alex, but he tried to put these thoughts out of his head, since he worried he was thinking them only because Marcus was black.

Back in his office, Alex decided to get ahead of the problem. He opened his laptop, and typed out an email to Marcus:

Mr. Jones,

Shortly, you will hear from the registrar that you earned an F in Securities Regulation. I take no pleasure in this, and, in fact, deeply regret that this is the result for you. I would like to help you in any way I can. If you want to come talk to me about this, please let me know. I'm happy to try to work through this unfortunate result together.

Prof. J.

As soon as he pressed "send," Alex regretted sending the email.

CHAPTER 10

April 2015
Chicago, Illinois

The headlines of all the papers in the lobby of the Courtyard Marriott mentioned his brother. *The Chicago Tribune* declared "Prominent Professor Dead." *USA Today* led with "Friend of Court Nominee Kills Self." *The New York Times* devoted a story on A10 to "Apparent Suicide of Professor Reverberates in Washington." Royce swore under his breath, popped four Advil to make last night's sleeping cocktail go away, and headed for the exit. The day-two story was morphing from an apparent suicide of a professor of modest acclaim to *the* suicide of a friend of the future chief justice.

He called for an Uber using his personal cell phone, then checked email on the government-issued Blackberry to see if his investigation was live. It wasn't. Five minutes later, he was on Lake Shore Drive headed south toward Alex's home. The Uber exited at 47th Street and headed into the historic Kenwood neighborhood. The home was on two city lots in a comely neighborhood that felt more like the suburbs than the city. Streets were lined with tall shade trees, and the houses, all built right around the time of Chicago's World's Fair in 1893, evoked wealth and power.

Yellow crime-scene tape came into view. A single police cruiser was parked in front, and a middle-aged police officer sat behind the wheel looking at her phone. Royce had the Uber stop fifty yards down the street. He got out and approached perpendicular to the squad car and slightly in front so he'd be observable, even to someone lost on Facebook. The car's window was down.

"Good morning, Officer." He tried to sound cheery and benign, even though he wasn't feeling either.

She looked up momentarily, seeing a middle-aged man with a buzz cut in a Penn State sweatshirt and holding a briefcase. She nodded and went back to her phone.

Sloppy and lazy. The wrong guy, she'd be dead. He felt a muscle twinge in his arm, an automatic reflex from reaching for the Glock 9mm service revolver in the fanny pack slung on his waist.

"I'm Professor Johnson's brother. The deceased. I'm here to take charge of his affairs."

"This is a crime scene, sir, and I can't let anyone in the house. I can get you the information about where to claim the body. There's a contact number." Her answer was pat, eyes on her phone.

Royce flashed his badge through the open window.

"Special Agent Johnson, Federal Bureau of Investigation. I'm not sure you heard me, I'm here to take charge."

The officer barely looked up, and Royce could tell she was a danger to her fellow officers, in addition to being rude.

"Are you asserting jurisdiction here? 'Cause if you are, that's the first I've heard of it." She knew the FBI didn't come to take over crime scenes like this.

Busted. His tone went from bold to begging in a flash.

"I'm not here in an official capacity, but obviously I'm not going to contaminate the crime scene. I lost my brother yesterday, and it would be helpful to be in his house for a few minutes. You can come with me if need be."

"Sir," she said with the most disrespect possible, "We don't give guided tours of crime scenes." She didn't even look up at him. "Even for feds."

This wasn't a fight worth picking, so he walked over to the low stone wall in front of the neighbor's house, sat down, and pretended to look in his bag for something in case the officer tried to shoo him away.

His phone dinged—an email from his ASAC. The National Security section chief had approved the NSL an hour earlier.

He knew not to go right back to the officer and pull rank. Better to wait for a shift change when he could start fresh.

There was other work to be done. Chicago PD would have already taken statements from the neighbors, but they weren't looking for what he was looking for. They were worth a visit. The investigation began now.

He started with the house closest to Alex's, a white-brick house that looked a bit more run down than the others on the block. The planters in front were empty and the window frames were molting. Royce pushed the bell, but heard nothing inside, so he raised the brass pineapple knocker, and let if fall heavily to the door. Thirty seconds passed, and then the door creaked open. Talk about the fattening of America; he'd taken down some giants, but the man standing before him was bigger than anyone he'd ever seen. The man took up the entire doorframe.

"I'm Alex Johnson's brother, uh, Royce."

"Oh my God, yes, I recognize you." Within seconds, the massive arms of Alex's neighbor enveloped him. The behemoth patted him on the back and whispered in his ear, "I'm sorry, I'm so sorry," over and over again. When he finally released his grip, it was like surfacing after holding his breath under water.

"Thanks, that means a lot to me." Royce said through gasps. "I didn't know you and Alex were so close."

"We weren't, I mean, no more than neighbors typically," the neighbor said through gentle sobs. Tears ran down the side of his nose. "Please come in."

The house was filthy and cluttered, but the moldings were broad and carved with careful detail, and there were several stained-glass windows within eyeshot. The man waddled through the mess and sat down on a large leather couch. He pointed to a wooden chair.

"Please, make yourself at home."

Feeling at home would have included picking up all the dirty dishes and newspapers off the floor, and an army of workers with garbage bags and Lysol to purge the place.

The man tried to sit forward a bit to show his sincerity and empathy, but his girth made this difficult. The fat rolls bulged like...Robert Earl Hughes—the fattest man in the world, according to the Guinness Book of World Records 1979. As a child, Alex had talked about him so much that forty years later, Royce could recall that his record-breaking weight was one thousand sixty-nine pounds. The way the neighbor looked right now was just how Robert Earl Hughes looked in that grainy, black-and-white photo on a dog-eared page in the book Alex carried with him everywhere as a child. Royce smiled at the thought but suppressed it so as not to offend his host.

A half-hour later, Royce had no new information to help the case, but the big man had exonerated himself as a suspect. Tears, sobs, and massive quivering showed how much the lonely giant depended on the occasional smile and kind word from next door. He would never have killed a source of emotional sustenance.

Royce moved on. He visited several other houses that morning, talking to nannies of Polish, Guatemalan, and Swedish descent. He learned nothing more than Officer Dziewulski told him on the phone—a few people heard a loud bang around 11 a.m.; no one saw anything suspicious.

A few blocks away on 53rd Street there were places to eat. An hour and a bowl of ramen later, he was back in front of the house and ready for a confrontation with Officer Facebook. But she was gone, and all that remained was the yellow

police tape tied to the low wrought-iron fence that surrounded Alex's property. Ducking under the tape, Royce walked up
to the front door. An antique mailbox was stuck to the house
next to the door, and in the lid he found a spare house key,
right where Alex had always told him to find one in an emer-
gency. He broke the police seal on the front door, and keyed
in. The alarm keypad hung by a wire, disarmed by police after
they forced their way in.

French doors separated the entryway from the living room.
They opened noiselessly. There weren't even any signs anything had happened there the day before. The wood floors
were cleaned of any blood or skull fragments, and the place
tidied up as if company were expected any minute.

Pulling latex gloves out of his Filson bag, he wiggled them
on. The centerpiece of the living room was an oval walnut
table. It was a gift from his parents. Now it stood where his
brother must have fallen and bled to death.

Circling his fingertips slowly around the table's edge, he
tried to get a sense of what Alex might have been looking at
or doing when he died. Two people had been in the room at
the time, he was certain. At this point, he couldn't be sure
which way Alex was facing when he fell—was he walking toward the front door or the kitchen at the back of the house?
Since the murder happened in the front room of the house, it
figured that Alex let the person in—he knew him.

Royce scanned the scene, running through scenarios and
looking for anything out of the ordinary. There appeared to
be a bullet hole in the wall separating the living room and the
kitchen. Black spray paint made a crude circle around the hole
about one foot below the ceiling. The ceilings were at least ten
feet high, which meant the bullet impacted the wall about
nine feet off the ground. Alex was about six-foot-eight, so this
was not impossible to imagine, but the location suggested that
even for someone that tall, if it were suicide, the angle of the
pistol had to be aimed upward. *Did a typical person shooting*

in the temple aim parallel to the ground, slightly up, or slightly down? He didn't know.

In the kitchen, Royce opened every drawer, every cabinet, and every container. Not looking for anything specific, just something that might inspire an idea. He opened every bottle and used his phone to google everything he didn't immediately understand. Book titles he didn't know, messages scribbled on unpaid bills, and matchbooks from local eateries. Moving on, he examined everything on Alex's DVR and in his computer browser's history.

On the top floor, the library was a treasure trove. Royce knew Alex spent a lot of hours here, reading and writing constantly. The room was a mess. Books and artifacts and just junk were piled everywhere. On Alex's desk there were stacks of paper piled high. Royce could tell police investigators had been in this room and rifled through papers. There were forensic footprints all around. But why? Were they looking for a suicide note two floors up? Weren't they usually found near the body? Suicide notes were designed to be public, not hidden.

Half an hour later, Royce wandered into the bedroom Alex and Claire had shared. Looking at the unmade king-size bed and the socks and underwear strewn about was depressing. And not just because of his penchant for order. The room smelled of his brother. Royce wanted to lie there with him, but there wasn't time. He paused brother mode and hit play on investigator mode.

What was Alex thinking when he went to sleep two nights ago? Did he know his days were numbered?

"Who was after you, buddy?" he whispered in frustration, bouncing on the edge of the mattress.

The single drawer in the bedside table was, no surprise, filled with junk. Batteries and coins sifted through his fingers until he felt a prick. Pulling back, blood was pooling under the glove on the tip of his index finger. He squinted into the drawer to find the culprit. Under several pieces of paper—a few bills and scraps with hand-written notes—were dozens of used syringes. He picked one up and held it up to the light. Empty. Of what he couldn't be sure.

He bolted down to the kitchen for a Ziploc bag. The local FBI crime lab was a quick Uber-ride downtown.

CHAPTER 11

June 1998
Chicago, Illinois

Alex sat in the bathroom tugging on the end of his flaccid penis. Nothing seemed to work, despite the fact that twenty yards down the hall Claire was naked and open to accept him. She was lying there vulnerable and totally exposed, cursing his stupid anxiety. Alex got up from the toilet, flushed the empty bowl to maintain the illusion he "had to go to the bathroom," and walked into the library. He woke the computer and googled "hardcore orgy xxx." Not even the graphic movies on the screen could make him hard.

"I don't feel very well, honey. I think it might be food poisoning," he shouted down the hall to his wife.

The next morning, they both pretended that nothing happened, but the space between them at the kitchen table while they drank their morning coffee was full of unasked questions and disappointment. They each were thinking of steps that would make sure this didn't happen again—Alex planned to email his doctor to see if he could get a Viagra prescription; Claire planned to make an appointment with her therapist, as she needed someone neutral to tell what an ass her husband was.

On several occasions Claire did get pregnant and they made it to six or eight and even twelve weeks. But miscarriages came on top of miscarriages. As their friends became pregnant one after the other, month after month, they turned to science.

The process was simple in design, but in retrospect, so was the Bataan Death March. Alex administered shots of hormones to Claire's backside nightly for weeks to stimulate egg production, then, when a sufficient number of follicles appeared, they were harvested surgically. He just had to add some of himself to the mix.

Of course, all this was easier said than done. When Alex first went to the clinic and saw the room where he was to do his part, he couldn't pull the trigger. It was right on the hallway just paces from the waiting room. There were just few inches of cheap wood between him and dozens of nervous professional women in their late thirties. The last image before going to masturbate was of the other couples holding hands nervously waiting their turn. The husbands seemed anxious and the wives distraught. It was like a nightmare version of group sex.

Inside the room, skivvy magazines and VHS tapes of artificial-looking couples copulating weren't enough to overcome the reality of a white-coated nurse on the other side of a revolving plexiglass window waiting for his bodily fluid. Beaten by the scene, Alex walked with his head down to the front counter.

"Um, I was wondering if I could, I don't know, do this at home, and deliver it?"

"Mr. Johnson, right?" the nurse was definitely a girl, not a woman, in Alex's eyes. She couldn't have been more than twenty, probably an intern.

"Yes. I'm Alex Johnson. Is this possible?"

She handed him a small container in a sterile package. "No problem. We get this a lot. Use this. Just be sure that you keep it, that you, ah, catch it all, seal it up, and bring it back within thirty minutes. Be on time. The...it goes bad after that. Good luck." The "good luck" stung.

Alex drove the six miles to his house, and fifteen minutes

later was back in the driver's seat, headed back to the clinic. About a thousand yards short of the clinic entrance, the line of cars abruptly stopped. It was a semi-residential street on a Wednesday afternoon, but it was one-way, and something was blocking the traffic ahead. After a few minutes of toe-tapping frustration, Alex got out. He could see the flashing lights of a police car and what appeared to be a few folks arguing over a fender bender.

"What's going on here?" Alex shouted as he approached them on foot.

"Go back to your vehicle!" the officer turned and shouted at Alex.

"Officer, I'm making a delivery to that clinic right over there," Alex said pointing madly. He couldn't imagine Claire's rage if he had to tell her that he couldn't jerk off in the clinic, had to do it at home, and, as a result, a fender-bender killed their baby, or, at least the hopes of one. "It's a matter of life and death. I've got five minutes to make it. Can't we just move this to the side so the traffic can get through?"

"I'm sorry, we really can't disrupt the scene until we've taken photos and statements."

"Are you kidding me? For this?!" Alex shouted, pointing at the dents and dings on two relatively shabby cars. "I'm walking it in."

"Sir, if you don't stay with your vehicle…" Alex threw his hands in the air and stomped off. Back at the car, he pulled around the vehicle in front and squeezed carefully between stalled cars and parked cars on the left side of the road. By the time he approached where the officer was standing, he was driving faster than he meant to. The brown bag in the passenger seat urged him on. He clipped a sideview mirror or three and didn't even think about stopping to leave notes. The officer didn't see him coming until the last second, so his only course was to jump to his right to avoid the on-rushing car. The last thing Alex saw in the rearview mirror was the officer, back in the middle of the road shouting in his direction.

Alex left the car running and rushed into the clinic carrying the paper bag with two hands like it contained nitroglycerine. He was petrified.

"Here…Johnson," he panted. "My, uh, delivery."

The same teenage attendant stared back him, bewildered.

"I'm sorry, what exactly is this?" she gestured toward the brown bag.

"It has my, you know, the sterile container is inside. What, ah…"

"Take the container out of the bag and hand it to me in the sterile bag we provided you please."

"Sterile bag? I'm sorry, there was a…"

"Yes. I gave you a sterile bag in which you were supposed to deposit the container. You don't have it?"

Alex shook his head in shame, but at this point, he honestly couldn't remember any such bag.

"Why don't we do this, Mr. Johnson. Go to room…" She looked at her computer screen, and Alex wondered for a second how those rooms were monitored. "…room 4. Take the container from this and put it into one of the clear bags in the room by the door. Then, open the partition on the far wall, like we told you when you were in there earlier. Slide the bag into the lab. Okay?"

Alex looked at his watch. Thirty-two minutes. He suspected thirty minutes was a guideline more than a rule but felt his father's gaze. The old Navy captain wouldn't have approved of any of this. Any of it.

"It better work," he mumbled to himself as he exited the clinic. The cop was nowhere to be found, but on his car was a two-hundred-fifty-dollar ticket. It seemed like a fair resolution.

Five days later the phone rang. Claire picked it up. At the sound of her voice, he wheeled toward her. She was in a pile next to the dishwasher, a look of absolute joy on her face. She nodded her head and smiled at Alex, a deeper smile than he'd ever seen, as tears fell from her eyes directly to the kitchen tile. He was pretty sure they weren't even touching her cheeks. Alex raced over and embraced her while she muttered into the phone.

"Yes...yes...Wednesday...no eating or drinking..." Alex held her as he never had and didn't ever again.

After their divorce, a hired woman came to clean out the house. She was a demon—throwing out old toys, clothes that hadn't been worn in the past year, DVDs and CDs, hundreds of books, magazines, and newspapers, and everything of Claire that remained. Alex bit his lip as he watched but never intervened. But when she stood in the kitchen over a giant trashcan holding a bag full of used hypodermic needles, Alex ripped the bag from her hand and held it close.

"No!" he shouted angrily such that the woman froze in terror. Realizing he'd gone over the line, his tone softened. "Not these."

He took the bag up to the bedroom, opened the side table drawer, and dumped them back in. Then closed it up like a vault full of diamonds. "Not these," he said again to no one.

CHAPTER 12

April 2015
Chicago, Illinois

Progesterone. Royce starred in shock and disbelief at the piece of paper the lab technician handed him. He was relieved in a sense. Alex wasn't a heroin addict and he wasn't shooting up experimental drugs to relieve the suffering of ALS or some other dreaded disease. The lab report revealed trace elements of blood from an unidentified female and the hormone progesterone.

"Are you sure this is the right result? You didn't give the needles to anyone else or mix them up in any way?"

"No, sir. I performed the analysis myself." The lab tech's voice cracked. Royce loomed over her.

"What about the chain of custody?"

"I took them straight to the lab, like you said."

Royce grunted. "It's just that I found the needles in my brother's night stand, and he lives alone."

"The blood and the hormone traces were dried, suggesting they had been there a while. If I had to guess, I'd say these were used years ago. We could do more precise tests to get a better estimate, but we'd have to send them to HQ. Want me to send this to Quantico?"

A quick mental calculation—Alex's youngest, a precocious little girl named Caroline, was three. They must have spent tens of thousands of dollars on drugs and procedures not covered by insurance. A professor and an under-paid pediatrician, a vast house remodeled to this side of perfect, and at least four rounds of IVF, likely many more. Just shy of one million dollars in cash expenditures on top of the mortgage, cars, private schools for the kids...*Money troubles?* He crumpled the lab report and tossed it a good fifteen feet into a trash can. Perfect shot.

With his best lead dead, Royce headed back to Kenwood in search of more clues. Someone was burning leaves, and a light breeze was coming off Lake Michigan. Royce wandered into Alex's backyard and breathed in memories of his childhood. They had raked leaves before Steelers games with the Captain. That smell of burning leaves always brought him home. He lingered, letting the wave of nostalgia wash over him. It was Alex's gift to him.

He pulled out his phone and flicked through pictures Alex had texted last week—pictures of his kids playing soccer in the backyard. Holding the phone up, pointed at the back of the house, Royce admired the shot. Alex's son, perfectly balanced in midair, shooting a neon yellow ball toward a small net at the base of the back porch. It touched his heart in all the right ways.

Then he noticed something. He lowered the phone, then raised it up again. Something was different. To his right, straight ahead next to the porch, there was a large blue spruce tree. But there was no tree in the photo. He lowered the phone—tree; he raised the phone—no tree. Time of the text: 5:16 p.m., two days before Alex was murdered. This meant the tree had been planted recently.

In a moment, he was inside and rifling through a desk looking for a canceled check or bill from a landscaper. Here! "Fernandez Brothers Landscaping Services." This had to be it.

"Fernandez Brothers, can I help you?" It was a young woman's voice.

"Hi. I'm looking for the man who works for Alex Johnson.

On Greenwood Avenue in Kenwood."

"That's my dad. He's out on a job. How can I help you?" The call was not ordinary but not suspicious either.

"I'm Alex's brother. Can you reach him?"

The person on the other end was quiet for a long moment. He could hear her swallow. "Can I tell him what this is about?" She was starting to get curious.

"I just need to ask him some questions."

"Okay." She paused again. "Is it about the bill?"

"No. Actually I work for the FBI. Your dad might have information about something that happened at Mr. Johnson's residence. I think he was working here at the time."

"I see."

Noncommittal answer. He could play it soft or hard. He decided to try both at the same time.

"Your dad isn't at risk and I don't want him to be an official witness. I just need his help. It is important. But if you can't help me, I have other ways of finding him. Do you understand?"

"I'll see if I can raise him on the radio." She sounded resigned and a bit scared.

He heard her put down the phone and pick up a walkie-talkie. She spoke in quick and muffled Spanish. Then she was back.

"Sorry about that. He's finishing up a job and can stop by when he's done. Would that be okay?"

CHAPTER 13

Jorge Fernandez rang the bell, but no one answered. He checked the text message from his daughter to be sure he had the right house. He turned back toward his truck, which was idling out front, and saw his son playing a game on his phone. He turned back.

"Señor? Hello, mister!"

No answer.

Fernandez was not close with his customers. He'd never seen Mr. Johnson's brother or heard about him. He wanted his thirty dollars at the end of every cut and to be left alone by everyone. This was a delicate situation he was walking into, so he didn't want to do the wrong thing. He rang the bell again and picked up the large brass knocker on the front door and let it fall heavily several times. He shouted again.

The door opened and a man stood there, straightening his blue blazer. He walked out with his arm extended. *Yup, this is the cop*, Fernandez thought to himself.

"Are you the FBI man I'm supposed to see?" Fernandez asked in a whisper.

"Yes, but I'm really here more as his brother." He touched the lapel of the blazer reflexively. "I'm Royce Johnson."

"Oh. Nice to meet you." He seemed relieved.

"You too. Thanks for coming."

Fernandez's hands were large for a man his size, and the dirt and grass stains were woven deeply into the cracks. Royce instantly liked him. Tough, hardworking, and polite. The Captain would have put Mr. Fernandez up on the highest pedestal. So, Royce did too.

"What can I do to help you, *señor*?"

Royce motioned to the front porch and a small white-metal loveseat with cushions covered in spider webs, then thought better of it.

"I need your help, Mr...I don't know your name. Is it Fernandez?"

"It is okay that we keep it that way, *señor*?"

"Of course."

"*Mi hija* tell me that I not in trouble, but still, I worry."

"Yes, yes, yes. I just wanted some information."

"Do I need a lawyer?"

"No, definitely not."

"Good, because your brother doesn't pay me enough for one." They both laughed.

"Can I offer you some water? Glass of wine? *Cerveza*?" Royce regretted the Spanish as soon as he said it.

"Thank you, but I am okay."

"Alright then." Royce swallowed, then spat: "Alex, my brother, he was found dead inside yesterday."

"Oh, no, *señor*, I had not heard that. *¡Dios mío!* I'm so sorry."

"He was shot." Royce made sure he had eye contact.

"Shot?" the man shook his head and squirmed.

"Yes. In the head. Right over there." He motioned over his shoulder through the open French door toward the living room.

Fernandez looked around. He crossed himself.

"Were you in my brother's neighborhood yesterday morning?"

"What you say I do? You say I—"

"Stop." Royce held up his hand. "Of course not. I saw that my brother owes you about two hundred dollars. I'll make sure you get paid."

Fernandez relaxed a notch.

"I will take that *cerveza, señor.*"

Royce went to the kitchen and was back in a minute with a bottle of Chimay, the only beer he saw in the refrigerator. He came back, handed the beer over, pushed the cobwebbed cushions off the loveseat, and motioned for Fernandez to have a seat. He lowered himself into a cast-iron rocking chair.

The gardener eyed the beer skeptically, then took a long drink. He glanced curiously at the bottle and mouthed the word "Chimay."

"Very good. Thank you."

"So, as I was saying, were you here yesterday?"

"Yes, planting a new tree, to give back porch some privacy. He had a magnolia there, but it no survive the winter."

"What time were you here?"

"We start about eight or eight-thirty, and we finish cutting grass and cleaning around…before eleven, I say."

Royce sat forward on the edge of the rocking chair, tilting toward the man.

"Did you see anything unusual?

"Am I going to be in trouble?" It was a whisper.

"Why would you be in trouble?"

"Well, I, ah, I no want to talk to *policia.*"

"I'm not following you."

"I can't give statement to *policia.* I'm sorry. Mr. Alex was a nice guy. He make us coffee, always nice to me. I am very sorry he is gone."

"Think of me as Alex's brother. No one will know we talked. Did you see him that morning? There may be more to the story than the police think."

"I see him on the front porch, drinking coffee and reading the paper. He was always reading something when I seen him. He had to let us in the side gate. We had to park the truck up the street because a delivery truck was taking the space in

63

front of the house. So we were working hard to carry that big tree down the street. Your brother offered to go get us donuts."

"That sounds like Alex." It made Royce sad. "You said you were done around eleven. Did you hear the gunshot or see anything suspicious?"

"On your word I not be involved, *señor…*"

Royce held up his hand again, as if testifying.

"I did. I did, *señor*."

"Hear the shot or see something suspicious?" Royce's heartrate quickened.

"Both, *señor*."

Another thing the police missed.

"What can you tell me? Between you and me. I promise."

"Like I say, *señor*, there was a truck in front of your brother's house, so we park up the street. Follow, I show you."

The two of them walked silently out to the street. The light was fading. To the west between the brick mansions, the bright orange and purple of the sunset painted the sky.

Fernandez propped one cowboy boot up on a fire hydrant. He gestured to the north side of the yellow no-parking line.

"Our truck's here, because on the other side of the line is delivery truck." He pointed back to Alex's house.

They were a good forty or fifty feet from the front porch, and from the sidewalk there wasn't a clear line of sight. Royce wondered if the truck was parked where it was for a reason. It made for a nice barrier. Maybe they were pros.

"Like I say, we here, packing up our tractors and mowers, and taking a smoke when we hear the shot."

"You knew it was a gunshot?"

"No, not until you tell me about Mr. Alex. It sounded like a backfire or an engine blowing."

"When was this?"

"I not sure. About eleven, I think."

"Okay. You said you saw something too? What did you see?"

"Well, when I hear the backfire, or what I think is backfire, I go to see if one my machines causing trouble."

The man took about ten paces down the sidewalk.

"I was here, and I see someone walking fast down the sidewalk in other direction. There!" He pointed to in front of Alex's house. Royce started walking in that direction. When he was on the far side of Alex's house, he turned back to the man.

"About here?"

"Yes, maybe closer a little than that." Royce walked back to the gardener amazed at his luck.

"Tell me who you saw."

"They look suspicious, *señor*. Not sure why, but I thought they look like trying to get away from something, not running but hurry, you know?"

"Could the person you saw have come past you on the sidewalk?"

"No. I don't think so. We all sitting here in the grass drinking coffee and having a smoke. He would have walk over us."

"So he came from the house? Right?"

"I don't know. Is possible."

"What did the person look like?" Royce tried to calm himself. Inside, he was frantic.

"Black. A black man."

"How can you be sure, at this distance?" Royce looked down the sidewalk in the direction of where the person would have been standing.

"He wear shorts. He was dark skin." Fernandez walked to where he remembered the man standing. "About here. You see my skin, right?"

"Anything else?"

"He wearing a green sweatshirt, and hood pulled over his head."

It was impossible good luck. Royce typed "Rockefeller University sweatshirt" into Google on his phone. He clicked on the first result. When the sweatshirt came up, he held it out.

"Like this?"

"Color the same. His had a hood." Fernandez knitted his brow, concentrating. "As I watch him run away, he reach into his pocket and pull out what I think was phone. I don't think he call anyone—he just look at the phone and put it back in his pocket."

Royce held out his hand and gave the gardener a two-handed shake. He knew he was right to like him.

CHAPTER 14

Rockefeller Law was a gleaming six-story glass tower among the Gothic architecture of one of the world's great universities. It looked like investment bankers should be walking the halls talking about reverse triangular mergers instead of avowed Marxists and critical race theorists debating the role of the patriarchy in modern political discourse.

The security agent at the reception desk was distracted by computer solitaire, so Royce could have walked right past him. But he stopped. Every conversation in Alex's world was a potential lead.

"I'm Alex Johnson's brother," he said to the top of the man's balding head. Seeing his nametag, he added, "Sidney." The man didn't look up but motioned toward the sign-in sheet that was set cockeyed on the shelf in front of him. It wasn't exactly tight security in what was a tough part of town.

"I'm here to pick up his things. I don't know if you've heard, but he passed away." This got Sidney's attention.

"Oh, yes. I'm so sorry to hear about Professor Johnson. A nice man, always very nice to me." He fumbled with a directory while he talked. "Let me...just give me—" holding up a finger as he dialed the phone. Royce stepped away and gazed out the floor-to-ceiling windows at the vast zero-depth fountain that covered the entire courtyard in front of the building. The Captain would not have approved. A building like this

67

and a fountain like that was a sign there were too many law-yers making too much money.

"Mr. Johnson," the guard shouted over. "The dean will see you now."

He got up from his station, put on a green blazer with a Phoenix emblazoned on the pocket and led the way down a long hall, through the student lounge, and over to the dean's office.

"Good luck," he said.

It was an odd remark. Royce kept seeing the word "Dean" circled on his desk blotter back in Pittsburgh.

Dean Ostergaard appeared and held out her hand to em-brace his with a grip that betrayed her blue-collar roots.

"Sylvia," she said forcefully, maintaining fierce eye contact and flashing a bright, pearly white smile. Despite her Ivy-League pedigree and the fact she'd lived far from Parkersburg for decades, the hollers of West Virginia were still in her voice. Pittsburgh was just over the hill from West Virginia, and Royce could identify a Mountaineer in even the slightest twang.

"Please. Come in. We are all heartbroken. Can I get you anything?" It ran together awkwardly.

"I'm fine. Thank you." He was far from fine.

Royce took a seat at the marble side table.

"How can I help you? What can we do for Alex? For you and his family?" Before he could respond, she added with a sense of urgency, "He really was one of our beloved faculty members."

She put her hand on Royce's shoulder, and gave a warm smile and a wink. She was trying to charm him, but it was awkward and inappropriate. "Alex was special. We started here just a few years apart, so we went through the trials of the academy together. I really loved him, if you don't mind me saying so." Her words were like bullets from a machine gun. In his mind's eye, Royce tried to dodge them.

The dean reached to the center of the table, took a piece of black licorice out of a Chinese bowl, and put it in her mouth. She chewed on the stringy candy expectantly.

"Well, I'm here for a few reasons. My brother's things, pictures...knickknacks. His files. That kind of thing." A bald-faced lie. He wanted the computer. But honesty rarely served the investigative purpose. "Also, I wanted to come and see this place so I could say goodbye. Losing him has opened him up to me. I'm finding I understand him...that I'm closer to him now. More than ever."

The dean tilted her head and smiled broadly.

"What a wonderful sentiment."

"Thank you."

"We can definitely help you with his things. Give us a couple of days?" It was halfway between a question and a command.

Forcing a smile, he decided the woman was not all she seemed.

"Thanks but I'd rather take care of it now. I need to get back to my work. To my family. Is there any reason I can't just grab a box and get to work?"

"I can certainly find out for you. There are some administrative rules that we need to follow. Let me look into it." She rose and walked over to her desk. "I'll send an email to our business manager, and we'll see what can be done."

Royce didn't know the way universities worked, but he doubted the dean of a law school had so little power. She was deliberately not helping him—but why? *A murderer? Why would she want to kill Alex?* The stakes in the academy seemed far too low for murder.

"I'm not trying to be difficult." He was.

"Oh, no, don't get me wrong. I'm just...we do things a certain way around here, and my job is to make sure that I follow the rules to the letter. For all you've heard about this place, we are actually very conservative in the way we do things.

Change doesn't happen fast around here."

"I think I should be totally honest with you, Dean Ostergaard." He paused for effect. She turned from her computer, her fingers still on the home-row keys. "I'm an FBI agent.
I'm leading the federal government's investigation of my
brother's death." He let the statement hang in the space between them like a piece of meat hung in a tree hoping to at-
tract a bear. "This isn't strictly personal. I'm here following
leads that originated in Pakistan and ended in my brother's
living room."

The dean wheeled the rest of her body to catch up to
where her eyes were.

"What exactly are you implying?" Her mouth was like
sand.

"Do you know anything about my brother's recent travel?
I know he was in Lahore last year, Beirut the year before that."

"I don't." She seemed relieved, perhaps because it was a
question should could answer truthfully, he thought. "Each
faculty member has a budget for travel, and no one approves
trips in advance. Frankly, I don't know where any of them are
on a daily basis. They have to teach their classes and be 'in
residence—'" she made little air quotes with her hands, "—
whatever that means, but those are pretty trivial constraints.
I'm afraid I can't be of much help."

"Hmmm," he moaned, while pretending to jot something
down in a Moleskin notebook he'd pulled out.

"One thing I can tell you is that Alex seems like the least
likely person I've ever known to be involved in something…"

"It's way too early to jump to any conclusions. I'm just in
the data collection phase."

"Of course, of course. I'm just a bit rattled." She walked
back over toward him. "We are scrambling to arrange for a
suitable way to honor him, to set up counseling for students
and staff, and to find replacements to teach his classes and
fulfill his other duties. Plus, we all lost a friend. I'm sorry if

I'm not thinking straight or as clearly as I should." Sylvia was pleased with how that came out, and she couldn't hide the small smile that formed in the corners of her mouth.

"I do have one thing you can help me with."

She settled back into her chair at the side table but sat like she was on a porcupine.

"Yes, anything." She stretched her hand out as if inviting him to hold it. He didn't take it but smiled as though appreciating the gesture.

"I need access to all of your files related to Alex: student records, employment file, expense receipts, evaluations, his work files, that sort of thing. Basically, I need to paint a picture of his activities on campus for the past year or two. Can you pull these together for me? Maybe by the end of the day?"

"As I said…"

"Right," he nodded, "the procedures."

"Exactly."

"Then just point me to the relevant administrator. I'd be happy to go work with them to get what I need."

The dean stood and walked back behind her desk. By the time she turned around, he was also standing.

"I'd love to help you, but as you can imagine, the things you are asking for are private and quite confidential. We are bound by rules of our university, as well as state and federal law. I can't do it today."

He nodded understandingly.

She went on, "Let me confer with the lawyers in the general counsel's office, and I'll get back to you. Say, first thing tomorrow?"

Royce shook the dean's extended hand firmly. He squeezed and looked deeply into her eyes. He saw there what students, faculty, and donors saw—a reflection of their best selves. Sylvia Ostergaard was a blank slate of ambition. People wrote in dusty chalk whatever they wanted on her, and in doing so, saw the very best of themselves and their ideas. Her chameleonic personality enabled her to be a prolific fundraiser and effective dean. It might make her capable of murder.

"I'd appreciate it, Dean Ostergaard. The sooner, the better. I'm afraid there may be forces at work here that aren't as they seem, and the faster I have what I need, the faster I can stop them."

"Of course. I'll be back to you soon." He took a piece of licorice from the bowl on the table and put it into his mouth. He chewed deliberately, staring at the woman he was increasingly certain played a role in Alex's death.

Dean Ostergaard patted him on the shoulder and closed the door behind him. She waited until the outer door closed, then walked back over to her desk and picked up the phone.

"We have a problem."

CHAPTER 15

He wasn't going to hear from Dean Ostergaard ever again. Only a court order was going to get him what he wanted, and an NSL couldn't push that far. It was flimsy on its own terms, and the university's records were outside its obvious scope. The files from Verizon and Bank of America were on the way, but these companies were used to playing ball with the feds. Ever since 9/11, American corporations were practically agents of the government when it came to spying and data mining. But universities were another matter. Nope, they wouldn't play along, whether out of politics or principles or whatever. They'd have to be forced.

At the security desk, Sidney was doing a Sudoku puzzle.

"Excuse me, I need a favor."

"Sure, what can I do you for?" *So the dean hasn't called down yet.*

"I wanted to get a few personal effects from my brother's office—family pictures, that sort of thing. Do you think you can help me?"

"No problemo." Sidney jumped up from his puzzle and pressed the elevator button. "Follow me."

Minutes later they were standing at an office door where a child's drawing of Alex hung on the frosted glass.

Sidney keyed Royce in.

"I'll leave you alone," Sidney said in a caring tone.

"Thanks, appreciate your help." Sidney was going to be in

73

hot water and Royce felt a pang of guilt. He took comfort in the fact Sidney's union would stand up for him. Whatever happened, a greater good was being served.

He shut the door, walked to the center of the expansive office, and spun in a circle taking in the pictures, bobbleheads of judges, mementos from various universities, and piles and piles of books. There was also an incredibly gaudy and profane painting on the wall. It warranted closer scrutiny but he didn't know if he had minutes or hours. So he took out his phone and photographed everything, then walked over to Alex's standing desk, where his office computer was plugged into three large monitors. Royce hit the space bar, and a password prompt appeared.

"What's your password, bro?" He danced his fingers on the home-row keys. Then pulled away.

Combinations of children's birthdays came to mind, only some of which he could remember. The names of favorite things, his wife's name. The list quickly became long. The Bureau could access it, but the fewer resources he drew, the better.

He looked up in frustration. Stuck to the corner of the center monitor was a shriveling yellow sticky. On it was written, "Steelers6." Alex's favorite team and the number of Super Bowls they'd won.

He typed it into the prompt and the computer came to life. He stuck a flash drive into the USB port on the computer and dragged the Documents and Mail folders over to be copied. This was going to take few minutes.

His eyes scanned the office. On Alex's desk were pictures of the kids, and in an exquisite silver frame that undoubtedly used to hold a picture of Claire, there was a picture of Alex with five men with cigars and shotguns. He picked it up and looked closely while the flash drive hummed and blinked in the background. The six of them were standing in front of a sign that read: Quail Meadows Gun Club. There was a message written on the photo in a black Sharpie: "Thanks for the great event and your support of public interest scholarships!"

Every year Alex donated a shooting day to an auction where students bid to hang out with their professors. Royce snapped a shot of it and set it back down.

The file transfer was at fifty-seven percent. There were over a hundred unread emails on the computer and nearly eighty thousand saved messages. Clicking on the search bar, he typed in "kill." Over a thousand messages contained that word in one context or another. Invitations from criminal law conferences, recent case reports, and countless other variations of the word appeared at a quick glance. He even saw one from himself, dated about ten months ago: "I think the Rams are going to kill the Steelers this week—what do you think?"

Royce erased "kill" and put "discuss my grade." The mail program showed a few lines from each message, in addition to the sender and the subject line.

Quite a few students complained about their grades aggressively, but one stood out. Several months back, a student named Marcus Jones wrote multiple times regarding his performance in Securities Regulation. The first few were relatively benign—a disappointed student, "Student 1189," whatever that meant, writing to his professor to understand what went wrong. Pleading that there was some sort of mistake. They got more intense. Then they turned desperate, as the student pleaded with Alex to regrade the exam, to reconsider the grade after he had regraded it, to meet in person to discuss it, and to not to get an F. Alex had been firm but compassionate. He listened well, wrote many lengthy emails in response, and offered to help in a variety of ways. Royce smiled. His kid brother had been a caring professor.

The emails turned scary. Marcus told increasingly of his plight, his family's desperate situation, and the impact that an F was going to have on him and them. The emails got longer, more emotionally charged, and aggressive. The last one, sent shortly before Alex's murder, made his blood run cold.

Professor Johnson,

I'm sorry it has come to this. I do not understand why you have taken it upon yourself to ruin my life. I'm now deep in debt and unemployable. I will never be able to work myself out of this hole you've put me in. I was my family's hope, and now that hope is lost. I don't know why you've used me to send whatever message you are trying to send to the world, but I can't allow this to stand. I'm sorry that I have to take matters into my own hands, but this isn't just my life at stake.

Mr. Jones
Student 1189

Royce read it again. He pressed the printer icon, and heard the printer spin up and spit out a piece of paper on the table behind him. He could see the image in his mind that one of the Fernandez brothers painted for him—a black man in a green hoodie running away from Alex's house right after the shot.

"Marcus, if you killed my brother, I'm not going to be sorry for what I have to do to you," he said to the screen.

He pulled the flash drive and ordered an Uber to pick him up. Where he was hoping to go, it would be better to not be seen in Alex's car.

At the door he listened for noise in the hallway. Minutes later he was in a Nissan Altima that was waiting for him in the law school parking lot.

"Where to, sir?" the driver asked.

"Hold on for a second, will you?"

"It's your dime, man."

Royce picked up his Blackberry.

"Vasquez," he heard on the other end of the line.

"It's Johnson."

"Johnson who?"

"Very funny." Deep breath. "I need a favor."

"Hey, before that, I'm sorry to hear about your brother."

"Thanks. Screwed up."

"Yeah."

"Shit, man. Just shit. Why'd he do it?"

"I'm not sure he did it."

"What? I just saw…Your old ASAC told us all this morning—she said it was a seppuku."

"Well, you know me, never believing the chain of command."

Vasquez snorted.

"Look, I need a solid from you."

"Don't tell me—for old time's sake?"

"Yeah, for that, and for San Feliz. Remember?"

"You don't need to sell me brother. I'm just ridin' you. What do you need?"

"An address for a Marcus Jones in Chicago, probably. He was a student or maybe is a student at the Rockefeller University Law School. Twenties."

"Did this dude off your brother?"

"I don't know. It's what I've got right now."

"I'm on it."

"Keep this on the QT?"

"I'm not telling, homes. Be safe out there, man." Vasquez hung up.

Ninety seconds later, the Blackberry buzzed.

Royce turned to the driver. "Okay, ready. Forty-two-fifty South Cottage Grove Avenue."

CHAPTER 16

The Uber turned south on Cottage Grove Avenue toward 42nd Street. Within an instant, the neighborhood turned. On the campus, the landscape was dense and lush and well taken care of; beyond it, the environment was barren and scrub. Within a block, the sidewalks were cracked, the fences chain link instead of wrought iron, and the flowers were gone from window boxes. The streets were more crowded, especially with young men, which suggested the unemployment rate was higher than the official figures for the area. Walking around Kenwood or on the Rockefeller campus, one could be lulled into a false sense that the South Side of Chicago was a socially and ethnically integrated paradise on Earth. But here, in the few blocks between his brother's tree-lined neighborhood and the leafy campus and its idealistic undergraduates, the gritty reality of racial and economic segregation came into full view.

As he drove past the shrimp shacks and fortress-like liquor stores, it was obvious that to a Bronzeviller, Kenwood was a pot of gold to be plucked. If the brick mansions full of fancy things were based on institutional racism and a legacy of oppression and slavery, then the whole thing was illegitimate. It was easy to imagine the gangbangers convincing themselves they were modern-day Robin Hoods.

Murder was another matter, of course, and Royce had to plumb the depths of his imagination to fathom a justification for it. If Marcus blamed Alex for exiling him back to

Bronzeville and ruining his and his extended family's lives, he might lash out in desperation. Maybe the murder was simply a scream from Bronzeville to the world about the state of things. A painful and costly scream for help.

The Blackberry buzzed. The Uber driver's eyes met his in the rearview as he answered the call.

"Agent Johnson, my name is Mark Drier, and I'm the Midwest supervisor for national security investigations. How are you doing today?"

"Great. I'm working. What can I do for you, Agent Drier?"

"I hear you are working a case involving a live NSL in my jurisdiction, and I was hoping we could talk about it. "

Drier was investigating his investigation, not offering to help facilitate it. Royce expected pressure, but not this soon. Usually he'd have a few more days before anyone even thought to ask about an NSL or a new investigation. He needed to play along to find out what was going on.

"Of course, of course. I was meaning to write you an email today. This investigation just started this morning."

"That's fast. What's the story?"

"Well, I had a CI murdered in Pittsburgh the other day, and while reviewing the evidence, I came across some strange financial transactions."

"Drugs?"

"Yeah, the CI was a petty dealer for the main distributor of heroin in the Ohio Valley. Anyway, one thing led to another, and, well, I traced some money going from Mexican cartels through banks that might, *might,* have Middle-East connections."

"This is big. Are you suggesting a link between heroin distribution and terrorism? On U.S. soil?"

"I'm still fishing."

"Right, okay. But, if this is what you think it might be, you need help. I need to get a team on this."

Royce needed to change the subject.

"So, I'm starting to put this thing together, and the next thing I know, my brother, who lives here in Chicago, ends up dead."

"Shit. I'm sorry, Agent Johnson." He sounded sorry, but Royce knew not to trust his ears.

"Yeah, terrible. He was...well, thanks. Cops think it's suicide, but I have my own reasons to doubt that. Anyway, I find out my brother is going back and forth to Pakistan, Beirut, and so on, and while he's over there, meeting with some shady characters."

"Wait, you are...are you suggesting that your brother is involved in some way?"

"I don't know. He was a law professor involved in some consulting on the side. I didn't know about any of this, but going through his papers, I found some documents that make me believe he might have been killed for what he knew. I don't think he was deeply involved, but he might have stumbled into something."

"I see," Drier said. Royce could hear him paging through a file. "You're a public corruption and narcotics guy. What are you doing not calling in the pros here? Let me get you what you need."

"I didn't want to waste anyone's valuable time on my wild goose chase. After 9/11, our ASAC told us that every investigation was a national security investigation. Well, when my drug investigation has hints of national security, my orders are to follow the breadcrumbs."

"But we have a protocol in these situations for a reason, you know that."

"Give me seventy-two hours at the outside. My draw of resources will be extremely limited. If this turns into something more than a hunch, I'll turn it over."

"Okay, Agent Johnson. I'll expect a sit rep from you in twenty-four hours at the latest. Clear?"

"Yes, sir."

The Uber pulled in front of forty-two-fifty South Cottage Grove Avenue, a shabby yellow Chicago two-flat with faux rock pieces scattered in among the bricks. Royce held up a finger to the driver, while he finished his conversation with Washington.

"Now, do you need anything in the meantime?"

There it was: the empty promise designed to give the pretext for the call some legitimacy.

"No, thanks." He hung up before Drier could finish his goodbye.

CHAPTER 17

The clock was ticking faster and faster. Royce walked up the crumbling stoop. He pressed the buzzer next to "Jones." They lived in apartment A, the lower floor, and Royce could see the entrance to it through the glass in the vestibule. An orange eviction notice was plastered to the front door. He couldn't make out the date, but it was weathered and frayed at the edges. The Jones paid it no attention, realizing that the powers that be didn't know or didn't care what they were doing in apartment A. They weren't the only ones. No one knew where Royce was or what he was doing either, and no one would have supported him if they did.

"Who's that?" a woman said with a smoker's voice that carried easily through the cheap walls.

Inside, Marcus Jones was sitting at his mother's kitchen table feeding his sister's baby some applesauce. A treatise on international relations law and a yellow pad sat on the table, both smeared in the faded pastel colors of baby food. Despite his F in Alex's class, Marcus was pressing on with law studies. He'd left Rockefeller University for the Joseph Story Law School— it was a big step down, but he told himself it was a better place for a street-smart city kid anyway. The transfer would allow him to do his third year of school again and to make a fresh start. He convinced Rockefeller Law to transfer only his first two years of credits, and Story to ignore his regrettable third year at Rockefeller. He was pleased with the deal and was beginning to conquer the demons that still came to him at night and in times of stress. But he couldn't stop thinking about that punk professor, with his fancy Range Rover and his Nantucket pants embroidered with seasonal motifs—pheasants for autumn, snowmen for winter, orioles for spring, and whales for summer. In fact, Marcus's mind was on Alex, as it often was, when the buzzer rang to their apartment.

His mother pressed the intercom. "Hello?"

"Hello. Is Marcus home?"

"He ain't here."

"Ma'am, Marcus isn't in trouble. I need his help. He may be able to do some good." The voice sounded ominous as it echoed through their apartment, betraying the words.

"What bill you collectin' for?"

"Nothing like that. It's about the unfortunate death of—"

The intercom went dead. Royce instinctively put his hand on his service revolver. He waited a beat, then bounded down the front steps, trampling through barren flowerbeds to the corner of the building. He peeked his head around. About forty yards ahead, he saw a young black man running away in a big hurry.

"Marcus!" Royce shouted. The man turned his head ever so briefly to look back, and Royce knew it was his man. He drew the Glock and took off running after him.

Marcus was younger, faster, and on his home turf. He sprinted for a good three hundred yards, under the El tracks and down streets dotted with vacant lots. Royce was keeping up but he wasn't going to catch him, jumping over chain-link fences and dodging traffic. In an alley behind a Thai restaurant, Royce stopped running and raised his pistol. A gunshot was unlikely to injure a bystander back here. When Marcus was next to a dumpster, he pulled the trigger.

The shot rang off the metal dumpster, and Royce flinched

at the thought of it ricocheting into an apartment. The man froze. He put his hands up and turned around. Royce kept his weapon pointed at chest level.

"Don't move!" He walked forward. "Marcus Jones? Is that you, Marcus?"

The man's hands were clasped behind his head. He'd obviously been in this situation before or had heard enough stories from people who were. The look on his face was resignation.

"Yes, it's me. Ever since the day I was born." He stood motionless, avoiding eye contact.

"Okay, turn around and get down on your knees." Marcus did as he was told; Royce pulled a quick-tie plastic cuff from his pocket and tied them tightly around his wrists. He stood Marcus up and walked him over to the back of the Thai restaurant, pushing him hard against the wall.

"Don't move a muscle."

Taking a seat on the edge of a trash can, Royce breathed heavily. The smell of rotting pad thai was stomach turning. Now that the adrenaline was subsiding, pain was leaking from his knee and lungs. He caught his breath, then tugged out his phone and dialed the FBI field office.

"Suspect in custody, need transportation. I'm in an alley behind a Thai restaurant on 39th Street, between…"

"Between Drexel and Cottage," Marcus said over his shoulder.

Royce snorted. That was a first.

CHAPTER 18

About an hour later, Marcus sat in an interrogation room on the twelfth floor of the Federal Building. Royce walked in holding a file. It wasn't a file on Marcus. It was a file on a petty bank robber they'd brought in earlier in the week. But that was going to be a secret.

Royce dropped the file hard onto the metal table. The scene was straight out of every bad cop show he'd ever seen. "Sorry if I scared you back there in the alley. Why were you running?"

"Am I under arrest?"

"No. Like I said to your mom before you took off running, I just have a few questions for you."

"Is that why you tried to kill me?"

"If I wanted to shoot you, Marcus, I would have shot you. When I shoot to kill, I don't miss."

"So you've killed people, Agent Johnson?"

Royce admired him right away. Most people chained to a desk are too nervous to remember the agent's name, let alone joust with them. Marcus was cool, but the kind of cool that gave you a headache.

"I'm not the one in federal custody. I'll ask the questions, not you."

"Do I know you, man? You look familiar."

"Nope. And, like I said, I'm the one asking the *fucking* questions." Marcus smiled. Royce realized too late that he sounded like he'd lifted that line right out of an episode of

Law & Order.

"Get on with it then."

"Where were you yesterday? Give me a rundown of your day."

"Listen, I'm not sure why you were chasing me like some kind of fool, or shooting at me. I've done nothing wrong, and I think I'd like to talk to a lawyer. I'm pretty sure if you aren't going to charge me, you've got to release me."

"Come on, Marcus. This will go much better for you if we can talk without getting all formal and involving lawyers. I need your help."

"Lawyer." Marcus crossed his arms and glared.

Royce breathed deeply. "We don't need one."

"Lawyer, lawyer, lawyer."

This wasn't going as planned. Time to change tactics.

"I've got an idea. Let's go downstairs to the Starbucks and talk over coffee. I'm sorry I shot at you. If it makes you feel any better, I was just trying to get your attention."

"It worked."

"I know. Again, I'm sorry. I'm going to catch a lot of hell for that. But it was worth it, because I need your help."

"If by 'a lot of hell,' you mean a civil rights lawsuit, then you are right on."

"Well, we'll see about that. Can I buy you a coffee?"

The look on Marcus's face suggested he was disarmed by this offer. Perps were usually racking their brains trying to think of a lawyer to call, running through countless bus station ads and TV commercials they'd seen from two-bit hucksters. That was the time to throw a curve ball.

"I guess that would be okay. I'm really unclear what's happening here."

Royce seized the advantage. Pleased with himself, he walked around and uncuffed him. Marcus rubbed his wrists and said a polite thank you.

They walked side by side through the corridors of the FBI

building toward the elevators looking like partners, not cop and perp. Marcus felt Royce's unease. He had half a mind to just walk away when the elevator got to the ground level, but the other half thought he could talk his way out of this. While his friends used violence and aggression to navigate Bronzeville's perils, Marcus used words and arguments. Everyone called him Counselor, a name given to him by the head of the Reyes Negros gang, who baptized every little neighborhood boy with a nickname as a way of recruiting troopers. But the names were also predictions. And at eight, even a ruthless street thug could see Marcus was one in a million.

When they got to Starbucks, Marcus ordered a double espresso under the name Oscar and took a seat across from Royce at a table in the corner by the bathroom. From a distance, they looked like friends or, at least, work colleagues.

"Let's start over," Royce said, between sips of sweet tea.

Marcus eyed him skeptically. His coffee sat untouched.

"You aren't under arrest or going to be charged with anything. I want to talk for a few minutes, then I'm going to give you money for a cab and wish you on your way. All right?"

Marcus was expressionless.

"Okay. Listen, I'm working on an important case, and I have reason to believe you may be able to give me information that may be helpful to the investigation. It is a national security investigation."

This got his attention. "I'm not a terrorist and I don't know any terrorists, if that's what you are asking. I love my country, even if it doesn't always love me back."

Royce shook his head vigorously. "No, no. I didn't suggest that. You aren't a suspect; you are a potential witness."

"Do you think I'm stupid, Agent Johnson?"

"What do you mean?"

"At Quantico, they taught you to shoot at witnesses?"

Royce heard his brother's mind in that comment. The kid came away with something from the class.

"You have two choices: answer my questions here or answer my questions upstairs in cuffs. Which is it going to be?"

Royce knew nothing he learned would be admissible in court, but he wasn't trying to build a case. He didn't have the authority or the time or the chance to do it the right way. But the right way was all he knew. This was virgin ground.

"I think you've got the wrong guy, Agent Johnson. I'm not involved in anything that would even be close to being on the FBI's radar screen. But if you want to hear about my exciting day yesterday, knock yourself out. We both know nothing I tell you will ever be admissible in court."

"I do, Marcus, I do."

"I got up at around eleven, eleven-thirty, and made myself some breakfast. I was out late the night before celebrating my friend's birthday. I hung around my mom's place—where you were today—for a few hours, then met up with some friends to play basketball at the park. That was about two. We played for a few hours."

Royce nodded along, scribbling in his Moleskin.

"I came home and took a shower. I read sixty or eighty pages for my classes tomorrow. International relations law. Exciting stuff. Then we went out for some food and drinks. We partied for a while, and I got home, I don't know, about one-thirty in the morning." Marcus paused and took a sip of his espresso. His lips flinched and he swallowed hard. "Is this what you're looking for?"

"Exactly. Go on."

"There isn't much more I can tell you. I can give you specific places and people if you need them, but, as you can see, I didn't do anything exciting. I didn't see any crimes. I mean, any crimes you'd be interested in. Walking around in my shoes on my streets, I see lots of crimes, and not just ones committed by criminals. The cops commit a few crimes a day just on my block, you know what I mean?"

Royce let the question hang in the air, as he wrote mindless doodles in the notebook. He knew where Marcus was at 11 a.m. yesterday, and it wasn't "hanging out at his mother's house."

"That's helpful. Thank you."

"Okay, man. Whatever. Are we done here?"

"One more thing."

Royce reached into his bag and pulled the printout of the email Marcus sent his brother. He held it up and looked at its chilling contents. He shook his head and slid it across the table.

"Does this look familiar?"

Marcus was stunned. His look was shock and embarrassment, like he'd been shown a photograph of himself masturbating. He held it up against the light as if to verify its authenticity.

"Where did you get this? What's going on here?" He started to stand up, but Royce grabbed his wrist.

"Sit down! You aren't going anywhere. Unless you want to go back upstairs and make this official."

Marcus sat down reluctantly and stared at the printout. He was afraid to make eye contact.

"What's the point of this?" he asked sheepishly.

"Your securities professor, the one you sent this threatening note to, was found dead yesterday."

"Holy fuck!" Marcus rocked back in his chair.

"The cops think it was suicide, but I don't. You see, my job is to second-guess stupid cops. I think he was killed."

"And you think I had something to do with this?" Marcus half stood, then plopped back in the sturdy wooden chair.

"Guy gets killed, not a thing is taken from his house, and someone makes it look like a suicide. It was a job." Royce took a drink of his tea and sneered. "So who wants a law professor dead? Well, most people are murdered by people close to them. My first thought was the ex-wife, and if she did it, would you blame her? Guy probably slept with all his students and I hear he was rough with her. But she's got an air-tight alibi—five nurses put her in the hospital treating kids with cancer all day. I checked her bank records. She didn't hire a hit man either. Cross that one off." The lies were coming faster and easier now.

He made a crossing off motion in his notebook and looked closely as if it had a list of possibilities.

"Next on my list? Disgruntled student. Did you know that there have been about ten professors killed in past decade by students upset about their grades?"

"I didn't," Marcus said under his breath.

"Yup, one a year. Well, my guess is this was the one for this year. So I start looking at this professor's emails, and I come across a few from one of his students, a guy who flunked Securities Regulation and got kicked out of school because of this asshole. A student with access to weapons and killers. A student with more to lose than just disappointing mommy and daddy and their friends at the country club. This isn't exactly a love note, Marcus, is it?"

Royce snatched the email from Marcus's hands and read: "'I'm sorry that I have to take matters into my own hands.' What matters did you take into your own hands? Why'd you kill the professor over a fucking grade?"

Marcus was speechless. He looked around at the other tables. A few students were poring over medical books at one table, and two tourists were looking at a map of Chicago at another. There was a line of business people ordering chai lattes and macchiatos, all of their faces illuminated in the blue glow of their phones. Baristas moved in an organized chaos behind the counter, blending, grinding, and brewing. None of them noticed the FBI agent interrogating his prime suspect at the table in the corner. None of them noticed the kid who studied while his friends sold pot or worse, the valedictorian of his high school class, and the guy who earned two varsity letters in track and graduated with honors from the University of Illinois, being accused of murder.

"Listen, Agent Johnson. I had nothing to do with…"

He stopped mid-sentence and glared. Royce saw the realization in his face. The corners of his mouth ticked up, then widened into a smile, as Marcus put it all together. It wasn't hard. Royce and Alex shared a last name and looked like brothers. Johnson was common enough that it took a few minutes, especially given the stress of the situation. But now Royce could see it all over his face. Most times, two plus two equals four.

The two men stared intensely at each other, their hands on the table littered with Splenda and stray straws. Marcus was practiced at the art of escape and evasion. But it wasn't running from gangbangers that taught him this, it was an ancient strategy game called Go. It was his favorite game, other than basketball. The Japanese name for Go, *igo*, literally means "encircling game," and the whole point of the game is to surround your opponent while not letting him surround you. He was one of the top ranked Go players in the Midwest. When cornered in Go, Marcus's favorite response was called sente, a play that forces the opponent to respond. Right now, he needed the best sente of his life. And the best sente is one that finds and exploits the opponent's weakest spot on the board.

He was certain Agent Johnson was not authorized to be leading this investigation. The FBI didn't have jurisdiction over a dead law professor, wouldn't assign the brother of a murder victim to his case in any event, and no one would interrogate a witness in a Starbucks. You didn't need to be a law student to know this. Marcus decided to call his bluff. He rose to his feet and stood tall.

"This," he snatched the email back and waived it at Royce who remained seated, "this, is the stupid rant of a frustrated kid. Maybe I had to tell the dean what a prick your brother was; maybe I had to report him to the ABA for coming to class smelling of booze; maybe I had to tell his feminist colleagues that he routinely propositioned and fucked his female students; maybe, hell, maybe I had to punch him in his spoiled, cynical, stupid fucking face. I don't remember what I 'had to do,' but I know it wasn't to kill the guy and then stage it as a suicide. Come on, Agent Johnson. Do you really believe that? I made a mistake, but I didn't kill your brother."

Special Agent Johnson looked frozen in his seat.

"Yes, I know he was your brother, and I also know you are flying solo here, Agent. I am not the stupid street nigger you think I am."

Still no reply. Royce couldn't muster anything.

"I am sorry for your loss, and I see why you think I had something to do with it. But I didn't. I wish I could help you, but I can't." Marcus half turned, ready to declare victory and go home.

"Then why'd you run?" It was a half-court shot at the buzzer.

"Really? You never saw an innocent black guy run from the cops?"

Marcus turned back and put both his hands on the table, palms down flat and fingers spread wide. He leaned in close, using a half-whisper. "Listen, I live in a tough neighborhood. You were there, you saw it. There are black kids—good kids—running from the cops all over my neighborhood. I ran. Well, I'm not perfect. I have over a hundred grand in debt to a school that basically kicked me out. I'm now at a school where I don't know the kind of job I'll get, if I even get one. My mom, sister, and niece live off my support. I'm the only guy in my family who isn't high all the time." He shifted his weight off his palms and stood straight. "So, when Whitey McWhite shows up at my mom's door, and I'm the only thing between my girls and the street, well, I'm not sticking around to find out why."

He raised his voice. "I didn't kill your brother. He screwed me over but didn't deserve to die. I'm sorry he did. Goodbye,

Agent Johnson." Marcus turned and walked out into the street.

"Fuck!" Royce said it loud enough that the med students looked up from their anatomy texts for a moment. He crumpled the email and threw it toward the garbage can near the door. It missed by a mile.

CHAPTER 19

Royce stood in the middle of the sidewalk on Clark Street in front of the FBI's Chicago Field Office. A stream of men in suits and women in dresses and running shoes flowed around him like he was a rock in a stream. He didn't feel like a rock, more like a leaf being carried by the current.

"Maybe I can't do this," he muttered loud enough so that a woman pushing a stroller turned for a second, thinking he was talking to her.

His pants buzzed. It was an FBI number, the lab tech from that morning.

"This is Emily from the Chicago Lab—we met earlier about the needles."

"Of course. What's up?"

"You asked me to follow up forensic evidence from the *incident* on Greenwood." There was that word again.

"Murder is the word you were looking for, Emily."

"Yes, okay, the murder over on Greenwood."

"What did you find?"

"Well, they sent over the evidence over this morning, and the preliminaries are back. We did a GSR examination on the, excuse me, your brother's hands, and we didn't find anything. This means I think you are right—he probably didn't pull that trigger."

"Wait, didn't the M.E. look at his hands?"

"The initial tests were inconclusive. Given the lack of other clues or obvious motive, suicide was a logical conclusion."

"I'm confused, what did they miss?"

"They didn't miss anything per se, Agent Johnson. We just have better equipment than they do. We use scanning electron microscopy and energy dispersive x-ray spectrometry so we can pretty much find *any* amount of gunshot residue. We didn't find a trace. Zip. Nada. Zilch."

"So I was right, he didn't fire the gun."

"I can't say sure, it's against our code. You know, the CSI code." Royce could see her smirking through the phone.

"Well, what's the probability that my brother shot himself with that weapon?"

"Less than point-oh-one percent."

The street noise around him zeroed out as the impact of her statement hit.

"One more thing. We looked more closely at the weapon found at the scene."

"And?" His voice was hoarse.

"We have a match."

"What?" He raised his head triumphantly. He was standing in the late-afternoon shadows of the city's famous skyscrapers, but the sky was a deep blue. It looked like hope.

"We can't be one hundred percent certain. Ninety, ninety-five percent."

"Ninety, ninety-five percent?" he repeated. He'd sent people away for life on far less. It was way beyond good-enough-for-government work.

"I couldn't believe it either." She sounded truly surprised.

"And the Chicago PD missed it?"

"They probably looked. But, like I said, we look better."

"Go on."

"Well, we used a high-powered microscope and we saw something. The serial number. Not full numbers but fragments, an arch here, a line there. Computer simulation was able to recreate possible combinations from fragments we could see.

We ran those through the databases and tracked down a few candidates. Only one was in the Chicago area—a hunting club in southwest Michigan called...let me see..."

"Quail Meadows Gun Club?"

"Yes, exactly. Quail Meadows. How'd you know that?"

"Even a blind squirrel..."

"Well, enjoy the nut!" She laughed. "Is there anything else I can do to help?"

But Royce didn't hear her. He was holding his phone up to see the last photo he'd taken of Alex's desk at the office—the picture of five men at the Quail Meadows Gun Club. It couldn't be a coincidence. He zoomed in and shifted the center to the right so he could focus in on the picture of Alex and his students, arm-in-arm holding weapons of choice. The resolution was too grainy to make out much, but one of the students staring back was black. There was no doubt about who it was.

He dropped his hands to his sides and scanned the crowd. Alex's murderer had just walked away from him and disappeared into the crowded streets of downtown Chicago.

CHAPTER 20

At first light, Royce climbed into Alex's Volvo 850 station wagon, the one with the faded Reagan-Bush '84 bumper sticker and headed for the Quail Meadows Gun Club.

Just eighty miles from Chicago, the Quail Meadows Gun Club was on two hundred acres of rolling grass and marshland. A single muddy lake was located smack dab in the center of the property. The entire topography was artificial. The precise combination of marsh and open water was designed to provide ducks a pleasant spot to land on their journey along the Mississippi flyway, one of the four great duck flyways running from Canada south through the U.S. and into Mexico. The locals made money not by charging the ducks for a place to rest and to drink, but charging the hunters to kill them while they did.

Pulling into the gravel driveway of the club, the sign welcomed him to "Lake County's Premier Shooting Destination." From the outside, the club looked like a model home in an upscale subdivision in Missoula, Montana. Its broad beams and ultramodern log cabin feel looked out of place in the rippled and rusty plains of southwest Michigan. Inside, however, looked just as one would expect from the geography. Overweight and underworked men nursed beers at an ill-kempt bar and a scattering of round tables, under the watchful and frozen gaze of taxidermy. Royce was instantly transported to his grandfather's Elk Lodge in Wheeling, West Virginia circa 1980.

"I'm interested in some shooting," he told the bartender, a middle-aged man in his fifties who was pouring a whiskey for a customer reading Fox News on his iPad.

"Over there," the bartender pointed to a set of French doors that led out the back of the lounge. Twenty yards toward the marsh and down at the bottom of a small hill stood a wooden building with a duck decoy hanging on an old iron sign. The gun range had a modest shop selling Quail Meadows merchandise, as well as firearms, ammunition, and hunting gear. Royce didn't see any pistols for sale or rent. He wandered around for a few minutes, tried on a hat, and examined a leather shotgun satchel. It was the kind of thing Alex would buy on a whim, then carry to a Bears game as a conversation starter. Royce put it back on the hook. He made his way over to the counter, which was manned by a barrel-chested man in his mid-twenties. Tattoos covered all his exposed skin except his face. Ink crept up his neck like ivy climbing brick walls.

"I don't have a reservation or anything, but I'd like to do some shooting—clays if possible." The thought of killing anything, except Alex's killer of course, made Royce's stomach turn.

"We have two ranges to choose from. Both are available this morning."

"What's the difference? I've never done this before." While it was true he'd never shot sporting clays, he spent a few hours a week firing weapons of various calibers at a range in the basement of the FBI building in Pittsburgh. He wasn't exactly sure how he was going to play this and wanted to keep the options open without making his hosts raise their guard. It was also high time he blew off some stress.

"On the first range, we shoot from a single position, and the targets are a mix of sizes. There you can choose from a range of weapons: shotguns, of course, pistols, semi-automatic rifles, and so on."

Royce smiled. *Pistols.*

The man went on, "On the other range, there are twelve different stations scattered across the property. At each one the setup presents the shooter with a different scene and scenario. On both ranges, scoring is automatic based our new electronic tracking system. You just take this iPad—" he held it out, "—and the software takes care of the rest."

"It sounds like golfing. With an iPad." Royce stumbled over his words. Knowing, no, loving, the victim worked a double whammy—it sharpened the desire but dulled the instrument.

"Whatever works for you, man."

"Let's go with the second one."

The man handed over a twelve-gauge shotgun and a bag of shells.

"You okay with this?"

One handed, Royce snapped the shotgun up, closing the breach, still empty. He aimed it up at the ceiling, looking as if he'd done it a thousand times. He couldn't help himself, feeling the familiar weight and texture of his weapon of choice.

"Guess so. Follow me. Let's go kill some Frisbees." The man bounded off and Royce trailed after him, shotgun slung over his shoulder.

At each station, the pair shot at ten targets, earning one point for each hit. There were stations at the end of walkways that went out into the marsh, stations set in among tall oak trees, and stations up in the very same trees. The clays came from different angles and at different speeds at each station, sometimes from behind and overhead, sometimes from the left or right, and sometimes bouncing along the ground, as would a rabbit or squirrel.

As they approached the final two stations, the iPad showed Royce trailing ninety-six to ninety-three. His guide was impressed, and said so at every station as Royce wielded the Italian-made shotgun like a pro. The crack of explosions overpower-

ing the chirps of birds and the squeaks of crickets was exhila-
rating. For an hour, Royce forgot about Alex.

At the next station, they were shooting from the prone position from an elevated platform at clays skimming along the
waterline. Royce fired as soon as the clay came into view, and
it exploded into tiny red fragments that splashed into the water.

"No way you've never done this before. You shoot like a
pro." The guide's tone was accusing. Royce was giving himself
away. Raising his weapon confidently and into just the right
position time after time, exploding, not just glancing, the clays.
Plus, he didn't exactly look like an accountant. His military-
style haircut and his strong hands, shoulders that would have
fit in on Solider Field on a Sunday afternoon in November.
He was keeping pace with the man widely regarded as the
best shooter in Lake County.

"Honestly, my job requires a lot of weapons training. We
never shot clays before."

"Military?"

"FBI."

Royce caught a sideways glance with full eyes.

"I'm not here by coincidence," he added drolly. He looked
out at the air where the target would soon be. "Pull!"

The news that he was shooting with an agent here on business made the guide go quiet. The silence hung over them like
a fog as they walked between stations.

The score going into the last station was tied at one hundred three. As they approached an open field at the edge of an
apple orchard the guide stopped, turning ninety degrees. He
gazed at Royce. "Is there something I should know about
here, man?" The guide's voice was shaded with guilt, as if the
only uncertainty was which of many wrongs he'd done had
been found out.

"I'm just here as a regular guy, not a cop. You know what
I mean? Sorry if you got the wrong impression."

"Oh, no problem, man. We're cool," he said, turning back

to the path. Then, looking down at his boots kicking up dust, he added nonchalantly, "The way you said that back there, I just thought you were going to tell me what was the other reason you are here—maybe I can help you."

The man's breathing relaxed considerably. He was off the hook, but Royce thought it would be interesting to find out what he was hiding. Knowing the area, it was probably just petty narcotics, which was pretty low on everyone's list of targets these days. But it could be more serious—a gun shop this close to Chicago could make a tidy profit serving the black-market demand for a city of eight million people who weren't permitted to own most firearms. Or maybe he was part of one of the right-wing militia groups that operated in Michigan. Both interesting to the average G-man.

"Help me? Interesting." Royce let the words hang between them like the mounted deer heads on the walls of the lodge just over the rise. "Let's finish the last station, then we'll talk. Deal?"

"Deal."

The last ten shots were known as "bouncers"—simulated rabbits that rolled and bounced along the ground. They were thought of as being the most difficult on the course. Royce knew these shots were right in his wheelhouse. He'd trained heavily on tracking running objects. He could win the day but wanted the guide's help. Having him be in a good and agreeable frame of mind would be valuable. If he threw the last ten shots, and the contest, he'd put his guide in a position of superiority that he could exploit.

He lost by one shot. Kept it close and made the win that much sweeter.

Back in the club, the guide put away their gear and cleaned out the shotgun barrels with a long brush. Royce casually held up the image from Alex's desk.

"Recognize this photo?"

The guide smiled. It wasn't about him and the network of

trailers he and his friends had strung through the thick woods a few miles away.

"Recognize it? I took it."

"Remember any details about the people in the photo?"

"Of course I do. We're open to the public but we don't get a ton of walk-ins. Most of our business is members. Summer season is when all the FIBs are here—"

"FIBs? You mean FBI agents?" Royce was nonplussed.

"Oh, not FBI. F...I...B. It's just kind of an expression we use around here to describe the seasonal crowd. 'Fucking Illinois Bastards.'" He paused. "You aren't from Illinois, are you?"

Royce managed a half laugh.

"Pittsburgh."

"Steelers?"

"Big time." He held up six fingers.

"Anyway, what was I saying? Oh, yeah. When we get a group from a university from the city here for a shooting day, it is something you remember. Plus, we don't get a lot of black guys coming around here. It ain't that I'm prejudiced—I'll take everyone's money and every excuse to shoot I can—but just an observation." This day and age, even in places like this among guys like these, people watched their words. "Heck, I wish we had more of every color around here, I could use the cash."

"Tell me anything about the people in the photograph?"

"Why? Any of them in trouble?" This question was instinctual—it was a guy who'd been asked about empathizing with guys being asked about.

"Just trying to track down a firearm used in a recent crime. One of these guys might be involved."

"A firearm? Can you be more specific?" The man raised his arms, and as the sleeves of his tattered button-down shirt slid down his forearms, Royce could make out tattoos that on another day would have piqued his interest. "We've got a few of those around here," he gestured in sweeping motions around the room.

"A pistol. Glock, 9 mil."

"I've got a dozen of those back there."

"I have a particular one in mind." The guide cocked his head to one side and squinted at Royce. "I know you had one stolen a few months ago, and I'm wondering if there might be a connection with any of the people in this photograph."

"You are being quite...What was your name again? Agent..."

"Everyone calls me Royce."

"Well, Agent Royce, I don't see how you know that, without a warrant or something, and I don't know what you are getting at. If I thought one of my customers stole the weapon, don't you think I would have called the police right then and there?"

"Of course, of course." Was the man being cagey or was he going for obtuse? Maybe he'd underestimated this yokel. "What I mean is, I think one of these men stole your pistol."

"Is that so?" The guide sounded doubtful.

"We found it at a crime scene in Chicago, and one of these men is involved in that crime."

"Really?" He wiped his brow. "That's shocking. These guys were the nerdiest people in the building in the past ten years. One of them...what, what did they do?"

No reason to reveal more than necessary. "It's true. The pistol and the guy are both in my custody," Royce lied. "Can you think of anything connecting one of them with the missing piece?"

"Well, I took this picture a few months before we noticed the pistol missing from our stock. I'm not one hundred percent sure, but doubt it could have been stolen that day and no one have noticed for months."

"Could one of them swipe it while out of sight?"

"Doubt it. I was with them almost the entire time from the time they arrived until the time they left; I mean, they weren't out of my sight more than a few minutes. The new ones are like just-hatched ducks—they stick very close to the mother duck, that's me, while they're around dangerous stuff for the first time."

"So, they didn't use pistols?"

"No, we did the course you did today. Twelve gauges. And I put those away myself."

"Where do you store your weapons?" he followed up, trying not to lapse into interrogation mode.

"In a secured room when they aren't being used."

"And where is that?" The tone and paced intensified, despite attempts to hold back.

"In the back, through the store room and down a flight of stairs."

"I see."

Royce let the silence between them linger. The best way to get someone to keep talking was to give them silent air to fill. The guide was going along, so it was time to hold back.

"No way one of them did that that day. They would have needed to have been here before and had a lot longer than a couple of minutes alone to steal a pistol from our cage. That was the only way."

"No pistols were out and around that day? Maybe out on the course or being cleaned?" Royce pointed at the shotguns the guide had put down on the glass top case as they talked. Several were now strewn around, more or less available for the taking. "How can you be sure?"

"It was a Sunday, and we don't shoot pistols on Sunday."

"Sorry? Is that a religious thing?"

"It's because, well, I'm not actually sure I know the reason. We just don't. Club rules. So, there wouldn't have been anyone on the range with a pistol. Mondays are our days we don't shoot shotguns, and Sundays no pistols or other weapons on the range."

"Interesting." Royce made a note in his Moleskin notebook, and as he wrapped the elastic band around it, he said,

"So, you mentioned it would take more than one visit. Did any of these guys visit after that?"

The guide paused. He blinked for a beat longer than normal, like he was about to give up a secret or a friend.

"The black guy. His name was Marcus something or other. Marcus...oh, I forget. I just called him 'Big M.'"

"Big M?"

"Yeah, little guy, but big personality. The kind of guy you want to give a nickname when you first meet him."

"Are you sure it was him?"

"Positive."

"How can you be so certain?"

"Like I said, we don't get many guys like that. So, he was interesting to me. We talked."

Royce nodded along. He could see Marcus doing that. The description fit to a t. Royce liked him too, even though he was increasingly convinced he murdered his brother.

"Anyway, during that first shoot, he was just in awe that this place was so close to his neighborhood. Everyone enjoyed the day, but you could tell that he was a different person when he left. Like he found a part of himself out here that he didn't know existed. I felt it too, the first time I stepped onto a range."

"I know what you mean. The smell of gunpowder in the morning." They shared a laugh.

"Exactly. So right away, I liked him. He came back here maybe ten times in the next couple of months. We shot birds, clays, targets, bottles, pretty much anything that would take a bullet. I'd call him a regular."

"How can a guy from the South Side of Chicago afford to come do this ten times in six months?" Royce held up his receipt from the morning. "I mean, one hundred fifty dollars isn't exactly bus fare."

"Like I said, we kind of became friends. He'd take the train down to Michigan City, and I'd go get him. We'd drink some

beers and shoot. Being friends with the shoot boss has bene-
fits." There was hope in his voice, and Royce sensed he was
begging off giving away too much.

"And none of the others ever came back?"

"Not that I know of."

"Did you guys ever shoot pistols? You and Big M?"

"Shotguns at first, but eventually he became interested in
target practice, so, yes, we shot pistols a bunch of times. But,
truthfully, I don't think he stole the weapon," the guide said,
shaking his head. "I'm not certain he was here the day it was
stolen, and I don't see how he could have gotten into our cage
without someone noticing. If he really needed a weapon for
something, I..." The man caught himself. His defense almost
turned into admitting something there was no reason to admit.

Royce let it slide. He had everything needed from the Quail
Meadows Gun Club. The murder weapon was stolen from the
club; Marcus was a frequent customer of the club; he trained
on the exact weapon used in the crime; and the club employees could not definitively rule him out as involved in the theft.
There was one last angle to play.

"What day was the pistol in question first noticed missing
from the cage?"

"We check the cage every night. We don't do inventory per
se, but we don't have that many weapons, so things generally
stand out when they aren't in place. Phil, one of the guys here,
noticed it missing on July twenty-fourth, a Wednesday, I
think."

"Okay, July twenty-four. You reported it stolen that night
or the next morning, I assume?"

"I didn't do it, but I think they did a search of the shop,
the main club house, the whole place. It probably took a few
days. I'm sure you can find that out by just, you know, pulling the records."

"Thanks. One last question: can I see your customer receipts
for July twenty-fourth?"

"It'll take me a minute—I've got to go to the back and dig them out. Why don't you go to the lounge and get a drink? I'll be up in a minute with the receipts."

At the bar Royce took a seat and ordered two ryes, neat. He swirled one in his hand and put the other in front of the empty bar stool next to him. He clinked glasses and downed his in one shot.

A while later he felt a tap on the shoulder. "I've got 'em," the guide said.

"The receipts?"

"The ones from Marcus Jones—July twenty-fourth, three receipts: shooting on the pistol range, a hamburger and a beer for lunch, and a Quail Meadows polo shirt."

"Can I take a picture of this?"

"Sure."

"Going to have one with me? Bartender, two more over there."

"Sorry, gotta skip the drink." He laid the receipt on the bar. "I've got to get back to it."

"Thank you." Royce reached into his back pocket, fishing for some money to tip the guide.

"Nah, man. Keep your money. It wouldn't feel right."

"For the shooting..."

The guide shook his head. Then sighed.

"Keep it. I'm sad to see Big M in trouble, but if he stole from us and did some other bad shit, you know, in my world, he deserves what's coming to him. But..." He trailed off, shaking his head. He turned like a military man and headed back down the hill.

Royce took the pictures, left forty dollars on the bar, and headed for the Volvo. Back on Interstate 94 headed toward Chicago, he dialed in a favor.

"Sally, I think you saw the NSL and my request for a phone location search for a Marcus Jones." His breathing quickened and he could feel the adrenaline course.

Sally Morovich was a fifteen-year veteran of the Bureau; a competent but undistinguished agent. But Royce's life depended on her at that moment, and not for the first time. The Bureau needs more than just cluesmiths, sharpshooters, and people who can kick in doors. For better or worse, the federal bureaucracy had doubled in size in the past few decades, and if it didn't have people like Sally—public-minded people who got things done and could navigate Washington's dangerous shoals—the government would grind to a halt or, even worse, be directed toward even more malevolent ends. Tens of thousands of well-meaning, nine-to-fivers were one of the great bulwarks against tyranny. Sally was one of them. One of the best.

"In fact, I've got your files right here. Sending those to you via secure email. You should have them inside the hour. There's a lot."

"Great, Talk to you later. Thanks a mil."

"One more thing. Your hunch about Marcus Jones' cell phone was a good one."

Royce sat up and gripped the wheel with both hands. He turned down the radio and swallowed hard.

"What do you mean?"

"His phone was on and GPS location services were active on various applications during the time in question."

"Seriously?"

"Yeah, who knows whether he was aware AT&T and Facebook and Google were tracking him, but they were."

Could it be true?

"Between ten-forty-five and eleven-fifteen, two days ago, he was in the vicinity of Greenwood Avenue between 47th Street and 50th Street."

"Fuck." Marcus deserved to rot in prison, or worse.

"What?"

"Nothing."

"The only active use during this time was at 11:02 a.m. He

sent a text message from near the corner of 50th and Green-wood."

Royce pulled onto the shoulder as an eighteen-wheeler roared by, shaking the rusty old Volvo. He closed his eyes and air poured through his nostrils in a long and deliberate release. He did it. Inside of the forty-eight-hour window, he'd actually done it. He patted the dashboard—it was as close as he could come to his little brother now. It was time to hand everything over to the one person who had jurisdiction to follow the evidence and make an arrest.

CHAPTER 21

It was early, and Officer Dan Dziewulski was in his underwear as he walked toward the front door of his apartment, taking sips of Folgers out of a Northern Illinois University mug. DZ, as his friends called him, was eager to see if the White Sox broke out of their slump, and the answer was in the *Sun-Times*, which was waiting for him, as it was every morning, on his porch.

Before he got to the door, DZ saw a large manila envelope on the tile floor in the entryway. He wiped the sleep from his eyes and tried to focus on the envelope, set askew next to an umbrella that had fallen over onto the floor. Someone must have slipped it through the mail slot in his door during the night. He walked back toward the kitchen and retrieved his service revolver, which was in a holster slung over a recliner covered with popcorn crumbs. He drew the weapon and walked cautiously down the hallway toward the front door.

DZ picked up the envelope and rotated it in his hands. It had no markings and based on its feel, seemed to be filled with papers. He put the pistol in his waistband and carried the envelope back to the kitchen table. He had no big cases these days, and no one he could think of had reason to blackmail him or threaten him in any way. But the envelope scared him. It could be a bomb or laced with anthrax. But who would want to off a university cop? He took a deep breath, broke the seal, and spilled the contents on the table.

There was no note or explanation for what, at first glance, seemed to be a disorganized police file of some sort.

As DZ leafed through the file, he munched on a piece of carrot bread his mother brought over the week before when she came to clean his apartment and do his laundry. In DZ's five years on the Rockefeller University police force, he'd investigated a few serious crimes, but nothing quite like he saw sprawled out before him. His most heinous crime to date involved the investigation of two fraternity brothers who had been accused of sexual assault. DZ worked the case, but it was never his.

The envelope contained an orgy of evidence: cell phone records, forensics and ballistics reports, written statements, narrative summaries of testimonies from several witnesses, maps, drawings, copies of emails, dozens of photographs, and theories written in red pen on pages of yellow paper. As DZ read the details he saw the case form against Marcus Jones, whoever that was, in the murder of Professor Alex Johnson. He held up a picture of Marcus, who was wearing a University of Illinois tie and looking distinguished. Not a usual killer.

Looking at the photographs and reading the notes, he remembered the morning he'd pushed open the door to the professor's three-story, red brick house. He'd expected another case of an old lock and a gust of wind. But then he saw the soles of Professor Johnson's stocking feet. Then there was the blood. The brain bits on the wall and ceiling. So much blood and bits of bone and flesh that DZ had to step outside and catch his breath. Nothing about five years of being a university cop prepared him for that.

After reading the file, he pushed his chair back in amazement. The case was compelling and built on data—cell phone records, bank account information, Google searches, travel, credit card purchases, and countless other details of the lives of Alex Johnson and Marcus Jones. He could see their lives proceeding in parallel, intersecting a few times in classrooms and on the hunting fields of Michigan, before they crashed violently together on that morning several weeks ago.

DZ decided to make this his case. He wrote out the story on a yellow pad and studied it so that he knew it like he built it. In no time, it was time to bring this to his captain. It was time to get off the campus and onto the streets of Chicago.

CHAPTER 22

Ever since Marcus had been arrested for murder, the apartment was in disarray. Dorothy Jones could barely even keep up with the dishes. She was embarrassed but too overcome to do much about it. She picked at the fraying edge of the linoleum table in what passed for the dining room and dabbed at tears with a handkerchief. It was hard to remain focused on what the two men at the table drinking her watered-down coffee were saying. Their words were important.

Across from her was one of her idols, the Reverend Taliaferro Lincoln. He was the founder and president of Operation LIFT, an advocacy group devoted to ending racial subordination and segregation in all aspects of American society. Dorothy Jones never thought she'd get a chance to meet him, let alone have him sitting at her table. She'd seen him on television leading march after march, and she'd stood on countless occasions at the back of the Greek revival church where he held rallies and gave political sermons, chanting along with the faithful. She even voted for him in the Democratic presidential primary, twice. She never thought she'd be within ten feet of him.

Then one Saturday afternoon, right after the news broke of Marcus's arrest in the slaying of his former professor, Reverend Lincoln called and offered his unqualified support. When she got over the shock it was him on the phone—*on her crummy flip phone with the missing seven key*—she told the Reverend her boy was innocent, he was one of the good ones, and this was a wrong only he could right.

"It's an old-fashioned lynching, Mrs. Jones. They might as well go get a rope and a tree and hang your boy up by his toes, 'cause he ain't getting no fair trial in this case. No, ma'am. A poor black boy and a rich white man. Nooo waay."

Mrs. Jones didn't know that the Reverend's father was a doctor and prominent landowner in Virginia and raised his sons to speak the Queen's English and have the manners of landed gentry, so when Reverend Lincoln talked like this, it was an act. He was more Martha's Vineyard than Mississippi, but no one who had summered in Chilmark could do what he had done without creating a persona. He was a politician, so that meant acting and reshaping the truth were tools of the trade. If George W. Bush could be from Texas, by golly, he could be from, well, wherever he needed to be from to get the job done.

The first order of business, the Reverend told Mrs. Jones, was to engage a legal team. Getting Marcus out of jail was step one. Step two was getting out in front of the news cycle with their story. So that meant hiring a PR team as well. Step three was to build their defense, which meant private investigators. As the Reverend set out the strategy, Mrs. Jones could barely keep up, and she couldn't imagine how she was going to afford any of this. She looked around at the stained walls and peeling fake tile floor.

"Reverend, I'm so grateful for your help, but I ain't got no money," she told him. "I'm getting evicted as soon as my number comes up, and I am going to be on the street. I can't afford no lawyers or investigators."

She was irritated at the suggestion but tried to hide it in her voice.

"Oh, you dear," the Reverend intoned in his deepest baritone, "I'm here to take your burden. Marcus's case is now our case. My case. Operation LIFT lifts people up who are down

because of their race. Your situation is not your fault, and
Marcus's situation isn't his fault either. We are here to lift you
up."

He could hear her intoning breathy amens as he spoke.

This was Reverend Lincoln's favorite part of every day.
The chance to help his brothers and sisters fight against cor-
porate power, against corrupt public officials, against judges
and juries who were biased by skin and class. It was a fight
that made him feel much younger than his seventy-three years.

"You're paying for…for all that stuff for my boy?" Mrs.
Jones was incredulous.

"I'm not paying, ma'am. Your brothers and sisters are.
Thousands of black souls across this land have given money
to me so I can fight for those who can't fight for themselves.
I'm just the messenger of their faith and fellowship. I'm connecting you to them and their deep well of support. Can you
feel their love?"

"Praise Jesus! Thank you, Reverend. Amen, amen." She
hung up the phone and collapsed on the floor of her kitchen.
Her boy had a chance.

Twenty-four hours later, he, it was actually him, was sitting in her kitchen. He brought a lawyer. The lawyer introduced himself as Winston Ellis. Mrs. Jones didn't know him,
but she trusted Reverend Lincoln without question. Her trust
was well placed. Ellis was one of the most prominent civil
rights attorneys of the past thirty years. Even in the dingy
apartment, he cast a regal aura. He wore a bespoke royal
blue, pinstriped suit and bright pink tie. The cuff links on his
five-hundred-dollar shirt were encrusted with diamonds. And
as the Reverend Lincoln spoke, he twirled his large fountain
pen in his graceful, well-manicured hands.

"Mrs. Jones, I just want to reiterate what I told you on the
phone."

Reverend Lincoln reached out and took her hand in his.
He looked deeply into her eyes. She would have followed him

anywhere and done anything he asked. Especially for her boy.

"This injustice will not stand. We cannot let them put another talented brother in prison for a crime he did not commit. This will not stand. We will fight for Marcus in the streets, in the courtroom, and in the court of public opinion. This will not stand. We will bring his case to the mayor, to the governor, and to the president. This will not stand. I will not stop until your boy is free and back here in your home where he belongs. I promise. This will not stand."

Mrs. Jones nodded along to the Reverend's rhythmic cadence, whispering amen at intervals. She was sweating profusely, as the window fan tried to keep up with the early summer heat that was blanketing the city. But her concentration was broken not by the heat but the pain of thinking of Marcus sitting in jail awaiting trial.

"We are putting together teams of volunteers to make sure we let the voices of the people be heard, Mrs. Jones. This will not stand..."

"If I may," Ellis said. "We need to do some paperwork here to get the process started." He'd been to this show before, and he was anxious to move on with his day.

He reached into his bag and pulled out a blue file folder. He set it on the table and tapped it with his index finger. She was in awe and noticed the perfect shape of his fingernails and cuticles. It made her feel safe.

"In here, Mrs. Jones, is a contract between you and me. It says that if I agree to take the case, I will represent Marcus and to use whatever resources are available to me to ensure his acquittal. By signing, you are agreeing to giving me a first chance to take this, do you understand that?"

"I do," she said, although in truth she knew that she did not know exactly what that meant for either her or Marcus. But she trusted Reverend Lincoln, and she'd seen the results he'd secured for others wrongly accused of crimes. Just last month, he'd led a march on city hall on behalf of two young boys accused of attempted murder in a West Side turf dispute that left two other gangbangers dead. The boys, both honor students at a local high school, were playing basketball in a park near where the shooting happened. They were in the wrong place at the wrong time, the Reverend argued. But the D.A. used eyewitness testimony and some grainy surveillance footage to justify charges against them. The march on city hall drew thousands, but, more importantly, public attention to the boys' cause. A few days after the march, other witnesses came forward and provided testimony that exonerated the boys. The Reverend could count many victories like this among his accomplishments, as well as pressing for more black access to positions of power in government, academia, and the private sector.

With the signatures he needed, the lawyer turned to the Reverend and nodded. He rose, buttoned his jacket, and wished Mrs. Jones a good evening.

"We will win this case. You have my word. I'll get your boy home for you."

Ellis shook the Reverend's hand and left the apartment as fast as he could. Once outside, he dialed his paralegal and asked her to arrange for a loan to post Marcus's bail and to prepare a motion for his immediate release, as well as for the prosecution to turn over any Brady material. Ellis climbed into a black Escalade that was waiting outside the apartment on Cottage Grove. It was cooled, as per his explicit instructions, to sixty-eight degrees, and a bottle of Fiji water was in a cooler of ice by his seat. In a minute, he was gone, headed toward the University Club, where his squash partner was no doubt already getting dressed.

Reverend Lincoln wasn't in such a rush to leave. He asked Mrs. Jones for another piece of peach pie and pulled his chair closer to her. The pie was too watery and the crust store bought, but the Reverend was an accomplished liar. He'd blessed unions he knew had no chance, presided over negotiations he knew were shakedowns, and made countless public arguments that were simply cover for what he thought was the right result. Flattering an old woman who was going to lose her only son about her cooking was the easiest lie he ever told.

"The Lord is on our side, Mrs. Jones."

"Amen," she whispered.

"The brothers and the sisters are on our side, Mrs. Jones."

"Amen."

"And when we are done telling your boy's story, the people will be on our side."

"Amen, Reverend, amen."

"So here's what we are going to do, my dear. I'm headed back to headquarters, and when I get there, I'm going to tell my army of God's warriors the work that has to be done. I'm going to inspire them, like Marcus has inspired me. I'm going to mobilize these brothers and sisters to take your son's burden off his shoulders and off your shoulders and off your daughter's shoulders, and put it on to our shoulders. The shoulders of the mighty and the strong and the powerful. The seas are rough for you; we will be your boat. The forces of darkness are against you; we will be your light. The privileged man wants to keep your boy down; we will lift him up!"

Tears rolled down Dorothy Jones face. It was a speech Reverend Lincoln would give to inspire a crowd of thousands in Ogden Park at the Bud Billiken Parade. But he was here, in her kitchen, delivering it to her alone, about her boy.

Reverend Lincoln rose and put his hand on top of her head.

"Bless you, child."

She closed her eyes and felt his power. She forgot for a minute what he was talking about. He was talking to her, and she felt joyous, like she was at one with Jesus.

"In two days, you come to our sanctuary, you know, over on Martin Luther King Drive. You come to the Temple after lunch, and I'll introduce you to God's army, to Marcus's army. They will be working tirelessly to free him."

"I will, Reverend."

"Oh, and don't you worry about that eviction notice. It's been taken care of. No one is going to take anything else away from you. You are under my protection now."

He turned and walked out.

CHAPTER 23

Reverend Lincoln strode into his expansive office on the second floor of the Temple, saying "Good morning," along the way to each of the dozens of staffers who hung on his every word. He knew them all by name. He greeted his assistant, as he did every morning, with a broad smile and a dozen doughnuts from the Abundance Bakery. She handed him a stack of messages and a pile of printed out emails for him to review.

"There is someone waiting in your office, Reverend."

Reverend Lincoln stopped in mid-stride and gave her a puzzled look.

"Did I have an appointment?"

"No, sir. He came unannounced and insisted that he wait in there." She pointed to the large burled walnut door that always remained closed. "He, well, he said you'd understand the need for discretion."

Reverend Lincoln frowned. She was reliable and he trusted her without doubt. Until now.

"Can I take your hat?"

He handed his Homburg to her and keyed into his inner office.

The man sitting at his desk was no stranger. It was the president's chief of staff, Mike Schafer. He was known around Washington as a smooth operator and a master of political strategy. He had sad brown eyes, fingers like rolls of quarters, and a jaw a carpenter could use to square a corner.

He was from Texas. But his folksy, good-ol'-boy manner belied his win-at-all-costs approach to everything in life. He admitted no possibility of losing.

When Reverend Lincoln entered, he stood and strode to him like a charging bull, hand out with fingers spread wide. They shook, vigorously.

"Mike!" the Reverend said with fake enthusiasm in his voice. "To what do I owe the pleasure?"

Reverend Lincoln plopped into his high-back leather chair and crossed his hands on his desk like he was about to pray.

"I'm here on business, Linc."

"I figured you didn't come all this way to make a donation."

Schafer smiled. "We need to talk."

Reverend Lincoln knew Schafer was not someone who talked; he was someone who gave orders, and, if you were smart, you followed them. He wasn't to be trifled with.

"I'm listening, Mike."

"We need your help, Reverend." There was no doubt that he meant the president. "This case your involved with, this kid from the neighborhood who is in jail awaiting trial..."

"Marcus Jones is his name." Reverend Lincoln hid his shock. Why on earth would the chief of staff care about this kid? And how did he know about Operation LIFT's involvement? It had only been a few days.

"Yeah, right, Marcus Jones. Well, we need you to not be involved."

Reverend Lincoln stared at him in disbelief. He could still taste Dorothy Jones's watery peach pie on his lips.

"Whatever do you mean? Why on earth is the president interested in this case?"

"She is, which is all I'll say."

"He didn't do it, Mike, and I'm not about to let them sell that boy down the river."

"No one is asking you to do that, Linc."

"But he'll go down if we don't help."

"You don't know that. If he didn't do it, the jury will see that without you."

Reverend Lincoln rose and walked over to the window. He surveyed the vacant lots of South Ellis Avenue. They were overgrown with grass and weeds, littered with pieces of garbage that looked like chocolate chips baked into a muffin. He closed his eyes and rubbed his hands on his head. He turned back toward Schafer, who was scrolling through messages on his Blackberry.

"You don't believe that, Mike. No Chicago jury will give that boy a chance."

"I do believe it," he said unconvincingly without looking up from his phone.

"Well, I guess we'll have agree to disagree. I just can't take a chance. Not with Marcus."

Schafer looked another minute at his phone. The silence raised the dramatic tension. Phone down, he looked up at the Reverend, then stood and put his hands on his hips.

"He did it, Linc. He killed that professor. We have proof."

"What are you talking about? What proof? How?" Reverend Lincoln was incredulous.

Schafer walked over toward the window. He put his hand on Reverend Lincoln's shoulder.

"There are things I can't tell you. But we know what happened." He tried to sound as condescending as possible. It was time to end this without escalating to threats.

"Why is this something that is on your radar? I don't get it. Help me out here, Mike."

"This professor, he wasn't just some right-wing crank. He and Judge Pham go way back. They've been friends since childhood."

"I saw the news reports. What does this have to do with Marcus?"

"When the professor died on the eve of his testimony, we had the vetting team—my personal guys—look into the case.

You can understand that. There was a chance we could get some blowback."

"But wasn't the professor going to support the nomination?"

"We know that now. We didn't know it then."

"I see." Linc saw where this was going.

"So, we did our due diligence. You can appreciate why I can't tell you what we did or how we learned what we did, but you can trust me when I say that the kid killed him. I'm certain of it. I've seen the evidence." He held up his hands.

Reverend Lincoln knew Schafer to be a straight shooter, but he also knew he was willing to bury some bodies to do what he thought was right.

"So we shouldn't fight? Just because you think this boy did it."

"You shouldn't fight *this* fight, Linc. There are other fights. We'll fight those with you. Ending racial discrimination. Raising the minimum wage. Investing in education. Building some social infrastructure around here—" he pointed out at the lots that had caught Reverend Lincoln's attention. "The president is with you one hundred percent of the way. You know that."

"I do. But this boy is one of the good ones. I know that too."

"You are wrong, Reverend. He was, but he made a tragic mistake. Now, if I wanted to, I could make an argument. The system of racial subordination puts this kid in a position that was untenable, and the culture of violence he grew up around gave him the ability to do something that some kid from Glencoe, some kid that is just like him in every other way, wouldn't ever do. I can make the argument, Linc. But is this what you want to be crusading for? To let a killer loose because he didn't have a real choice? There is no the-streets-made-me-do-it defense to first-degree murder."

Reverend Lincoln nodded, but he couldn't speak.

"Maybe there should be, but there isn't," Schafer said.

They sat down, exhausted from the passion they both

brought to the issue.

"So, what, we just walk away from him and his family?" Reverend Lincoln resigned himself but couldn't let go just yet.

"Yes. As hard as that may seem, it is the right thing to do."

"That's a big ask, Mike."

"I know." Schafer reached down and put a leather satchel on Reverend Lincoln's desk. "You've been inconvenienced. You've made a bet on a horse that you didn't know was lame. You've spent some of your reputational capital. We understand that. So this will defray those costs."

Reverend Lincoln ignored the bag.

"You told me why you think you know he did it, but you haven't told me why you think I should care."

"Assuming you aren't interested in justice."

"Don't lecture me about justice, Mike. Don't tell me my people get justice in your system, Mike. Don't tell me that not fighting for this boy, whether he did it or not, is in the interests of justice for the black man."

"Save it for the adoring crowds and the talking heads. We need this to go away."

"You said. Why?"

"Are you being deliberately obtuse, Linc?"

"Maybe I am. Explain it to me, Mike. You owe me that."

"Think about what happens if this boy gets off. You work your magic, and the jury acquits him, even though he did it. But imagine that no one ever knows that, so you aren't tarnished with getting a killer back on the streets. Let's just pretend."

"Sounds good to me."

"For you and him, maybe. But think about it from the president's perspective. She doesn't care about Marcus or this dead professor. What she cares about is the future of our country. All three hundred plus million of us. Her legislative accomplishments, the ones that are going to give hundreds of thousands of Marcuss a better life, are being evaluated by a

Supreme Court that is stacked against her. And then, fortune gave her a chance to nominate a new chief justice and finally swing the balance of the court back in our favor. Judge Pham is that chance. And what do you think will happen to his nomination when it turns out that Professor Johnson was murdered, but just not by this Marcus kid? The press and the public and some fence-sitting senators might start asking who else might have done it. That isn't exactly the story we want in the news in the lead up to the confirmation vote. We need some Republican votes, Linc, and we don't need any doubts."

"But I thought the professor was going to support—"

"I hope you don't think I'd put my faith in that. We're talking politics here, Linc. Conspiracy theories are already flying around the internet. We need this kid to go down. It is fortunate that we know he did it."

"Seems convenient."

"Look, Linc. If it is up to me, I don't care if the kid did it or not. I'm with Dr. Spock—the needs of the many outweigh the needs of the few. I'm not happy he is one of yours, but if you ask me if I trade the freedom of Marcus Jones for a chance to preserve what we've built—a new social safety net for working Americans—and to put a reliable vote on the court that will make the close cases five to four in our way for a change, I'll take that deal every day and twice on Sunday."

"I've never doubted your ruthlessness," the Reverend said.

"But it isn't up to me, Linc."

Reverend Lincoln put his head in his left hand. His breathing slowed.

The chief of staff ignored him and went on. "The president wouldn't make that deal. She sent me here only after she was convinced the boy did it. I wouldn't be here if she wasn't completely sure this was the right thing to do."

Reverend Lincoln leaned back in his chair and gazed up at the ornate tin ceiling of his office. He had to admit that Schafer's concern about conspiracy theories derailing the nomination,

while somewhat far-fetched, was not outside the realm of possibility. And in politics, possibilities like that mattered. Schafer
was who he was because they mattered to him. He took care
of things before they became things.

The Reverend leaned forward and saw the bag sitting on
his desk.

"What's in there, Mike?"

"A bright future for Operation LIFT and the causes you
care so much about."

Reverend Lincoln fingered the handles. He looked back up
at Schafer, who was looking again at his Blackberry.

"I don't understand the logic here, Mike. I mean, I just
don't think this is going to matter so much to Judge Pham's
nomination."

"Take the bag, Linc. The boy did it."

Reverend Lincoln reached forward and pulled the bag
toward him.

"I've got another appointment in town," Schafer said as he
rose and put out his hand. "Can I tell the president that she
can count on you?"

Reverend Lincoln stood up and grabbed Schafer's extended
hand.

"You can."

"Great. Thanks, Linc. You did the right thing."

Schafer was gone in an instant. When the walnut door
slammed behind him, Reverend Lincoln opened the bag. He
gasped at its contents. At least one million dollars in bundled
one hundred dollar-bills filled every inch of the large bag. It
was the biggest donation in the history of Operation LIFT,
and yet no one could ever know it happened.

Twenty-four hours later, Dorothy Jones walked into the large
open room of the Temple, expecting to find hundreds of volunteers making signs and manning the phones. The halls were

empty and not a staffer could be found. The tables were there to hold the brothers and sisters who were going to shout from the plazas and the streets that Marcus was innocent. So too were the reams of paper for flyers and the poster board and markers for signs. But not a one contained the message— "Free Marcus!"—she expected to see. The banks of phones sat silent.

Dorothy Jones found her way up to the second floor to the office of Reverend Lincoln. His assistant told Mrs. Jones that the reverend was out of the office for the next few days and couldn't be reached. When Mrs. Jones asked about her son's case—"Do you know about Marcus?" she pleaded—the assistant handed her a note and started to escort her toward the exit. When Dorothy Jones found herself out on Martin Luther King Drive, she opened the folded note. The message from Reverend Lincoln, written in a graceful hand, was simple: "I regret that Operation LIFT cannot assist you any further. We wish you and Marcus well. God bless you, Reverend T.D. Lincoln."

CHAPTER 24

Mike Schafer headed just down the street to the Rockefeller University Law School, satisfied that he'd avoided one potential disaster but knew he needed to avert another. Schafer's black Chevy Suburban pulled into the parking lot, and Secret Service agents went about clearing a safe path for him. Chiefs of staff didn't always travel with entourages, but Schafer did. Ensconced in the comfort of the SUV, he listened to Alan Jackson and typed out instructions to his team back in Washington. A dozen emails went out in the few minutes while the agents did their work; one went to the president. All it said was: The Padres won. When Schafer got the all clear from the Secret Service, he strode from the SUV with confidence, and headed straight for the dean's suite. His old friend Sylvia Ostergaard was expecting him.

When she saw him cross the threshold, Dean Ostergaard felt herself flush. She wanted to run across the room, put her mouth on his, and take him right there in her office. It had been a long time since she felt that about anyone, far too long. And she'd longed for Mike Schafer to be inside her for the better part of two decades.

"Mike!"

"It's been too long." He embraced her, kissing each cheek.

"It feels like the first time I saw you, that first day in Griswold Hall."

"I remember that day." He pulled back and stared deeply

into her dark eyes. "You were wearing a black dress and black stockings, and with your jet black hair, you looked like a character from *The Munsters*. A beautiful, charming, intelligent Munster." Ostergaard smiled the biggest smile she could remember. He smiled back.

Schafer didn't remember any of that. In preparation for this meeting, he'd studied a picture from their first day at Harvard Law School that one of his aides found in their class yearbook. She was standing aloofly in the corner while a dozen or so students posed arm-in-arm for the camera. She was blurry and distorted in the blown-up picture, but Schafer got what he needed out of it.

"Sit down," she pointed toward a chair at her marble side table. "Can I get you something?"

"Tequila."

"I guess that can be arranged."

"I'm joking, Sylvia. I'll have a coffee, black."

While she went to see about coffee, Schafer checked his Blackberry. The president had written back: the subject line and the message content were blank. It was her way of saying she'd received the message, understood it's meaning, and had no further instructions.

"Your coffee, sir." The dean's assistant handed him a tall green mug. "Cream or sugar?"

"No thanks. Just black."

Dean Ostergaard closed the door behind her assistant and walked back to her chair, running her hand along Schafer's broad shoulders as she did.

"I've missed you, Mike."

"How have you been, sweetie?" he played along.

Back in her seat, she spread her arms and glanced around her large office, filled with books and memorabilia from her time as dean.

"Pretty great. Pretty damn great. How about you?"

"No complaints." He typed out a quick message on his

Blackberry as he answered. He looked up as he pressed send. "I feel like a firefighter battling the Great Chicago Fire, but how can I complain about that? The work is always interesting and we are all that stands between millions of people and misery."

"That's what I like the most about you, Mike, your modesty!" She reached out and held his hand.

Schafer squeezed it affectionately and met her eyes again. He could see in them a yearning, and with his look he let her know that he felt it too. He held onto her hand and stroked her pinkie gently with his thumb.

"I'd love to spend the day with you, Sylvia." He let her savor the comment for a few seconds. But before she could formulate a response, he added, "But I needed to be in Washington three hours ago." He looked down again at his Blackberry. It was an email from his assistant rescheduling a relatively trivial meeting, but Schafer pretended it was important. "Excuse me for a second." He got up and walked out of the room. He stood outside, in view of the dean's window, pacing back and forth for a few minutes, talking to no one on his cell phone. A few moments later, he was back in her office. She was sitting at the table, her hand still extended to where his had been.

"I really need to get back. The president...I just have to get back."

"I understand," she said forlornly as she pulled back her hand.

"So, what was so urgent that I had to see you?"

"Look, Mike. I am extremely grateful for all you've done for me, and I am not sure I'll ever be able to repay your kindness and support."

"No problem, babe. You earned it."

"Thanks. I'm certain I did, but I'm also certain I wouldn't be here if it weren't for you."

"Hopefully you didn't make me fly here to tell me that."

"No, you know I didn't."

"Good."

She paused and shifted in her seat. "I'm worried, Mike."

"Don't be."

"Murder? Fucking murder?"

"Calm down, Sylvia." His voice was steely. "We have this under control." He looked over his shoulder.

The dean stood up and walked to the other side of the room and sat behind her large blond wood desk. It was her position of power. She knew that Mike hadn't asked for Alex and for Marcus because he wanted to nominate them to cabinet positions or send them Christmas cards, but she had never expected it to go this far or this way.

"It feels like this is spinning out of control. You asked me for a favor...a *big* favor, and I delivered. You asked me for a way to get to the professor, and I gave you a way in. I even paid for business class so he'd be more likely to take the trip."

"And we appreciate what you did. That plan worked perfectly."

"Then you asked me for a vulnerable student; I gave you a name. I rigged it. The kid didn't fail. Bright kid. I altered the exam. I deleted an entire answer. I demanded a hard line on the grading so you'd have someone who...*fit your parameters.* There is no way I'd have let him flunk that kid. Do you know the blow back I've gotten for that? Hell, if I were the head of BLSA, I would have been mad as hell too." She took a deep breath and let that sink in. She went on, more calmly, "I've done everything you've asked of me, not just because I owed you but because I was sure you'd take care of things. Now I'm not so sure."

"I'm taking care of things, Sylvia. Nothing has gone differently than we expected. We didn't have one plan, we had many. When one didn't work out, a backup was ready. That's how we do things. How we make sure we protect ourselves and our friends. That includes you. We are right where we want to be."

She nodded along but wasn't reassured. It was just the

force of decanal habit.

"Well, not where we want to be exactly, but we are not in jeopardy. I've deployed the power of the presidency to ensure this doesn't go sideways. Trust me."

He reached out for her.

"What am I supposed to do?" she said. "If you tell me to sit tight and keep my mouth shut, I'm going to freak out. I can't just sit here calmly with a dead professor and a former student about to be tried for a first-degree murder he didn't commit. I'm involved in this, whether you want me to be or not, Mike."

Schafer paused long enough for it to be awkward. But he was really lost in thought. He'd never known her to be weak minded or weak willed; if he had, he wouldn't have chosen her for this important job. But he could sense her loyalty cracking.

"The president of the United States of America chose us— you and me, Sylvia—for the most important mission of her second term."

"I know."

"When I called you several months ago and asked for help, it wasn't your old law school friend calling, it was the president asking you to serve your country. Just as if she were asking you to take a machine gun nest. The president doesn't send troops into battle lightly. You know that."

She nodded.

"I've been in that room. I've seen her struggle and I've even seen her weep. But I'll tell you that her resolve is sure and her decisions are always motivated by the welfare of the American people. She isn't a selfish person, Sylvia. You know that."

"Well, not personally."

He smiled at her, and they shared the moment.

The dean went on, acknowledging the point. "When I voted for her, twice, I assumed that to be true."

"This appointment isn't about her or her legacy. It is about not allowing a bunch of right-wing judges to undo what we've accomplished for the American people. Every president dreams of changing the ideological balance on the Supreme Court, and we have the chance to swing it to our side for the first time in more than a generation."

"I know what's at stake, Mike. You don't need to—"

"This isn't just about our accomplishments being at risk, although the current court could undo them all, but about ten, twenty, fifty years from now. What will *those* presidents be able to do as a result of our work? The Constitution can start being about what we can do instead of what we can't do. Isn't that worth a few casualties?"

"I know...I know."

"I don't think you do, Dean Ostergaard. I don't think you do." Schafer was tired of fake flirting. "If you did, I wouldn't be here."

"What should I do? I'm afraid the truth will come out."

"You did the right thing. Marcus will be tried and convicted of the murder of Alex Johnson, just like we've designed this from the minute we learned, well, you know, the story about Pham. It would have been better if his brother didn't get involved and it was ruled a suicide like we planned. But this was a good backup plan, and I always wear a reserve chute. A couple, in fact."

"I wish I didn't know it. The story about Pham and all this, you know. I wish the whole thing..."

She trailed off like a balloon deflating. It was a pathetic comment, and Schafer didn't respect her for it. But he understood where it was coming from. He knew the comment also probably contained more regret than just knowing what she knew. It was also the first sign to either of them that she regretted the Faustian deal struck with Rockefeller University Trustee Michael Schafer. Sylvia Ostergaard's ambition had always been a force pulling her toward self-improvement, but for the first time, she could see how it could be her undoing.

She was right where she wanted to be, but West Virginia's gravity was pulling her back. It was like she'd fooled everyone long enough, and now she had to be returned to rightful place so the balance of the universe could be restored.

Schafer knew she needed a pep talk.

"Do you know how we got here, Sylvia? How the president got in this pickle?"

"Pickle? You sure are downplaying this mess." She was starting to get irritated. But she was curious as to the answer, and at this point thought if she didn't get back on board, she might be the second Rockefeller Law professor killed by Schafer's boys. "Go on."

"When Chief Justice Rabinowitz died it was our chance. Our chance! Pham wasn't the president's first choice. He wasn't in her top ten, well, maybe in the top ten. In any event, when Malin Olsen had to withdraw on the eve of the senate vote because our own party viewed her as a lightweight, it was a real blow to the president. Then the first couple of potential replacement nominees ran into difficulties in the vetting process. The president couldn't chance another failure, so she put together a top-flight vetting team—do you know Bob Gerhardt?"

"I don't, should I?"

"Well, they turned over every leaf and looked under every stone in researching these guys. Susan Christensen's husband had some shady real estate deals that she couldn't distance herself from; Richard Fong was thought to be too soft on crime—one of the killers he let go because he excluded evidence killed someone the day he was set free. I think it was a little girl. The cops didn't dot their Is or cross their Ts, so it was legit. But still. There were more stories like this. Everyone had a weakness of one kind or another that the team was uncomfortable with."

He knew that she knew the stories more or less, but the look on her face suggested that hearing Mike tell them made her feel better.

"The president started to get frustrated. The clock was ticking to get a nominee confirmed for the upcoming term. The entire Fair America plan is being challenged, and we lost several of the cases in the courts of appeals. This means with a deadlocked Supreme Court—four of ours, four of theirs—the lower court rulings would most likely stand. And you know what this means, Sylvia. It means millions of Americans will lose access to cheap, quality health care; it means retirement will be less secure and that Wall Street will continue to earn profits they don't deserve; it means regulation of the environment, working conditions, bank risk taking, and a whole host of other areas will be reduced or even eliminated; it means...do I have to go on?"

"I know all this. You don't have to read me the talking points. I get MSNBC at my house. What I don't know and would like to know is why we are risking this all for *him*?"

"Well, I was getting to that. As I said, the president was worried we wouldn't get someone in time to hear these cases, so she pressed her team for a name. Javier Aldeanueva over at Justice threw Pham's name into the ring. It wasn't a crazy choice. I guess Javier knew him from some work they did on voting rights and immigration. We all knew Pham was solid as they come on the merits. Plus, an Asian-American justice would be a huge win for the country and for the president. We'd lock up even more of the growing Asian-American vote. The vetting was pretty clean relative to the other candidates. So I call him up and tell him to come to the White House to meet the president. I still remember the meeting. I thought the two of them were going to head up to the residence for some extra-curricular activities they got on so well. Judge Pham said and did everything like a pro, and halfway through, I was completely sure the president would choose him. Especially with the clock ticking."

"Then what, Mike?"

"Then the judge dropped a bomb. He told the president that the only thing she should be aware of is that he had, you know, something in his past that might be a problem if it came up. He doubted it would...come up, that is. It happened four decades ago and the only other person who knew about it wasn't likely to talk. I'm sure you can guess who that is."

"Alex Johnson."

"Alex Johnson."

Sylvia got up and started pacing.

"Well, apparently our good friend Professor Johnson is the only person who was privy to the particular facts, but Pham said he was certain he wouldn't sing. First, it was apparently pretty embarrassing for Johnson, so he wouldn't want the world to know; and, second, he wouldn't be credible, since he was a known opponent of the president and Judge Pham."

"So what happened? I'm not seeing where this is going." While he was talking, she'd made her way back over to the marble side table where he was sitting.

"Well, Bob's team did their due diligence, and the guy comes up pretty freakin' clean, especially compared with our other options. He had no money problems, no drugs, no angry ex-wives, no professional missteps. The guy is a saint, pretty much. With the clock running out, the president smitten with the guy, and him being a homerun on the merits, the next thing I know I'm sitting in the Rose Garden watching him being announced as our nominee. I wouldn't have picked him, but I didn't get seventy million votes, she did. I told the president it was a risk, but she took the chance. I don't leave anything to chance, so I had some of Bob's guys start running the what-ifs and the backup plans. If Johnson decided to talk, we couldn't be caught flat-footed. So we developed a series of plans, several of which required extensive planning and a couple of which have been deployed. Of course, if the president knew Johnson was going to sing, she would never have picked this guy. But at the point we learned that he would, our fate was tied to

Pham."

"How'd you..."

"Let me finish."

"Okay, sorry," she said meekly.

"Once we learned Johnson was going to the press, we had no choice. If we cast Pham overboard, the bloggers and right-wing websites would never have accepted a cooked-up story about spending more time with his family or the like. They would have dug, found the truth, and no one would have believed we didn't know the story. The truth would have come out, and the president would have been tarnished by his past. Heck, even if we successfully played the fool and threw Pham overboard, the political winds would nevertheless have changed. Our next nominee would have been much less reliable on the merits. At that point, with two nominees in the can, we would have been at the whim of a bunch of fence-sitting senators. Our whole agenda would be in peril. So, you can see the problem we faced—we didn't make the bed, but we had to lie in it, and the people who would suffer if we didn't solve this problem were hard-working Americans, struggling Americans. We just couldn't let that happen."

Sylvia could see the events unfolding as he spoke. She could visualize the anxious meetings and the screaming matches, the plotting and the scheming. She imagined herself in their shoes and wondered whether she would have made the same calls. The argument was one every tyrant in history used but that was because it made sense and described a lot of human behavior: we sometimes have to sacrifice one to save many. Soldiers sometimes have to fall on a grenade.

"How'd you know Alex was going to spill the beans? I read his prepared remarks, and they didn't say anything about skeletons in Pham's closet—in fact, just the opposite; it sounded like Pham's mom wrote it."

"It is my job to know things that no one else knows." Schafer tried not to make it sound condescending, but he

couldn't. "You don't need to know how I knew. It is better
for you, for me, and for the country that you don't. Trust me."

There was a long silence. Sylvia leaned forward and tried
several times to formulate a response, but she couldn't think
of anything to say. She wanted to hire Superman to spin the
globe backwards to turn back time and undo all the damage
done. As she saw it, her life was ruined. There was no way the
story wouldn't eventually come out.

Sylvia Ostergaard looked across the marble table at the
man she'd loved since the first day of law school. He'd ruined
her life, along with who knew how many others. He'd sacri-
ficed Alex and Marcus for the greater good. *The trolley problem comes to life*, she thought. She remembered thinking that
problem through for the first time with Mike in the common
room of Hastings Hall too many years ago to count.

"What would you do," she could hear Professor Mueller
intone, "if you saw an out-of-control trolley headed toward
twenty people standing on the track, all of whom will be
killed, and you could throw a switch and divert the trolley onto
another track, where only one person is certain to be killed?"

"Flip the switch! Of course," was the first answer out of
the gate. Most of her class, nodded along, although some
rumblings of disagreement could be heard too.

"But wouldn't that make you a murderer? You flip a switch,
and someone dies. Sounds like pre-meditated murder to me."

An eager 1L, Ostergaard couldn't remember who, pushed
back.

"But not acting would be worse. Once you find yourself in
that position, the question isn't whether you are going to
participate in death, but just how many deaths are going to
happen."

"Interesting." Professor Mueller had them right where he
wanted them. "Try this one: a patient comes into the ER with
a sore throat, and the doctor knows that there are twenty
people waiting in the ICU for organs, all of whom will die if

they don't get them today. The doctor can kill the patient and save twenty lives. Should she do it?"

"That's a different case, I think." The answer was unsure.

"Why is it different?"

The Socratic dialogue went on like this for an hour. She remembered some seeing a difference between acts and omissions. Others worried about slippery slope problems: Mueller asked if it made a difference if there were only two on the other track instead of twenty? Then he varied the facts about the people: What if the one person is a baby and the twenty people are all in their nineties—should it be the number of lives or the number of life years saved that mattered? What if the one person is Mozart or Shakespeare and the twenty people all have Down syndrome?

This was all blood in the water for the sharks of her 1L class at Harvard, and the conversations and debates spilled into the halls and long into the night. She remembers sitting on a ratty couch, looking at awe as Mike Schafer, the handsomest boy she'd ever seen, spin his arguments and tales like a master Persian weaver. She couldn't remember what side he took in those late-night sessions, but it was the side she believed. Looking across at him now, she could see he hadn't changed at all. And maybe she hadn't either. She felt like a pretender then, and she felt like a tool now.

She stared at him for a long time. Then something changed. She knew that she didn't believe him this time. The decision to sacrifice Alex's life and Marcus's life and who knows who else's life was a decision she regretted being a part of. Law school hypotheticals are one thing, but taking a life, ruining a life, all for the sake of what you think is good policy was just wrong. A surge of disgust rose up in her guts like magma searching for a way out. She was thankful her parents were dead, because what she now had to do would ruin them.

Sylvia Ostergaard stood up, straightened her skirt, and ran her hands through her graying hair. She reached out her hand,

as one would to a stranger, stiff at the elbow, and said goodbye to Mike Schafer for the last time.

"Good to see you, Mike. I wish things had been different."

"About this or about something else?"

"Both."

"Me too." He lied.

They walked out together. He peeled off to the Suburban
waiting to take him to Gary International Airport and a quick
G5 ride back to the White House. She carried her jurispru-
dence textbook under her arm and watched him go.

Out on Lake Shore Drive headed south toward Gary, Mike
Schafer sent the president another email. It read: Sylvia Plath.
The meaning was clear, but the way forward was not. Schafer
put down his phone, hoping he wouldn't have to find it.

CHAPTER 25

May 2015
Kiawah Island, South Carolina

On a long wooden dock that jutted out into the Kiawah River, Royce stood surrounded by Jenny and his girls, Claire, her children, and other family. He was holding Claire's hand with one hand and an urn containing his brother's ashes in the other. Jenny had brought them all back together. She had been the balm Claire needed to soothe her anger. A gentle plea to bring the children to Kiawah, close to the bosom of the family, worked magic. That Alex had been murdered, had not been selfish, and that Royce had caught his killer helped. The Chicago Johnsons would never be fully integrated with the family, but on this night, they were one.

The sun was setting over the marsh that the river created on the landside of Kiawah Island, and the night was cool and comfortable. They planned the ceremony at dusk because it was Alex's favorite time of day. The clinking of boat masts and the chirps of bugs in the marsh mixed with the wind rushing through the sweet grass to give the coming night a serenity broken only by gentle sobs of the mourners.

Royce and Claire raised the urn together and turned it over. The wind took the ashes and spread them over marsh grass, into the deeper water of the Kiawah River, and out toward the oyster beds on the bluff. As the family turned to watch them scatter, they all could see the plants and animals that Alex would nourish—herons and osprey fishing in the shallows, alligators lurking below the muddy water. Tips of shells could be seen from an oyster bed the collective family had harvested more times than anyone could remember.

Royce handed the empty urn to Claire and turned toward the family. He hadn't planned to say anything, and he wasn't a storyteller, but felt something needed to be said. Claire gave a gentle smile and said, "Goodbye, Alex. We will miss you."

The family left Rhett's Bluff holding each other against the chill of the darkening night and their own grief and fears.

CHAPTER 26

Jenny turned off her Kindle reading device, put it on the nightstand, and rolled over toward her husband. He was lying on his back, eyes glued on the ceiling. She curled in next to him, letting his warmth sweep over and envelope her. She breathed him in and nuzzled into the deepest part of his neck. If they had not just scattered Alex to the wind, she would have kissed him, signaling her willingness. But not tonight. Even Royce wouldn't be interested tonight. No, tonight she was pretty sure he needed her to just lie next to him so he could feel alive and safe. She wanted him to relax enough so he could fall asleep and start again tomorrow.

But after a few moments, she realized it wasn't working. He was still staring at the popcorn ceiling of the hotel room, hardly blinking. Jenny wanted to help him, but didn't know a way in.

"It was a beautiful ceremony," she said.

He looked at her without moving his head but said nothing.

Jenny stood up and went to the bathroom. She splashed water on her face and looked deeply into her reflection and through to Royce, who was on the other side of the mirror. Now that the ceremony was over, and the family saw him as a hero, he should be riding high.

As she started to brush her teeth, she shouted through the wall, her voice muffled by the brush and the paste, "I still can't believe he was murdered over the grade in a class. I

143

mean, two lives ended over something so…what's the word… trivial, that's what Alex would say. Trivial." She peeked around the corner, but saw Royce lying motionless, still looking up at the ceiling.

"Why'd he do it? I mean, why *kill* him? Why not, I don't know, just make him suffer some way—slash his tires or beat him up or spread some rumors about him on Facebook? Murder's a bit…extreme, don't you think?"

Royce sat up and scooted to the edge of the bed. He needed to snap out of it. He also needed to talk about it with someone. Crazy theories, forensic clues, intuitions, and testimonies had to be checked and double checked by multiple investigators, none of them with a personal attachment to the case. Definitely not by the brother of the victim. Ideally this would have been taken care of before the arrest but, if it had to be with his wife in a hotel room while Marcus was in jail awaiting trial, then so be it.

"Criminals are irrational. I don't know why he took that route. Dumb."

"Do you really want to talk about the case?"

"You brought it up. Do you?"

"I'm interested in what you do. This is the only case I've ever known about. It's my window into your world."

"Quite a window."

"Yeah."

"Should we go for a walk? The kids will be okay." The girls were in the adjoining room, the television playing to four sleeping faces.

Without answering, Jenny pulled on some sweats. Royce put on his jeans and slipped into his loafers. They were out by the marsh in moments, walking alone along the waters. They walked in silence along the estuary of the Kiawah River, almost as far as the Vanderhorst Plantation. Standing in ankle-deep pine straw among loblolly pines dancing in the wind, Jenny turned and gazed at him.

"Have you ever killed anyone at work?"

"I shot my weapon at a criminal for the first time that day. At Marcus."

She froze.

"I missed on purpose."

She kissed his shoulder. There were more questions, but she wanted him to lead. They walked back silently to the inn and strode up the stairs at the back that led to a large wraparound porch.

"Why does he make it look like a suicide?" It was an offhand remark, but it went off like a bomb.

Royce almost missed a step. "Obviously to throw off the cops. Right? He's a smart guy, he's not going to get caught."

She shrugged. They climbed the rest of the steps and took a seat on a porch swing. She thought about reaching for his hand but pushed off the floor with her feet to make them swing slowly together.

"Sure," she finally responded, "at one level I get it. But, then again, it doesn't seem that a law student could do this." She paused, waiting to see if Royce bit. "I mean, how many murderers make it look like suicide? Can't be very many, and the ones that do are probably more professional than...than students at Rockefeller."

They stared out at the marsh, swinging in silence for a minute.

"I guess that question never really...I didn't ask him why."

"Alex was a huge guy, and this kid, well, I only saw him on the news, but he seemed short and slight, more point guard than center. Assuming he gets in the front door, how does he make that shot happen so it looks like suicide?"

"There was an upward trajectory to the shot..." He stopped the swing with his feet.

She continued, "You've seen the photos." She shuddered at even the thought. "Thankfully, I haven't. But that would be quite a shot. Would he be able to pull that off? The entry wound must have had some signs that it was a close-range shot."

"Yeah, my recollection is that it did."

They sank into silence until Jenny took his hand. They got up together and made their way in silence back to the room.

Jenny decided she wasn't going back to bed and opted for a shower. She heard the television flick on when she stood under the steaming water.

By the time she was standing in her towel, one wrapped around her head as well, Royce came in.

"Why'd you ask me that? You know, back there on the path. Why'd you ask me if I ever..."

"Curious, I guess. Just wondering if having done it was necessary to get into the mind of a killer."

"What are you talking about, Jen?" He was standing behind her and their eyes met in the mirror. She went back to smoothing cream on her face, scrunched it up a little, and spoke out of the side of her mouth.

"Well, I bet it's like anything. Unless you practice, a tense situation will make you mess it up. I mean, if you aren't used to it. Like anything. If I handed you a golf club or a chainsaw and told you to use it in the pressure of a tense situation, could you really do it perfectly?"

"Huh?"

"Marcus. I mean, I bet Alex was the first person he killed."

"I don't know. He ran with some bad dudes."

"Yeah, maybe you're right."

The conversation trailed off and she pushed the door closed. When she emerged, dressed for a day that was still a few hours away, Royce was on his computer.

She picked up her Kindle and settled into the side chair. A few minutes later, he looked over from his laptop.

"So, what if Alex was his first?"

The more they talked, the more Jenny realized how this conversation should have already been had. She could see it in

Royce's eyes too.

"It just seems like a pretty incredible thing for someone to do. I know I couldn't pull the trigger, no matter how mad I was, let alone do it in a way that made it look enough like a suicide to fool the cops."

"You think?"

They shared a small laugh. Jenny felt she was making progress pulling him out of the gloom. They went back to their devices. A few moments later, he restarted.

"The way they found the gun was by tracing it to a shooting range, so he had some training, or, at least practice."

"I'm not saying he was like me; a rookie, an amateur. But shooting at a range is one thing. I would bet shooting someone in the head—sorry, I didn't mean to…"

"It's okay."

"You tell me. What must it be like when someone not used to killing actually gets there, standing with a weapon in their hand and looking at another life, seeing the photos of kids and grandparents on the table? Can they really pull it off so clinically and perfectly that it really looks like suicide to the trained eye? And not leave a trace?"

"This guy was great at everything he ever did."

"That's what I gathered but—"

"So I have no reason to think he wouldn't study up, make the necessary preparations, and perform under pressure."

"Okay, I…you are the…"

"Like I said, most criminals get caught because they're idiots. They can't make it in the real world, so they resort to crime. That's why we catch them."

"But Marcus was no idiot." It was an obvious point, but making it changed everything.

Jenny didn't see the trap she had just laid. But she saw Royce's shoulders edge forward and his brow furrow. He looked like an animal realizing it was caught, the tension in the trap's spring, steel clamping around his ankle.

"From what I've read, he sounds like an impressive kid. But still. Being good at chess or whatever, and being about to sneak up on Alex, shoot him at just the right spot and angle to make it look like it was self-inflicted, then clean the scene and escape all in a minute or two...that's remarkable, right?"

She cast her eyes at the pineapple motif in the rug as Royce answered.

"I've seen some things that don't make sense when you try to piece it together like this. I mean, incredible things happen. All the time. I've seen some bank shots that juries had a hard time believing, even when we drew the picture for them."

She went back to her Kindle. Royce flipped through channels, finally settling on SportsCenter. They sat consumed by distractions for a while.

"Yeah, and a kid like that would be capable of lots of planning and attention to detail." She picked up the conversation right where they left off.

"That's what I was thinking, Jen. I mean, he is a smart kid. Real smart. When I questioned him, he tied me in knots. I'm actually surprised we got him. If it weren't for that x-ray-whatever the kids in the lab use, we wouldn't be here."

"So why does he use his phone?" Snap. The accidental trap slammed shut. The simple question that would change everyone's life. "He used it right after he...you know. Why would he do that?"

"Maybe he was..."

"No, I mean, why risk it? Why not wait until he's back at home or at least far enough away so as not to raise suspicion." Jenny didn't realize it, but she was torqueing the trap tighter and tighter.

"I think the..."

"I mean who was he calling?" She said it half-jokingly.

Royce caught an image of Marcus, the image that Mr. Fernandez, the gardener, painted for him—green hoodie, bare legs, eyes on his cell phone, running away from a murder—

148

and suddenly it made no sense. None at all. It didn't fit with the methodical and clinical nature of the murder. The conversation with Officer Dziewulski sprang to the front of mind. A contraband Glock and no suicide note were pieces that didn't fit together either. And now, two more incongruous pieces had been shoved together. His wife had just blown his entire case wide open.

Royce shifted uneasily. His case—it was *his* despite the fact it was credited to Officer Dziewulski—was a sham. He was a patsy. They both were. He caught a glimpse of himself in the mirror, and it was revolting.

Jenny put down the Kindle. "Are you okay, babe?"

He wasn't okay. And he didn't know what to do about it either.

CHAPTER 27

Royce blew reveille at o-dark-thirty, and while Jenny finished a cup of coffee on the back porch of the inn, he got the girls out of their PJs. An hour later they boarded a plane for Pittsburgh.

He wanted to think about the case or get some more sleep on the short flight, but his girls wanted to play "Pass the Pigs!" He tried to be in the moment, this moment, with his girls rolling two small plastic pigs like dice, instead of thinking about Marcus sitting in a jail cell awaiting the latest Trial of the Century. Or, on the people who, he was increasingly convinced, were sitting somewhere toasting themselves for duping him and the entire world and pulling off whatever it was they were trying to pull off. *What are they trying to pull off? Who would want to kill a law professor and pin it on one of his students? A poor kid from the inner city?* It made no sense. Royce stared out the window as the plane leapt skyward, then jerked back when Jane rolled a double leaning joweler.

He stewed all day. That night, when Jenny slackened beside him in bed, he eased the covers back and slipped into khaki pants strewn on the floor. Gingerly retrieving his gun and badge, he headed for the FBI field office. Winding streets lead out of his hillside neighborhood down to the Monongahela River, and as he sped along its shoreline, littered with carcasses of Pittsburgh's industrial past, he thought of his own transformation and the bodies he'd littered by the side of the road.

He made the fifteen-minute trip in ten and parked illegally in front of the Carnegie Building, letting the siren lights hidden in the grill of his bureau car flash without sound.

By the time he keyed into his office, he was enraged. He was coming around to the idea that Jenny was right, even though Jenny wasn't actually making an argument one way or the other. Someone had set up Marcus, then set up Royce to get him. Once the idea of a double setup was raised, it was impossible to see anything else. It was like a pointillist painting— from one perspective it was nothing but a bunch of dots, but once the image is realized, you can't unsee it.

But what if the FBI brother gets involved? That surely would have been asked at the planning meeting. He could see them, faceless men in suits—he was sure they were all men— sitting around a large, oak table, plotting his brother's murder. They had to set a trap if Alex's pesky bro walked that way. The filed-off serial number was sloppily done, which allowed the FBI, but not the Chicago PD, to ID the weapon. This required pretty advanced knowledge of the capabilities of the FBI, and this thought made him seethe. Whoever was behind this was knowledgeable and clever. Suicide was the first and most likely resolution, but if the FBI brother snooped around, he'd be led to Marcus. It was an ingenious plan. The timing of the hit to correspond with people being around to hear and see, but not to hear and see everything. The delivery truck, the shorts and the green sweatshirt, and, of course, the cell phone. All of this was deliberate. The entire scene was a stage, and Royce was the leading man. A leading man who didn't know he was even in the scene. He'd been played. Even Royce admired the craft. These were pros.

He pulled a banker's box labeled "Operation Slapbox" from his office closet and dumped the contents on the floor. Time for a fresh start. He looked at each hand-labeled manila folder, read every note, and looked at every detail twice. He sifted and sorted the evidence until the sun poured through the windows of his office, hours later. At one point he fell back onto the floor and lay among the photographs, scraps of paper, and bags of evidence. Officer Dziewulski, the detectives from the Chicago PD, and the state's attorney had similar boxes, but theirs didn't contain the false starts and bad leads this one did. He held up the bag of syringes and looked up at them from the floor, before letting them fall to the ground with the other evidence. *Poor Alex.*

Ms. Rachelle found him asleep on the floor a few hours later. She appeared at his door holding a steaming mug of coffee.

"What happened in here, child?" Ms. Rachelle said loud enough to raise the dead.

Royce jumped up. "Oh, just a case that took an unexpected turn last night. Nothing really."

"This is your brother's case," she said, picking up a glossy photograph of Alex from the pile. "I seen it all over the news and knew you were the brains behind this." Her tone was that of a mother who was both proud and a little worried at what her son had done.

Royce looked up at her massive frame looming over him like a hovering angel.

"Intuition, dear," she said. "All the women in my family got it. We see things others don't." She handed him the coffee.

He managed a half smile, then sat up. "I could use some of your powers, Ms. Rachelle." She saw the look in his eyes, like something had gone wrong.

"What is it? That boy, he's the one who done it, isn't he?"

"Maybe. I..." He took a deep breath, "I don't know anymore." He took a big sip of coffee. "I'll pick up this mess." *My mess. Yup, that about sums it up.*

"Pardon me, sir." It was the first time she'd ever called him that. "I have to say that if you think there's any chance he didn't do it...I've seen too many young men taken from their families. I know many of them did bad things or, at least illegal things. And I don't like those gangbangers at all, you know

152

that. But the thought of a young black man with so much promise going away..."

She bent down to hide her face and started putting the evidence back in the proper files. They sat together, legs crossed, putting the papers back where they belonged. Ms. Rachelle picked up a set of papers containing phone records. She began to collate them, then stopped and scanned the floor.

"We're missing a page." She held out the phone records. "Page eight, nine, eleven..." she counted. "Page ten is missing."

Royce confirmed the missing page but thought little of it. He hadn't focused Alex's calls. Before turning the case over to Dziewulski, he ran down every call Marcus made in and around the murder and found nothing. But, because the clues came in waves just around the time his NSL hit and turned in Alex's phone records, he never really examined them in detail.

Looking now, he saw nothing leap out, but page ten, the last of the actual calls in the file, was the last few days leading up to Alex's death. It could be a key piece of the puzzle, and it was missing. *Had someone gotten to his files? Or, did someone within the FBI instruct Verizon to omit this potential crucial piece of evidence?*

He heaved himself off the floor and laid out the phone records over his desk, scanning for any hints at what might have happened.

"Here it is!" Ms. Rachelle shouted.

Royce peered over the edge of his desk, "What?"

"Page ten."

She stood up awkwardly and walked over, holding out a single piece of paper, arm extended.

"It was stuck to a page of a—what is this?—a...a bank statement—something sticky, maybe honey or something like that."

Deflated, he took it and put it in its proper place in the file. As he sorted the pages, he noticed something odd about page ten. Setting it on his desk next to the other pages—all filled with numbers dialed by and dialing Alex—one number repeated again. On page ten, two four-oh-four numbers appeared over and over again, sometimes two or three times an hour for several days. He looked back at the other pages, and saw the number a few times, but not in the density in which it appeared at the end of Alex's life. And no other number appeared that often on any of the days in these records.

"Four-oh-four," he muttered to himself.

"Huh?" Ms. Rachelle looked up at him from the floor, where she continued refiling his mess.

"Where is the four-oh-four area code?" He was already firing up his computer.

"Atlanta. My sister lives there," Ms. Rachelle said without looking up.

He typed one of the four-oh-four numbers into Google and hit search. The first result was the web page of an Emory University law professor named Roger Havens. A click on the link, and he was looking at the picture of a middle-aged white guy who seemed like central casting's answer to a request to send over a typical law professor. He had thinning hair, small round glasses, and was wearing a tweed jacket. Neither the name nor the face was familiar.

Royce manhandled the bulky phone around on the desk and dialed the number. The phone rang and rang. Nothing. It was 8:30 a.m. on a Monday. Maybe he was teaching.

He tried the second number, not knowing whether they were connected. On the second ring he heard the voice of a young girl, maybe ten years old.

"Havens residence, may I help you?" she said with impeccable manners.

They were connected.

CHAPTER 28

One hour and forty minutes nonstop from Pittsburgh to Atlanta. On the runway at Hartsfield-Jackson Airport, the Embraer 190 taxied in as Royce googled "Roger Havens." He was about Alex's age and they were both law professors. They went to different colleges, different law schools, and worked in different fields. Alex studied financial and business law; Havens studied criminal law. They never coauthored a paper together, and the conferences Havens attended regularly were not the ones Alex went to. If there was an overlap, it wasn't obvious.

After picking up a cheap rental, he drove straight to Emory. The schedule on the flat-panel monitor in the entryway of the law school told him that R. Havens was at that moment teaching a seminar on Sexual Crimes in Room C. A perky student in sweatpants and flip flops—not the appropriate sartorial style for a law student—directed him to the classroom. Peeking through the door's thin rectangular window revealed a few wide-eyed faces and a bunch of people staring idly at their laptops. Havens, or, at least he assumed it was Havens, stood slumped in front, leaning on a half podium that sat askew on the table. He turned toward the white board behind him, and when he did, caught Royce looking through the glass. They made eye contact.

At precisely five o'clock, a group of backpack-laden students burst through the door, followed by Havens, who turned off the lights and closed the door. He paused unnaturally long with his hand on the handle, staring into the classroom. Royce was leaning up against a wall checking his Blackberry when Havens approached.

"You must be Alex Johnson's brother?"

"I am."

"My family told me you called. I didn't expect a visit."

Royce tilted his head in the direction of a long hall that seemed less densely populated with students. He tried to look unthreatening, but the look of fear on Havens's face was unmistakable.

Havens followed down the hall, then pointed to a service corridor that stank of garbage and toner. The professor keyed into an unmarked office, flipped on the lights, and closed the door, making sure it was secure. Royce extended his hand, but the professor walked past him, took his phone out of his pocket, and turned it off. He walked over toward a large copy machine in the far corner of the room, put a blank piece of paper on the glass, and keyed in a request for two thousand copies. When the machine hummed to the task, he finally turned.

"Alex spoke of you often." His voice cracked. "The look, especially the eyes, is uncanny."

They shook and Havens leaned forward.

"I'm so sorry." He almost ended on a whimper.

"Sorry that I crept up on you. I tried calling—"

"Why did you come here?" Havens's mood changed in a beat from sadness to accusation, then to panic. "Are you alone?"

Royce pulled back and leaned on the copy machine.

"I'm trying to get a picture of Alex's last days. You guys talked a lot in the past few months. Sounds like you were friends."

"We are...were, I guess..."

Havens's eyes filled with tears, but Royce saw that it

wasn't just sadness. The man seemed terrified.

"I need you to help me, Professor. To help me understand my brother a bit better. We grew apart, I guess."

"I asked why you came here. To my work. To Atlanta. You've done a stupid thing, Agent Johnson. You've put us both in terrible peril." Havens walked over to the door and peered out through the frosted glass window. "You don't know what we're up against."

"I'm a federal agent, Professor." Royce tapped his fanny pack. "We'll be okay." The professor was a bit over-dramatic it seemed.

"You think you can protect us? With, whatever you've got in there." He pointed at Royce's bag. Havens was rocking back and forth nervously. If he didn't know better, he'd think Havens was mentally ill.

"You seem like you know more than I do, Professor. Can you bring me up to speed? How did you know Alex? And why are you so afraid?"

"How do I know I can trust you?"

"You can trust me. I'm Alex's brother. I'm one of the good guys."

"Even if I can, what's the point?"

Havens stood there, mouth agape, as the copy machine counted down like the timer in a Bond movie. Eighteen thirty-six, eighteen thirty-five, eighteen thirty-four...

"We were."

"Were what?"

"Friends. You asked if we were friends. I think Alex may be the best friend I ever had."

"I...I didn't know." Royce felt regret at not knowing. "How'd you guys know each other."

Havens, now over by the copier, slouched down on the floor, resting his back against the giant machine, still counting, seventeen oh-four, seventeen oh-three, seventeen oh-two... rhythmically spitting out blank page after blank page, doing its job but producing nothing.

"We met at a conference a while back. At first I thought it was just chance. But he came there to find me. We ended up talking for hours."

Royce raised his eyebrows. He didn't want to read between the lines, but at this point, anything seemed possible.

"About what?"

"What's the point, anyway?" Havens sighed and slumped even more. He seemed headed for the standing fetal position. "Everyone in this building is not going to be here in a hundred years. I'm not sure what…"

"Come on," Royce said with growing exasperation. He didn't need any ivory-tower existential angst; he had a murderer to catch. "We are here now, trying to do right. This is what we can do."

"I was quoting Xerxes, the—"

"What?" Royce rolled his eyes.

"They killed him."

"Who killed him? Xerxes?"

"Alex."

"Who? Who killed Alex? You've got to tell me." Royce stepped toward him, putting his hands on Havens's shoulders, and propping him up. Their faces were inches apart. "Who?"

"I don't know exactly." He closed his eyes again and shook his head.

"That's why I'm here. My job is to find out who and bring whoever they are to justice."

"Your brother had secrets. They haunted him. Did you know that?"

"What secrets? Why are you being so damn coy?" Royce turned and paced to the other side of the small room and back. Ten sixty, ten fifty-nine, ten fifty-eight…

"The story is about…I shouldn't…I can't."

"Well, in that case, I'll just fly back to South Carolina, fish his ashes out of the marsh, have the boys down at the lab reanimate him, and ask him about the secret that got him killed. Let's go with that plan."

"I loved your brother."

Royce wheeled his head around, shocked at what he was hearing.

"No, not physically. It wasn't that at all. We were...we were just friends."

"I see." He didn't.

"My wife left me because of him. Did you know that?"

"She mentioned you were separated, but she didn't..."

"You talked?"

"When I called the house looking for you. We just chatted briefly."

"Well, she asked me to leave because of what Alex and I were to each other these past months and how messed up I am now as a result of...his loss and all this. And she just thinks, well, she thinks I've lost it. That I'm a danger to the kids, to her, and to myself. She actually tried to have me committed. Can you believe it?"

"I believe you, Professor Havens. And, as corny as this sounds, thanks for being such a good friend to my brother."

Havens began to weep. "I think you should leave. There is nothing we can do."

Royce moved closer. He put his hand on the professor's upper arm and squeezed gently.

"That's what they want you to think. Isn't it time to stop keeping secrets? Isn't it time you stop protecting them? The bastards who did this. To us all. Isn't it time for..." Royce looked around the room, lined with old case books. "...for justice."

Havens lifted his head up. He wiped his face with both hands.

"It's time."

CHAPTER 29

August 1982
Pittsburgh, Pennsylvania

Alex crouched under the pool table, trying to control his breathing. After running at nearly full speed from the starting tree in the yard about two hundred feet away, he was breathing heavy, and this was a sure-fire way to give away his hiding place. He could sense someone else enter the space under the pool table, although at the far side. It was a beautiful nine-foot Brunswick the Captain inherited from his father. Twelve-year-old Alex ignored the other person and hoped for the best.

Soon, there was noise—screaming and running—and Alex could see the beam of light here and there as the seeker's flashlight searched the backyard. This was two-hand touch, so the ousting of a hider was not the end of the game. Choosing the basement and this spot under the pool table meant evasion was less likely, but so was being found. Everyone made their own choice in the tradeoffs of flashlight tag. Alex was fast for his age, but not fast enough. He chose hiding, not escape.

With the seeker diverted outside, Alex felt the other person under the table move closer to him. They were right next to each other, when he heard a gentle, "Shhhh." Alex froze. He didn't know who it was or what they were up to—*Who would jeopardize a hiding spot by moving and talking?* That was just nuts.

Then Alex felt a hand on his leg. He had a mind to smack it away or ask the person what was up, but he didn't want to give away their position—I guess it was *their* position now. He thought the person might just be feeling around in the dark. But then the hand started stroking his thigh and moving up toward his groin.

Over the next thirty years, Alex thought a lot about those minutes under the pool table. During those years, when he was afraid of being gay, or anytime someone jokingly called him a fag, he told himself he was probably thinking it was a girl's hand that gave him his first erection induced by another person. But there was only one girl playing that night, and, if he were being truthful with himself, he would have admitted he knew how Kimberly smelled—like fruity bubble gum—and that wasn't Kimberly giving him a hard on.

The truth was it didn't matter who it was—it felt good, and he didn't want it to stop. That message was not lost on the person groping him. Within a minute, his hand—Alex was sure it was a he at this point, since they were practically on top of each other—was rubbing his erect penis, which was deformed under his briefs and his tight jeans. Then, with a lurch, the boy was on top of him, kissing him on the mouth. Before Alex knew what hit him, the boy's tongue was in his mouth, and they were French kissing, or so he was told that's what that was. It was his first kiss, and man was it a doozy. Alex never imagined his first kiss would be from a boy, but it wasn't nearly as bad as he imagined it might be. In fact, it made him feel quite good, although he never told anyone that and would have denied it if asked. The "pool table incident" got no more graphic than that. The seeker found the hider, everyone came out and gathered at the starting tree, and Alex and Doug pretended that *that* never happened.

Doug was six years older than Alex. The families were friends too, which meant Doug was around a lot, and he was the kind of kid Alex looked up to. Actually, he was the kind of kid everyone looked up to. He wasn't tall, like the Johnsons, on the account of his Vietnamese heritage, but he was handsome and muscular, and he had a personality that was winning with the girls in his class. Doug was a stud, the girls would tell you. Alex liked him because he was a deadeye with a bow and arrow, and he knew a lot about medieval history, something that fascinated Alex from a young age. Doug also introduced him to Dungeons & Dragons, and although Alex was never invited to join the regular neighborhood game, which included beer he was told, Alex always admired Doug for teaching him how to play.

Alex thought a lot about that night, and he hoped it would happen again. It didn't take long. The next time they were alone was a few weeks later in the back room of the store owned by Doug's father. The Phams moved to America from Vietnam when Doug, then named Duc, was two years old. They came when Saigon fell. Quang Dũng Pham worked three jobs before he saved enough money to buy his own clothing store. Now, some sixteen years later, The Gentleman's Closet had six locations in the tri-state area. On that particular evening, Alex and his brother were helping the Phams do their quarterly inventory. While the Steelers played on the black and white television on a table in the corner of the store room, Alex sat Indian-style counting pairs of men's socks and underwear, recording the tallies in a large carbon-paper ledger book. After a while, everyone pitching in from the neighborhood went home, and only Alex, Doug, and Mrs. Pham remained. Alex volunteered to stay to finish up, while the rest of the crew left to celebrate a comeback win over the Broncos.

Alex and Doug sat across from each other, not saying much, other than an occasional remark about the frustrations of their task. But Alex hoped they'd find a way to be alone together. His body ached for it, and as his hands lifted and counted socks, his mind was focused on finding some way to get Mrs. Pham out of the store. When she came back into the storeroom to say she was going out for a few minutes to run an errand, for a moment Alex believed in the power of telepathy.

Seconds after the metal door to the back alley squeaked shut, they were on each other. The kissing this time was even more passionate, and their hands were going places and doing things that were new. Then, Alex felt Doug undo his belt and pull down his pants, revealing a bulge that at first made Alex nervous, but exhilarated at the same time. Doug kissed there gently, then gave him what Alex had heard was called a blow job. When Doug stopped after a few minutes, he took down his own pants expecting Alex do him the favor in return. Doug was much older and, Alex gulped, larger. It was thick and long and hairy. Something about seeing it frightened him that it would go in his mouth. He balked. But Doug put his hand on the back of his head and pulled him forward. Once it began, it wasn't the worst thing he could imagine, but he saw why they called it a "job." It was worth it, though; a pretty fair trade, he thought.

But, while Alex merely felt good and ended without a bang, Doug was demanding more. After about the time Doug had spent on him, Alex slowed down his rhythm looking to dismount, so to speak, but Doug used his hands to control the speed, holding Alex's ears like handle bars on his bicycle. Doug's moaning got louder and his thrusting more aggressive to the point where Alex felt uncomfortable and like he might get hurt. Then Doug let out a scream, and something wet and salty was in Alex's mouth. Alex spit it out on the floor, while Doug got up, put on his pants, and walked to the bathroom. Although if you'd asked him then whether it was worth it, Alex would have said it was, the night didn't go exactly as planned.

Over the next year or so, these rendezvous were a regular event. They each found ways of getting the other alone, and the location or time of day didn't really matter. They pleased each other or "messed around," as they came to call it, in the woods, after school in the basement, while their families were downstairs eating dessert, and in the garage behind Mr. Pham's Porsche 928. Although Alex desired, even craved these meetings, afterward he felt like he did after eating at McDonalds—the during part was great, but he always regretted the choice after the fact. Of course, he went back to both McDonalds and Doug's body repeatedly.

Like all physical relations among people, this one followed a familiar curve: passion, exploration, experimentation, boredom, and decay. Alex was a full-fledged and happy participant up to the experimentation stage. He was too young or too inexperienced to reach orgasm, so he never needed to go beyond the "basics," as he called it. But Doug wanted—*needed*—more. He urged Alex to bend over to accept him, but unlike the oral sex, it was not something Alex was remotely interested in. When it did happen, after many failed efforts, Alex felt as if somehow he'd made a giant mistake.

He'd told Doug no repeatedly, but this just increased Doug's need and his aggression. Denial was met with desire. The first time it happened, Doug pinned him to the ground with his weight, holding a hand over Alex's mouth. Alex screamed and bit the fleshy part of his thumb—enough that he tasted Doug's blood in his mouth as he felt the pain as Doug penetrated him. But Doug would not be denied his want.

It was at about this time that AIDS stories were appearing in the news every night. When Alex heard them, sitting with his parents at dinner, he clenched his butt cheeks with fear. The fears were enough to make him doubt the wisdom of his relationship, it was safe to call it that now, with Doug. They weren't dating—they did nothing together but have sex of one form or another—and the sex had gone from pleasurable to painful in ways that upset him. Alex cried himself to sleep every night after Doug took him from behind and thrust at him until he came. At night, Alex could feel Doug's cum inside him, and he wanted more than anything to get it out. When he did sleep, he heard Doug's grunting and snorting in his nightmares. Alex started looking for excuses for them not to be alone, and when they were, to keep things to the basics. Doug heard him say "yes" but never "no."

Then, it just kind of ended. They stopped being alone, whether by chance or on purpose, and within a few months, Doug was gone. The Phams sold all The Gentleman's Closet locations to a local competitor and moved to Miami. Doug went off to Stanford to college. Alex missed him, especially the early days when they were together, when Doug taught him about role-playing board games and when they used to kiss and stroke each other gently. But over the years, the main emotion he felt was fear. Fear and regret. As more and more people died of AIDS, Alex worried that he was a ticking time bomb. Every news story brought him sweaty palms and a dry throat. He calculated the incubation time, imagining how old he'd be when he could stop worrying.

But over time, Alex buried his conflicted thoughts about Doug under layers of history and memory. The pleasure surfaced on occasion, but so too did the pain and the feeling that he had in his entire body as Doug forced himself into him and thrust angrily until he came. Twenty years later, the layers of sediment had obscured the details leaving only the ossified bones of the experience. It was a fossil he lugged around, out of view. But it was excavated when the president announced that his rapist was going to be the next chief justice of the United States.

CHAPTER 30

June 2015
Chicago, Illinois

The For Sale sign in front of Alex's house had fallen from one of its hinges, so it dangled and twisted in the wind. Royce keyed into the house, which smelled dank and neglected. He went into the kitchen and poured himself a glass of wine. Then he went upstairs in search of the answers Havens told him were there, somewhere. Royce pulled the high-back leather chair tightly into position in front of Alex's roll-top desk in the library on the third floor. This was Alex's sacred space, where Havens said the information he needed to catch the killer was hidden.

Royce ran his fingers along the edge of the front of the desk with the care one would stroke a newborn's fontanel. His grandfather made this desk from wood the Captain cut down in the grove of walnut trees that shaded the pond where they all fished as kids. Those West Virginia trees, shaped by generations of Johnsons, now held Alex's secret. A secret that got him killed.

He woke the computer from sleep mode and opened an internet browser hoping to find some inspiration. The Google search bar stared at him, but he had investigators' block. Alex's bookmarks opened, and he selected Espn.com. The Pirates were losing five to nothing to the Nationals and were likely to miss the playoffs for the first time in a few years.

He leaned back and stared up at the ceiling, pushing the chair back to the precipice and feeling the tiny thrill of being about to tip over. Then he spun like a child on a merry-go-round, watching the clutter of his brother's library blur together like he was in a zoetrope. Maybe the books would animate and reveal a secret, he thought.

Getting up, he looked at the vast collection of books stacked three and four deep, and as many high on every shelf. The collection was disorganized, but Royce sensed there was some logic to it. He stepped into the middle of the room to see what sense he could make of the thousands of volumes.

On the far wall, there were lots of novels and non-fiction. He picked a few of them up and fingered their spines and ratty covers: *Animal Farm*, *Free to Choose*, *Atlas Shrugged*. They were the kind of books that would appeal to a high school or college student like Alex.

Toward the desk, there was a smattering of geology and medical books, then right next to the desk, lots of law. The organization in the disorganization was chronological, kind of. Alex's youth—Isaac Asimov's Foundation series, *National Geographic* volumes—were on the far wall, college and law school were in the middle of the room. Then the rise of Claire on the opposite wall, with chemistry and medical books, also chick lit, tons of art books, and a smattering of classics, Jane Austen and the like. Law books, the casebooks Alex researched and taught from, formed the library equivalent of the Berlin Wall. Beyond that wall of uniformly red and black legal casebooks were books about economics and law. A life lived in books.

Then Royce noticed an outlier. All the books near the desk were work books, except one. It jumped out at him, as if his brother were shouting, "Over here, you dumb lug!" Right up against Alex's desk, where one would reach to the left and find just the book for a key fact or citation, sat the *Guinness*

Book of World Records, 1979 Edition. It was as striking as if everyone in a picture were wearing tuxedos, except one guy in ratty old blue jeans.

He had been spinning slowly, like the library was in orbit around him as he divined his brother's system, but now he froze and he squinted at the book his brother carried around for years like a toddler's blanket. It was deliberately out of place. There was no doubt about it.

Royce pulled it from the shelf as one would a family heirloom. It was. He turned it over delicately and laid it on the desk so he could see the cover. That was it. The one Alex had his nose in at every sporting event and family outing, the one he quoted from endlessly, and the one that had become a running family joke. It wasn't just the book, but the actual one he had as a child, all ratty and faded and dog-eared. His memory of it was nearly perfect. Big Maddy Garlits's drag racer was right there on the cover as he remembered. The number 5.637 seconds burst into his mind. It frightened him. He found "Garlits" in the index, and there on page five-twenty-one saw his record-breaking time: the quarter mile in 5.637 seconds for a piston-engine dragster. How many times must his brother have read him that to remember it so clearly nearly four decades later? Once he pulled that book from the shelf, it was as clear to him as his own name. The book was a madeleine cake dipped in tea. It caused the past to leap forward to reveal itself, and Royce figured, Alex's secret along with it.

Royce flipped through frantically, looking for the treasure map, looking for Alex's message from the past. He paused at some of the pictures that reminded him of facts Alex obsessed about—the world's longest fingernails or the longest bridge span in the world. He turned the book on its side and held it by the spine with two hands, fluttering it back and forth. But nothing dropped out.

Frustrated, he closed the book and went to the window. Scanning the view in all directions, he stopped on the white-brick house just twenty feet to the left. It jutted out in the back further than Alex's house, so he could see down on the roof and through the window into what appeared to be a laundry or craft room. Junk was piled high. The image of the morbidly obese man who wept over losing Alex came surging back. He was the spitting image of Robert Earl Hughes. *The heaviest man in the world.*

Royce lunged for the book, flipped to the index, and found the name "Robert Earl Hughes"—page twenty-one. There, put firmly into the spine was a note in Alex's hand. The date on the top was April fourth, the morning he was murdered.

Pulling the page from the book carefully, Royce held it in his hand, feeling the texture and weight. Alex had written with a fountain pen; the letters were large and bold, and the ink soaked deep into the high-grade paper. He opened it, smoothing the page out.

Roy,

I don't have much time left, and so I'll keep this short. If you are reading this, I'm probably dead or missing or incapacitated in some way. Stop him, Royce. He is still doing these things, still hurting people. Take care of Claire and the kids for me. Tell them all my last thoughts were of them.

Here is what I know. I'm sorry I've got to tell you this. They killed me because...

CHAPTER 31

February 2015
Chicago, Illinois

The grandeur of the Union League Club ballroom in Chicago seemed an ironic setting for a panel discussion on inequality in the United States. Not many reminders of the Gilded Age were left in Chicago, but this was one of them. Sitting at the dais, waiting for his turn to speak, Alex imagined robber barons like Marshall Field and Charles Tyson Yerkes sitting in this room debating their latest business strategies. The men of that era, in their bowler hats and three-piece suits, would still find the tactics of business and politics discussed today familiar. Big business still influenced regulation although the presence of women, blacks, Jews, Catholics, and the lack of cigar smoke would have been notable differences.

When the panel was done, Alex shook hands with colleagues and beelined to the bar. He drank one scotch then retired to a set of plush chairs in the corner of the lobby area with his second. There were papers and magazines strewn about on the large marble-top coffee table, and Alex leafed aimlessly through *Crain's Chicago Business* and *The Economist* while he swirled and savored his drink. The clink of the ice, the slight smell of must in the drapes, and the bustle of business people moving around made him deeply relaxed.

He looked up to take in more of the surroundings, when he

saw Judge Duc Pham push through the revolving door entrance to the club. Pham paused in the grand foyer and turned to wait for his companion. Alex was fifty feet away and partially obscured by a large weeping fig tree in an ornate bronze planter, but he could see them as they approached. Pham was with a young man, or perhaps boy, of about thirteen or fourteen. Pham looked immaculate in a highly tailored pinstriped suit that hugged his muscular physique; the boy was wearing baggy jeans and a letterman jacket with HF emblazoned on the left chest. They talked as they walked, and both were smiling and happy. Alex didn't want to be seen, so he slouched in his chair and ducked behind a magazine. He lowered it when they passed and watched them enter the restaurant in the corner of the first floor of the club.

The first thing that popped into Alex's head was to wonder why Pham was in town and to marvel at the coincidence of him being at the Union League Club. A quick Google search answered his first question: Pham was a member of the Judicial Conference of the United States, a group of circuit court judges responsible for making policies for the administration of U.S. courts, and it was having its annual meeting in Chicago that weekend.

But Alex felt there was something strange about seeing Pham and that boy together. The boy looked like Alex at that age, although a bit more athletic and missing the glasses and the curly hair his mother insisted he wear on the long side. Alex couldn't help but wonder why the soon-to-be chief justice of the United States in town for high-powered meetings would be lunching with a high school freshmen or maybe even a middle schooler. There were innocent possibilities that ran through Alex's head: perhaps he is the son of a friend, and the judge was doing a favor; perhaps the judge was involved in an official mentoring program, and this was his mentee. Before he could think of other innocuous stories, Alex started to fidget in his chair.

He found himself standing behind the fig tree, looking in the direction of the café. He couldn't see them, and for a moment thought they might have gone to another part of the club. The scotches had worked to lower his inhibition so he went to the front desk, where a chubby man with a lazy eye told him there were no meetings of the Judicial Conference taking place at the Union League Club. Then, Alex went to the maître d' who told him there was indeed a reservation for Pham, but that both guests had arrived. Alex walked away and could feel the stare at his back. He walked along the hallway while scanning over the planters that separated the café's tables from the rest of the lobby area. There in the corner by the window, he spotted Pham and his guest in an animated conversation. Alex found a spot where he could stand by a pillar and be relatively unobtrusive but have clear view of their table.

The scene seemed completely innocent. Strangers would think a father and his teenage son were out for an executive lunch at their club on a nice Friday afternoon. Sure, the kid should have been in school, but father-son days like this were part of the social fabric today in a way unimaginable when Alex was a kid. The Captain would no sooner have taken him from school to go to lunch than he would have offered to buy he and his buddies beer. Times certainly had changed. But Alex knew this wasn't that, although he wasn't quite sure what it was yet. Pham had no children, adopted or otherwise; he was sure of that. He wanted desperately for it to be nothing more than it appeared. He hoped it for the boy, because he was that boy, and knew that despite his ability to function well in society, the costs were enormous. He hoped it for himself, as it would deeply complicate his upcoming congressional testimony. He promised to read what they wrote for him. He promised the president's men he would lie to Congress and to the American people. He promised...His mouth went dry at even the thought.

Alex also hoped it for the country, which didn't need to

hear about an accomplished man acting this way and a president who, whether she knew or not, was nominating him to be chief justice.

The waiter delivered a martini to the judge and what looked like a Coke to the boy. Alex breathed a sigh of relief. He wasn't plying him with alcohol, which was a positive development. It was unlikely the boy would pass as twenty-one, but private clubs were probably less strict about enforcing these rules, and if the waiter believed the judge to be his father, it wouldn't have been unthinkable for the judge to order him a beer. Maybe this was nothing. Alex felt himself relax as their lunches arrived.

The boy took bites of his hamburger and Pham pushed a salad around the plate with his fork. His eyes were wide and focused on the boy. He didn't look down at his plate. Alex gulped.

Then Pham offered the boy a sip of his martini, which the boy took. There were no other diners within twenty feet, and Pham was discreet. One sip became ten, and the judge ordered a second and third in due course. Alex fumed. He could feel his face redden and pulse quicken, and he wanted to go over to the table, grab the boy by the leather sleeve of his jacket and drag him to safety. But rage immobilized him. Rage and fear. The fear that they would do to him what they promised if he mentioned what happened to anyone.

So, he stood there shaking his head and thinking about the implications of what he was watching. But he also doubted what he was seeing. Alex tried innocent explanations but shot them all down. Still, he hoped for the best.

When he saw Pham pay the bill, Alex whispered, "Come on, go to the exit; drive the boy home." He was trying to will them to avoid the cataclysm about to happen. They stood together and walked slowly toward the lobby, and for a moment, Alex felt a sense of relief. Maybe he was going to rape the boy somewhere else, but if they walked out that door,

Alex couldn't be sure, and he'd fly to Washington and give his fake support to the judge in good conscience. He'd lie like they said. But, if, on the other hand...

As they walked toward the center of the lobby, Pham stopped and turned to the boy, leaned forward and said something into his ear. They paused, and Alex felt his life hung in the balance. Then they turned ninety degrees and headed toward the elevator. Alex's blood ran cold. He closed his eyes and blew a breath like a whale surfacing. Then he walked toward them. Alex walked full steam and they were standing still, so if one were watching, it would have looked like he was charging them and would have run into their backs. But in point of fact, Alex had no idea what he was going to do. He didn't face the choice, however, because the elevator door opened and they entered. Before they turned around, Alex darted to the side toward the front desk. He wasn't sure if he'd been seen.

The elevator's floor indicator, an old-fashioned model that looked like half of a clock, rose without stopping to the twenty-first floor, where the club had hotel rooms that members could use. Alex found a chair within view of the elevators and collapsed into it like he'd just run a marathon. His body ached and his mind swirled. He was briefly back in school, hearing Doug panting and groaning while he thrust at him from behind, Alex yelping softly "stop...no..." which only seemed to encourage him and make Doug moan louder. He tasted Doug's blood in his mouth and felt his semen dripping into his underwear.

Then, he was sitting at the table in front of the Senate Judiciary Committee staring at the microphone and looking down at his remarks wondering whether he would give them as written. Written not by Alex, of course, but by Bob Gerhardt and an associate he called Finny. Remarks they'd pushed across the table at Alex when they came to visit him in his office at Rockefeller.

Every time the elevator dinged, Alex looked up, but the faces were smiling and not the ones he was looking for. He sat their fretting and sweating for what seemed like hours but was actually only about thirty minutes.

Then he heard a ding and saw the boy. His face was ashen; he wore a look that Alex had worn at that age. It was like looking in a thirty-year-old mirror. The boy walked out of the elevator but was unsteady on his feet. He shuffled and looked this way and that furtively. Although it wasn't strange looking to casual observers, Alex had seen the boy bound into the lobby a few hours before as a different kid. Yes, there was no doubt he was now and forever a completely different person. Alex had half a mind to go up to him, put his arm around his shoulders, and have a heart to heart with him. He had this same talk with Roger Havens recently, and it did him a great deal of good. His life might have been much better had he had it with someone thirty years ago. Perhaps this was just what the boy needed. But the other half of Alex's mind, the half that told him not to intervene, to run and hide, and to pretend this never happened, prevailed. So, he stood there like Han Solo frozen in carbonite, watching the boy walk through the revolving doors and out into the street.

At that moment, Alex realized Havens was right. The sex he'd had with Doug wasn't a "relationship" and it wasn't even consensual. Havens called it what it was, rape. And he was still raping boys. Of course, Alex the lawyer amended his thought—*allegedly* raping *a* boy. He knew the conclusion and what he imagined were mere speculation. But Alex the victim knew them to be true. He wasn't looking at glacial striations and imagining Viking runes—those were the marks of a predator on that boy's face.

Alex stumbled over to the bar and ordered a double Dickel. He swallowed it in a gulp and quickly ordered another. Within minutes he was high but it only made his head spin more and his thoughts grow more paranoid and extreme. He thought about standing up on the bar and shouting to the lobby that the next chief justice was a rapist; he thought about storming the meeting of the Judicial Conference and telling Pham's colleagues what he'd just seen; he even looked up the phone number for the senior senator from Illinois, who he thought might be interested that he would soon be asked to vote to confirm a child rapist to the highest court in the land. But instead, he called Roger Havens.

"Roger, it's me, Alex." His words were slurred.

"Of course. Are you okay?"

"He did it again, Roger. He fucking did it again."

"Calm down. I can't really understand you." Havens heard what he said, but he wanted to hear it again.

"Pham. His holiness. I just saw him fuck a fucking kid. I'm going to be sick."

"What did you see, Alex? How did you see this?"

Alex told him every detail. When he was done, Havens was silent. Alex wiped the sweat from his brow with a Union League napkin. He could hear Havens swallow hard.

"My God, Alex. What are you going to do?"

"I don't know. I...Do you think they knew?"

"I'm sorry, I don't know what you mean. Who knew?"

"The president. The vetting team. His home-state senators recommending him. Do you think they knew he was a pedophile? They couldn't have known, could they?"

Havens went quiet.

"Roger? You still there?"

Havens's voice rasped like he was dredging the words up from the bottom of somewhere.

"They knew, Alex. They had to know. They knew."

Royce turned Alex's letter over, looking for a P.S. He went through the book several times. He walked back downstairs and out onto the front porch. The sun was setting behind the

Victorian mansions across the street. The sky turned from pink to purple to black. He didn't want to admit what was staring him in the face. Alex had damning knowledge about the president's pick for the Supreme Court and was eliminated when he didn't endorse the nomination. This meant the deed was done by employees of the federal government, just like Royce. There were plenty of party liners in the Bureau and elsewhere in the government who would do whatever they were asked to do, even kill innocent American law professors in their living rooms. The badge flashers, the evidence planters, the spotlight rangers.

He lurched forward on the porch and emptied his stomach into the hemlock hedge. He wiped his mouth, still hunched over the chipped cast-iron railing.

Back inside, in the powder room, he splashed water on his face and rinsed his teeth. He wanted to walk down his old street in Pittsburgh, burst through the door, drag Doug into the street, and punch his face into a pulp. He wanted to walk out to the living room, collapse on the couch and sleep for a week. But he could hear the ghostly hum of the photocopier at Emory counting down, and knew the only choice was to get them before they got him. He was outmanned, outgunned, outresourced, out-everythinged.

He needed help—a front man. Someone they wouldn't expect to do some dirty work.

CHAPTER 32

When Claire pushed through the doors leading to the cancer ward, trailed by a posse of interns and nurses, she caught sight of Royce, squatting in a chair several sizes too small, reading a picture book to a boy. Their eyes met. She barked out instructions and signed some forms before making her way over.

"Good to see you." Her voice was warm for a change.

"Can we find a place to talk?"

"Sure, sure." She took him by the hand and led him into a small conference room. The table was littered with half-eaten lunches of doctors called away. The two of them took seats, pulled them close, and sat face to face.

"I need your help."

"Selling the house? How's that going?" She was distracted by her pager.

"Claire."

She looked up and into his eyes.

"I'm not sure how to tell you this."

"Oh, God, what?"

"Marcus didn't do it."

"What do you mean? The DA said the case is open and shut. *You* told me he did it." Her tone became slightly frantic.

"I know, Claire." He exhaled heavily. "I was wrong."

"Then Alex *did* kill himself?" It was the only possibility she was open to.

"No, no he didn't."

"Then what? What are you saying?" She rose, involuntarily.

"Sit down. Please."

Claire wasn't used to following orders, especially from Johnson men, but she did.

"I understand this is a shock. It is to me too."

He put his hand on her knee, and she clutched his.

"Is everything...am I in danger?"

"No. But I need your help. And, truthfully, it won't be without risks."

She stared back at him. "I don't understand."

Royce told her: the missing phone records, Havens, the note. But mostly about what was done to their Alex.

"I knew Alex better than anyone, you know that. We had our problems, but we didn't have secrets. Not like this. Not something worth dying over. If there was something...something so serious in his life, you think he wouldn't have told me?"

"This isn't about your marriage. This is about Alex's demons. He hid this from everyone except some law professor in Atlanta. I don't know why he hid it from me and you, but he did and it got him killed."

"Poor Alex," she closed her eyes and shook her head slowly. "Poor, poor Alex."

"I'm glad my parents are dead. This would have..." Royce gulped.

"Where do I fit in here?" She sounded defeated.

"Pham is the key to this, and we need to find out what he's doing. Alex's note said he decided to come forward because Pham is still doing it. The only way I know to find our way to them is to follow him. He's our only lead."

"You want me to tail him like some kind of private investigator? What are you talking about?"

"You love kids. You care. What about the children he might be hurting right now, just like he hurt Alex?"

"I can't do it."

179

"Yes, you can. *I* can't do it. Pham knows what I look like."

"Oh, you—"

"He'll never expect you, Claire. You're a pediatric oncologist, for Christ's sake. No one will suspect you of anything other than being a saint."

"You want me to film him—I wouldn't even know how to—"

"No. As it happens, he's coming to Chicago in a few days to give a speech at Northwestern Law School. What I want— what I need you to do—is to go to the speech. Take the day off work. When the speech is over, follow him to wherever he goes. Maybe we'll get lucky and get some proof about what Alex was talking about or who he's working with. If he checks into a hotel, go into the lobby or watch him from the street. I'll back you up from outside. I'll follow where you go. We need...we need proof. We need the next piece of the puzzle."

"I think you're fucking crazy. And I can't believe you are asking me to do this. And what makes you think he'll be so sloppy—that we'll get so lucky that we'll catch him in the act? With so much at stake and the hearings around the corner..."

"I don't think the probability is high, Claire. But this is how the game is played. You can't find the evidence if you don't look."

"But..."

"Look, I know the type. We have profilers give us lectures from time to time, and there is a pathological type that just can't help themselves. It doesn't matter if it's insider trading or raping kids. You'd think they'd be rational, they'd be more careful over time, they'd stop themselves when the odds turned against them. But the opposite is true. The more they get away with it, the more arrogant they become. And arrogance leads to sloppiness. Cops just have to be there when that happens. We count on it; we don't catch them unless they get sloppy or we get lucky."

Claire nodded along. "Pathological arrogance. Sounds like

most of the surgeons I work with."

"Plus, this guy is probably drunk on power. Pathology mixed with power is the world's most dangerous elixir."

"Okay," she said in a resigned voice.

"So, you'll do it?"

"I'll go to the speech. That's all I'm promising. But I'll do it. What kind of person would I be if I said no?"

CHAPTER 33

Royce sat in a Chevy Malibu rental at the corner of Sheridan Road and Chicago Avenue in Evanston, watching the service entrance to Cahn Auditorium where Judge Duc Pham was speaking about his heritage and his judicial philosophy to hundreds of students and faculty. Claire had rented the car and bought him several burner phones plus four boxes of shotgun ammo. She was already sitting in the auditorium, playing concerned citizen.

A small entourage of SUVs and Secret Service agents milled about in the chill of this late spring evening, bumming cigarettes and talking trash about those they vowed to die protecting. Royce tuned in the Cubs game on the car radio.

Thirty minutes after the speech was scheduled to end, the agents stamped out their smokes and secured their earpieces. Royce turned off a two-two game in the seventh and shifted the car into gear. He didn't see Pham emerge but watched as the SUVs turned out of the alley onto Chicago Avenue. Then he saw her, just the side of her face, with her blonde hair pulled back tightly in a ponytail, as she piloted her Audi wagon after them. He could see the tension in her jaw and her hands, which were strangling the glossy wooden wheel.

He turned out behind her, a few car lengths away, following from a distance. The small convoy turned left on Clark Street toward the lake, lined with grand homes. They all turned on Sheridan Road, which took them south to Lake

Shore Drive and the city.

Royce had expected this route and scouted it earlier that morning. He took two side streets between Evanston and the city, looping back each time to Sheridan Road and finding the conspicuous convoy and Claire's cherry-red Audi a few cars behind. He'd thought about planting a second car along the way and doing a switch, but decided against it since trailing Pham wasn't what they'd be expecting. If it were, Pham wouldn't be doing public appearances in Chicago. And, with Claire as his rabbit, he could keep far enough back to avoid detection.

The SUVs pulled into the turnout for the Sheraton Chicago, set on a high bluff overlooking the Chicago River. He parked across the street on North Water Street. It provided him an unobstructed view of the entrance to the hotel, and from there, he saw Pham leave his SUV, straighten his jacket, and head gingerly into the lobby. He also saw Claire pull in, leave her Audi with the valet, and slip him some money. Smart. *Keep it close.* The valet pulled the car out of the way and to the side. She followed Pham into the lobby, looking like a pro. He'd picked the right partner.

Royce's burner buzzed. *R U there? What do u want me to do?*

He typed back: *Stay on him. Keep in touch.*

He got out of the car and headed around toward the back of the hotel. But there was no rear access from the street, since the hotel butted right up on the river. He didn't want to risk going in the front, not knowing who was looking out. So he stood on the bridge, watching the Chicago River dance in the moonlight. The River Esplanade, as it was known, was a narrow path lined with trees and benches that provide an ideal escape from the bustle of the city. He eyed the walkway that led along the water, seeing lovers walking hand in hand, and an occasional biker or rollerblader glide by.

The burner vibrated again.

Claire: *He's headed out of the back of the hotel toward the river. Should I follow him?*

Royce: *Alone?*

Claire: *No.*

Royce: *Who's he with?*

Claire: *No idea. Looks like a kid. 12ish?*

Royce: *SS?*

Claire: *What is SS?*

Royce: *Secret Service.*

Claire: *Yes. Couple of big guys. Staying back. Waiting by the door.*

Royce: *DO NOT FOLLOW.*

Claire: *What then?*

Royce: *Go in to the lobby. Get a drink. Wait for him to come back.*

Claire: *OK*

Royce jerked his head up from the phone and spotted two men exiting the hotel's entrance along the esplanade. He couldn't be sure it was Pham, and he didn't want to use his pocket binoculars since agents might be watching. Instead, he walked to the other side of the road, pretending to talk on his phone. He looked up at the skyline, then down to the Esplanade in time to see the two figures emerge from under the Fahey Bridge. They were headed west, upriver away from the lake and toward the heart of the city.

A set of stairs led down to the esplanade, but he thought better of it. Claire said the Secret Service were back at the hotel, but he couldn't be sure there weren't others, and, in any event, Pham might recognize him, even in the dark. He wanted to race after them, grab Pham by the neck, and beat him to a pulp. Being a pro meant knowing when to press and when to sit back in a zone defense.

Squinting into the darkness, he saw the two figures, now

no bigger than Lego figurines, sit down together on a bench under the leaves of a large oak. They sat close, but he couldn't make out what they were doing. He needed his team— multiple eyes and ears on Pham from various angles. Photos, video, audio. And snipers. He could see where he would have deployed them, along the walkway on the other side of the river, posing as dog walkers and bikers, on foot on the various bridges spanning the river. They would be watching, listening, and, most importantly, recording every move he made. But instead he was alone, save a frightened pediatric oncologist sitting in the hotel lobby, nursing a vodka tonic.

Darkness fell. The traffic on the esplanade thinned, then he couldn't see anyone, including Pham. There were no lights, which struck him as odd, but having never been there, he couldn't reach any conclusions. Out of luck, he made his way back to the other side of the bridge, where the lights from the hotel illuminated that part of the esplanade. But he saw nothing. He was about to head back to the car when the phone buzzed again.

Claire: *They're back.*
Royce: *Status?*
Claire: *Waiting for elevator. What should I do?*
Royce: *Who's he with? The kid?*
Claire: *Does he have a kid? Is he going to...?*
Royce: *Stay put. Give it another hour. OK?*
Claire: *K*
Royce: *Can you get a picture?*

Claire didn't respond. He walked back to the car, turned on the ignition to get some heat, and grabbed a granola bar from his bag—it was the first thing he'd eaten since lunch. He wanted to google Pham again to see if he could figure out who the kid was but dared not turn on his smart phone. If they were tracking him, he needed to stick to the burners. So he sat there in silence, staring up at the Sheraton, wondering what Pham was up to. He was sure it was something.

About thirty minutes later, the phone buzzed.

"It's me." Claire's voice was hushed.

"What's up?"

"The kid just came down the elevator. Alone."

A young man exited the hotel and stepped into a waiting car. He was gone in an instant.

"Claire, are you there?"

"Yes. What do you want me to do? Should I follow him?"

"We're done for tonight—go home. And thank you."

"But I saw something."

"What'd you see?"

Royce heard a shuffle, some shouting.

"Claire? Claire? What's going on?"

The line was dead.

CHAPTER 34

Royce grabbed his shotgun from under the front seat and pushed five rounds into the chamber. He slipped it under his jacket and bounded across the street toward the hotel. He spun through the revolving door, hand on the weapon. Claire was standing on the marble floor of the lobby, head in her hands. Royce raced over.

"What happened!?"

She lunged into his arms.

"It's okay, you're alright, I've got you," he said as he patted her back.

Holding her tight, he scanned the lobby like a periscope. Nothing unusual. Tourists and business travelers milled about, a few looking askance at them. Thankfully no one noticed the weapon.

He practically carried her to her Audi, which was still parked out front, plopped her in the passenger seat, took the keys from the valet, and in under a minute they were on Columbus Drive headed out of the city.

Claire was a far cry from her normal, clinical self.

"The boy, that boy."

"What about him? Did you get a picture?"

"I couldn't."

They merged onto Interstate 55 South toward St. Louis, then to the interstate the locals call the Dan Ryan. They drove in silence, exiting at 95th Street in a neighborhood they were

sure wouldn't give them up. They headed west. After a few depressing blocks of junkyards and tattered buildings, they found
a nearly empty fast-food restaurant. Soon they were sitting in a
booth munching on butter burgers and frozen custard.

"What did you see? Tell me exactly."

"It was just, well, the kid had this look on his face."

"What do you mean?"

"I was sitting at the bar and had a good view of them
when they came in from their walk. I saw them walking together, practically arm in arm. They were chatting and laughing, smiling at each other. The kid was happy. He almost
looked drunk."

"Okay," Royce said between bites.

"I didn't think much of it. But then, the kid came down the
elevator, and it was like a different person. He was ashen. I
know this won't make sense to you, but it reminded me of the
kids about that age when we tell them they have cancer. They
come in with a bruise or a bump on their leg, and they're
laughing about texts with their friends, then, BOOM, I ruin
their life. As soon as they see me they know, but they don't
really know; they don't look like that kid until they hear the
C-word. Then, in a second, the blood is gone from their face,
and they look like, well, like they've seen death, I guess."

"And this kid, he looked that bad?"

"Yeah, like something terrible had just happened."

Alex's note came to his mind's eye, the elegant letters made
with deep blue ink: *He is still doing these things, still hurting
people.* The images, conversations, hints, and memories came
like a torrent, flooding his investigator's brain.

"Alex saw the same thing. Right before he died. Right before they killed him. Until he saw it happening to somebody
else, he likely thought what he and Doug did was as an innocent thing, that it was ancient history. But then he was trig-
gered to reconsider. Until he saw it with his own eyes, from the
outside, he thought it was two kids messing about. Then he

realized he was raped, that Pham was and remains a predator."

"Oh my God." Her head fell into her hands on the table. He reached over and touched her lightly on the top of the head.

"My sweet Alex," she mumbled. "That poor little boy. You know our son..." She couldn't finish the thought, but Royce knew that Alex's boy was now about the age he was when Doug raped him. The thought made him shudder.

"Your son is safe, Claire." Royce reassured her, but he couldn't know this for sure. *Was anyone ever safe from these things?*

"It must have...I can't believe I wasn't there to help him. Our stupid fighting, over what?" She shook her head, then looked up. Tears streamed down her face. Royce offered her a napkin, then used one to wipe his own eyes.

"I've got to confront him. I've got to tell him that I know what he did and is doing, and that he has to step aside or I'll go public." He clenched his jaw, going from sympathy to righteous rage in an instant.

"But they'll kill you, just like Alex. Don't be stupid."

"I don't think they will. Not an FBI agent. Not two brothers. They won't be able to explain that away."

"But how will you get close to him? They're already protecting him like crazy."

"There's always a way in. Always. You just have to look for it."

CHAPTER 35

June 2015
Pittsburgh, Pennsylvania

The auditorium of the St. John's School for Boys was packed, although by compulsion rather than choice. Several hundred boys stood and applauded, all clad in their maroon blazers with the crest of St. John on the pockets. Duc Pham, the day's guest speaker and member of the Class of 1983, had just given a speech, and it was a hit.

The headmaster rose at the conclusion of the clapping, and thanked Pham for his contributions to the school, noting that he was selected as lead boy a dozen times, a record that still stood. He also noted Pham's generous mentoring of St. John's graduates over the years, pointing out that he'd hired several alumni as law clerks during his many years on the bench.

At the end of his remarks the boys exited in single file by class and height, as they always had. The headmaster and Pham then came down from the podium and walked out into the leafy courtyard. Secret Service agents were in all the corners of the courtyard, but they gave the two a wide berth. They talked about the future of the school and what role Pham could play in it as they walked toward the headmaster's conference room. As a special treat, the headmaster had arranged for the judge to meet with several of the school's top students who expressed an interest in law. For the five boys, aged twelve to fourteen, it was the opportunity of a lifetime. As they came to the door, Pham sent the Secret Service agents away, telling them to wait outside. The headmaster excused himself, saying he had another commitment and, in any event, wanted to give the judge some time alone with the boys.

Pham opened the door and walked in. He was surprised that the boys were not there by the door waiting to greet him in the way he expected from St. John's boys. In fact, it appeared as if the room was empty. Pham turned to his right and looked down the length of the oak table that extended the length of the room. Royce Johnson, class of 1985, sat alone. His left hand lay flat on the table and his right hand was out of sight.

Pham thought about turning heel and retreating to the protective web of his security detail but recognized his old family friend. And not knowing the play, he decided not to panic. There was little danger in such a place, especially with his team just a shout away.

"Royce, I'm surprised and delighted. How have you been?" Pham said cheerfully. He bounded over to the other end of the table, hand outstretched. Royce pulled his right hand from under the table and set his service weapon down with a thud. He pointed to a chair and nodded for Pham to sit.

"I know what you did, Doug."

Pham glanced nervously out the large window to an empty courtyard three stories below. "Did what?" He sat down with a thump and pulled his chair in tight to the table. "And, for the record, it's been Duc for quite a while."

"I'm not a fool, *Duc*, and I'm not messing around."

"What are you talking about? And, for goodness sakes, put that away," he said motioning toward the piece.

"Alex left a note. He told me what you two...*did*. Or, rather, what you did *to* him."

"He prepared a wonderful statement. He did it on my behalf—"

"Cut the shit. You raped him, you son of a bitch!"

Pham shook his head vigorously.

"You're going to step down from the nomination or I'm going public," Royce spat.

"Don't be ridiculous. The confirmation hearings are over. The senate has scheduled a vote I'm predicted to get at least fifty-two votes. I'll be in place for the October term."

Royce leapt from the seat, and grabbed Pham by the hair, shoving him into the table. He put his Smith & Wesson .45 against his well-groomed temple.

"You're delusional! Get off me!"

Royce pressed down, smashing Pham's right cheek against the oak.

The man went rigid. There was a trickling sound. Royce looked down to see piss was streaming down Pham's leg.

"Tell me who killed Alex. Who pulled the trigger?"

"What?" Pham gave a strangled cry.

"Who did the deed?" Royce used his left hand to pull back the S&W mechanism, seating a round in the chamber.

"Take the gun away from my head and I'll tell you." Pham squirmed like an animal in a trap. "Just get that thing away from me."

The gun lowered as Royce slowly released.

Pham sat up in his chair, wriggling in his soaking wet trousers, smoothing out the wrinkles of his suit jacket with his hands.

"Okay. Here's what I know..." With a lurch, he dove to the floor and rolled out of reach. "Help, HELP! He's got a gun!"

Royce reached under the table and pulled his Mossberg shotgun free from the duct tape that held it securely in place. He fell to one knee and raised the twelve-gauge to the door to the conference room.

Crash! Two Secret Service agents burst through the door, weapons drawn. A round of buckshot let fly from the Mossberg, scattering at their feet. The agent on the left fell to his knees as some pellets struck him in the shin.

The other agent returned submachine gun fire, letting go a volley of 7.62mm rounds into the oak table. Royce ducked and rolled to his right, emerging on the long side of the table just long enough to fire off another round. This one he aimed high and slightly to the right of the stunned agent's head. The agent dove out of the room while the shot hit harmlessly into the drop ceiling of the conference room. Wheeling one hundred eighty degrees, Royce blasted out the window. In the split second remaining, he leaped—

CHAPTER 36

It was a hard landing. The slim jut of the administrative-wing roof was just below the conference room, but his knee still buckled. Royce went into a roll and came to a stop on his back, fumbling for the Mossberg, and glaring up at the window above. A face appeared, flashed a gun barrel, and then withdrew. Royce looked over his shoulder to see why, and the answer was plain—the courtyard was starting to fill with boys leaving the speech. He crawled to his feet and limped over to the fire escape, slinging the shotgun crosswise over his shoulder. It was his knowledge of the various escape routes that made the place ideal to confront Pham.

On terra firma, he headed along the north side of the Quad, hugging the ivy-covered walls of the classroom wing. A fire alarm started to echo across campus as he limped along, trying to hide his shotgun and his injuries. More and more people came from the buildings that surrounded on four sides. *The more bystanders in the quad, the better.* He tried to quicken his step, dragging his knee through flares of pain. *Almost there.* An alley separated Mellon Hall and the new art wing, dedicated this year to Pittsburgh native Andy Warhol. His car was there, parked behind a dumpster with the hazards on.

But as he turned the corner, two men in suits surfaced behind a window, and a Pittsburgh PD cruiser parked obliquely at the point where the alley emerged onto Darlington Road. They'd cordoned off the area quickly. In that moment, the officer in the police car caught his eye, saw either the shotgun slung on his back or recognized the look of shock on his face, and turned on the siren. The agents looked out the window as Royce broke into a jog. As he turned the corner, they blew out the window and shot recklessly down the alley.

He dove behind a dumpster and aimed the Mossberg back down the alley, firing three blasts in succession, before running along the building, away from sirens that were growing louder.

A helicopter chattered in the near distance, and a glance over his shoulder showed at least four agents in pursuit about a hundred yards back, weapons at their sides. His only saving grace was the boys running to and fro in the Quad, seeking shelter from the gunshots. In a few seconds they'd be gone, and he'd be a sitting duck.

Royce surged ahead, damning the burning and shooting pain. He bounded up the stairs of the Charles Adams Gymnasium and Natatorium. He vaulted the turnstile, and the kid at the desk didn't even have time to object. Turning sharply to his right, he slid sideways, careened off the wall, then raced down the hall toward the pool. Shouts behind betrayed the Secret Service bellowing at the kid on the desk. Twenty yards down the hall, he burst into the boys' locker room and a minute later was skidding on the pool deck.

A swim class was in progress. Boys in their maroon and white swim caps caught sight of the Mossberg barrel peeping out over his right shoulder. They stopped swimming to tread water. One kid looked panicky. Royce nodded at them and relaxed his body language. He even gave them a little wave. *What part of the pool was the mechanical room located in?*— it had been thirty years. In the far corner, he saw a door he remembered. He and his cronies—the Apostles, an ode to the patron saint and namesake of their school—used to come through it when sneaking into the pool after dark those many years ago.

He took off running along the long side of the pool, the

swimmers watching him stumble and slide along the deck. The swim coach shouted as he reached the end of the deck and grabbed a starting block. Swinging himself around to the left, he made the turn for home. The door to the mechanical room gave way with a kick, and he leaped through just as shouts heralded that the agents had found their way. He slammed the door shut.

Feeling along the wall, he flipped on the light and saw where the main pump was. Then flipped it back off. The pump was as big as a Prius and nearly filled the whole room. He leaped on top of it, turned sideways, and squeezed to the side, working his way to the back. Once there, he fell to his knees, and found a manhole cover. He said a quick prayer. That cover had waited thirty years to see him again.

Heaving and struggling, he kept an eye out for a beam of light to enter the dark room under from the door to the pool. After what seemed like hours, but was thirty seconds, he slid it to the side and dropped down into the hole. His feet struggled for purchase on the iron ladder that just had to be there. His toes found grip. With one foot on the rung, he pulled the cover back over the hole and let his body slide. Ten feet below, he landed with a thud. Pain shot out the top of his head.

He was in the steam tunnel. It ran in both directions. His mind cast back to when, as a senior, the Wolf Pack snuck out after curfew and found a manhole cover on Wightman Street. When the coast was clear, they dropped one by one down into the darkness. Dressed in sweats over swimsuits, and carrying one flashlight and two six packs of Iron City beer, they'd turned...which way had they turned? He spun around, trying to get his bearings, looking into the darkness. He was fairly certain they'd come from that way...*left*! Fifty paces down the tunnel he heard scraping and footfalls, like men were coming down the ladder. His breath stopped, heart thudding in his chest. Which direction would they go? His pace quickened, trying to be silent while his knee screamed. Every twenty steps or so he checked over his shoulder but saw no flashlights. Yet. They had gone in the other direction. But they'd turn back. He had to make it to the next manhole.

Thirty seconds later a shot echoed about a hundred yards behind. Pipes ran along the sides of the tunnel but he had no idea what was in them. If they shot the wrong pipe, they could all be cooked by a burst of hot steam shooting down the tunnel. But cooking to death was the least of his worries.

He lurched on, gripping the Mossberg like it had strength to give. Another twenty steps and he came to a ladder. He stepped up it and raised the manhole cover just enough to peek out. Cars zoomed by. But it was enough to get his bearings.

Below, distant flashlight beams flickered as he pulled the smartphone from his pocket. He hadn't used it in weeks; using it was suicide. He could be tracked, but hopefully not quickly enough. He willed his hands steady and turned off airplane mode. The LTE network engaged. Flashlight beams began crawling over the sweaty pipes. Echoes came within earshot. He flicked urgently to a taxi app and set the location for the American Legion Memorial Garden at the intersection of South Dallas Avenue and Forbes Avenue. He prayed that the weak glimmer of his phone wasn't visible.

He was ten feet underground, but the app saw only two dimensions. His ride, a green Civic driven by Frank, turned on-to Forbes Avenue about a quarter mile away. He flipped his phone back into airplane mode—they had only a few seconds to track him and that was all he needed.

He raised the manhole cover up again. This time, a blaring car horn leaked into the tunnel. The voices turned into shouts—they'd figured out it was him.

He threw the manhole cover over and popped his head out. On the street a few people sat at a bus stop staring at their phones. It was broad daylight, someone was sure to see him. Too bad. He climbed out of the hole and shoved it back into place. Cuddling the shotgun under his jacket, he ran in the direction of his ride. Seconds later he waved the Civic down and dashed over. He got in the back.

"You Royce?"

"Yup."

Twenty yards behind, the manhole cover raised an inch and then dropped.

"Where to?"

"Anywhere."

The manhole cover heaved again, higher this time.

"Company policy, I need a destination."

The cover slid half a foot into the street.

Royce wracked his brain. "Take off. Just drive."

The driver sat stubborn as a Buddha.

Clang! The manhole cover flipped back as unseen hands gave a mighty shove.

"The Double Eagle Pub in Braddock! Fifty bucks if you floor it."

The Civic accelerated so hard Royce was thrown back in the seat.

"Mister? Mister?!"

Royce jerked awake and wiped slobber off the corner of his mouth. He opened his eyes after what felt like a full night's sleep—it had been less than fifteen minutes. They were in front of a ramshackle corner building with a neon Yuengling sign hanging askew on a rusty chain.

Royce handed over a crisp one-hundred-dollar bill.

"I don't have change."

"None needed. The extra fifty's a request."

"What's that?"

"A request to forget. Don't give anybody anything. No details, just play dumb."

"Been doin' that my whole life." The driver laughed and tucked the bill into his shirt pocket. "Thanks! You made my week."

Cradling the Mossberg under his jacket again, Royce stepped out into a movie set of decaying industrial America. The streets were covered in a thin film of dirt. Litter dotted the landscape. A group of four young men walked past, aimless and arrogant. It was the middle of a workday. He was back in Bronzeville.

He pushed into the Double Eagle, bathed in darkness and the smell of stale beer and b.o. A Willie Nelson song played in the background, while a few old timers nursed beers, their eyes on the water-warped bar or *Jeopardy!* playing on an old tube TV. At the bar, he ordered three shots of whisky and a bag of ice. The smartphone switched off airplane mode again so he could log into a rarely used Facebook account.

"Bartender, can I get a piece of paper and a pencil?"

The barkeep delivered the shots and the paper and pencil, a stub with no eraser and chew marks along the shaft.

Downing the shots, he wrote out a note. Tucking it under the phone, he raised another hundred dollar-bill at the bartender. "Please leave this here? Some men in suits will be coming in a few minutes. I want to make sure they find it."

"Okay," the bartender said, curiously.

"This place have a back door?"

The bartender pointed. Royce laid down the money and walked out into the alley.

"What's it say?" a voice chirped from the end of the bar.

The bartender picked up Royce's abandoned phone. He pushed the home button. It was locked, but he saw a picture of two men in a kayak, soaked to the skin, raising a beer in a victory salute.

He unfolded the paper note. It read, *Alex Johnson sends his regards.*

CHAPTER 37

A few miles upstream from the steam tunnels, down Talbot Avenue toward the Rankin Bridge, this section of the Monongahela River used to bustle with activity. Now its shores were littered with only the footprints left by the giant mills, long since decamped for Alabama or Mexico. The mills left desperation in their wake, and rusting carcasses of days gone by. Royce limped up the shoreline and climbed through a hole in a chain-link fence that surrounded a yard full of tankers, eighteen-wheeler trailers, and cars in various states of decay. Among them was an unobtrusive Honda Accord with a faded Penguins bumper sticker.

Good ol' Claire. She'd come through again, arranging things long distance in advance of the Pham meet-up. Scattered around Pittsburgh, in practical reach of three possible escape routes, were various ways out.

Fishing beneath the front license plate, his fingertips detected a key taped in place. Inside the car, under a blanket on the back seat, was a small doctor's bag loaded with essentials—bandages, stitches kit, antibiotics—some spare clothes, and a bag of food. He wrapped the ice from the Double Eagle on his knee in an Ace bandage and popped four Advil.

Minutes later, the Accord cornered into a decrepit station with cheap gas, the kind of place with less-than-great video security. He headed for the restroom, taking along the spare clothes and a razor. A different person emerged wearing glasses and a Penn State hat.

Back in the car he opened the glove box and found one of Claire's burners. Dialing Jenny, his throat went dry.

"Listen, Jen..."

"Where are you?"

"It doesn't matter. I don't have time to explain. Get the kids from school and get out of town for a few days. Like we planned."

"What? What's going on?" She knew better than to ask where he was.

"Do as I say, for your sake and the kids. Go to the basement and open the gun safe. The combination is on the underside of the top right drawer of my desk. In there is a bag. Take it. Go to my parents' house in Deep Creek. You know how to get in. Stay there until I get in touch. Understand?"

"What's in the bag?" She choked a little.

"Things you'll need, and a few you won't, hopefully. Now hurry."

"But—"

"I love you."

He hung up, dropped the burner to the floor of the car, and sped out of the gas station. It was nearly noon and he was about fifteen minutes from the Greyhound station where a bus left every day for Arlington, Virginia at 2:45 p.m.

At a red light he texted Ms. Rachelle: *Meet me at the O in 10. Bring the ball. Bradshaw.*

When Ms. Rachelle's phone beeped and she looked at the message from an unknown number, she felt a chill go down her spine. Bradshaw, as in Terry, the famous Steeler quarterback, was a prearranged code name arranged with her favorite agent in the event he was in need of the utmost discretion. Already, rumors were circulating around the office secretarial pool. Soon, the ASAC would make the calls that would start processes that most agent didn't know existed. Ms. Rachelle found herself the sudden object of everyone's attention. She didn't know what to believe, having known Royce longer and better than anyone. A decision had to be made. Was he worth the risk?

She peered over the walls of her cubicle and, holding her phone under her desk, typed back: *Cheese fries on me.*

Fifteen minutes later, Ms. Rachelle pushed through the door of The Original Hotdog Shop in Oakland and saw him sitting at the back, a Penn State hat pulled low over this brow. He was reading the *Post-Gazette*, turned to the sports section. She worked her way through the lunch rush to the table where Royce was already noshing on a couple of fully loaded dogs. She pulled a black roller bag behind her like she was dragging a body.

"What's going on?" she said in hushed tones as she pushed the bag to him under the table.

"Talk naturally, act naturally."

"That's kinda hard, don't you think?"

"What have you heard? Grab a dog and eat. Eat."

"Just that the Secret Service is looking for you, that your badge and privileges are revoked, and that I'm supposed to contact the ASAC as soon as I hear anything from you."

"Wow, that was fast." His eyes were peeking into his go bag to make sure it was all there.

"What happened to your hair?"

"I lost it on the way here."

"Look...Royce..." she said with a mouth full of chili cheese dog, "...you've been there for my family many times. I'm just repaying my debts for what you've done for my boys."

"I did that because it was the right thing."

"Likewise, Agent, likewise."

They ate in silence, but the grease never tasted so bad. After a few minutes, Ms. Rachelle looked into his eyes.

"What now?"

"Find who killed Alex. I don't know who pulled the trigger, but I know why. The scrambling you see is them reacting."

"Good Lord, child. What's happening? The Secret Service killed your brother? Are you crazy?"

"Big things. Scary things. What I need you to do is to play the fool. You haven't heard from me, you don't know anything about Marcus being innocent, you haven't noticed any strange things going on in my work, and, most importantly, you have no idea where I or my family might be. Is that clear? Can I ask that of you?"

"I don't know nothing about nothing. Got it."

He got up to leave and placed his hand on her arm.

"Pray for me."

CHAPTER 38

April 2015
Arlington, Virginia

Every time Sean Flanagan walked through the heavy wooden
doors of Saint James Catholic Church, he felt physically sick.
The cross and the smell of the incense and the dank feel created
by the church's thick stone walls. But it was the sight of Father
Case in his vestments that caused Sean's heart to race, the
sweat to pool under his armpits, and his throat to dry up.
When he saw the collar and the priest's black frock, he felt
afraid. His mind replayed images that his consciousness was
trying to suppress. It was as if he were replaying the scenes of
decades ago on the television in his mind, but to keep from
seeing it, he tossed the television into the bottom of a swimming pool. While most people would only see blurry images
through stinging eyes and hear sounds warped by the density
of the water, this was a show Sean had lived through. Even
the distortions could not keep him from reliving the experience in full. He knew this script by heart and could say the
lines with just the slightest visual clues.

Sean was particularly nervous as he headed down the center aisle toward Father Case's office. Every time he stood at
the entrance to the church by the marble bowl of holy water,
he felt tremors. Although he hadn't been back a regular at
services since he graduated from high school, he knew the only

person he could trust to vouchsafe his secrets was a priest.

When he'd first thought this, he cursed himself. How could he trust those bastards? But he knew that whatever had been done to him, the average Catholic priest today was the most reliable confidant he was likely to find. Another lawyer would be duty bound to protect his secrets, but when push came to the point of a machine gun or a career-ending threat from the executive branch, Sean suspected that nearly every lawyer in America would fold. There were only two types of people willing to put their duty above all else—reporters and priests, and he wasn't ready yet to go to the press. It would have to be a priest, despite Sean's hatred of Catholicism and his fear of anyone purporting to wield divine power.

As he stared up at the altar, illuminated by the sun setting through the stained-glass windows depicting Christ on the Cross, he felt this would have to be one of his last drops. He looked down at the sealed manila envelope and hoped it would be enough. No, he knew it would be enough; he just hoped Father Case could protect it and get it to the people who could tell his story.

Starting the day Gerhardt told him to start planning a fake conference in Pakistan, Sean began copying documents that would be his insurance policy. He told himself then that he would get out just before his work became criminal, but he didn't. Instead, he participated in planning or covering up or dealing with the leftovers of two murders, the framing of an innocent man for murder, and countless other felonies and treasons. He told himself at every step that he would go no further, but he kept going. He wasn't sure why. Perhaps it was inertia or fear, or, most troublingly, because he thought that what they were doing in supporting Judge Pham was good for America. In his soul, he believed this unquestionably. It was a matter of faith. The Supreme Court had been the enemy of true equality and progress in America for too long, and this was the chance to change things for the better. He also told himself that every incremental step was necessary in light of the previous step, and that *this* one would finally get them out of the woods and reduce their risk. But every step made things worse; every cover up and lie led only to more lies and more chaos. Sean suspected that everyone who got in too deep, whether it was gambling or stealing or cheating or lying about anything, told himself the same thing and followed the same downward spiral of destruction. But even knowing this as he did, he couldn't stop it. He felt as powerless to resist it as gravity or hunger.

The only way he could live with himself was to ensure that the world would eventually know what he'd done. That there came a time when his soul could take no more.

He rapped hard on the priest's door and heard him offer admittance. Sean walked in holding the envelope in his outstretched hand. When he'd done this before, the priest knew to accept the envelope without question, to hardly make eye contact, and to file it away with the others. But this time was different.

"Is there something on your mind you'd like to share?" Father Case asked. He still didn't know Sean's name, or anything about him. Sean knew he'd noticed the Zegna suits and the IWC Schaffhausen watch—even priests were not immune to the allure of the finer things—perhaps he suspected his visitor was a lawyer.

Sean looked at him as if he were sizing him up for a fight. He wanted to scream obscenities about the church and what it had done to him, how it had failed in its earthly mission, and how the whole fucking thing should be dismantled and destroyed. But he realized in that moment the absurdity—that same church was the last thing he could really count on when he was facing the abyss.

"I..." Sean swallowed hard. His stomach turned and the hair on the back of his neck stood up. "The, well, I think the..."

What he wanted to say was, *You are doing a great thing,*

not just for me but also for our country. I realize now that I've participated in the worst crimes imaginable. I put aside all of my values because I was certain what was right for society and thought I could impose it on everyone else. What are a few cracked eggs when you're making the perfect omelet, right? I'm sorry, Father. I failed.

But he didn't say any of it. Instead, he dropped the envelope on the desk and walked out of the office. He walked quickly back down the center aisle of the church, not wanting the priest to catch him but secretly hoping he would. But Father Case didn't come after him. Sean walked alone, past a smattering of old women and a few men praying alone in the dark interior of the church. When he walked out the front door and into the night, he felt relief but also dread in the darkness. He scanned the parking lot and the surrounding area but saw nothing suspicious. So he walked casually to his car, started the ignition, and drove off toward a house full of people who still loved him.

CHAPTER 39

June 2015
Arlington, Virginia

The Greyhound bus ride from Pittsburgh lasted seven hours. Royce found a cheap motel and set up his base of operations. He dug a hole in the underside of the mattress on the bed he wasn't going to use, and stored his cash, documents, weapons, and ammunition in it. Then he set up the rest of his room like someone in town for a business trip. Cosmetics set out in the bathroom, book on the nightstand, and a laptop on the small side table. After staging the room, he fired up the laptop and got on the Wi-Fi to find out who was leading the Pham vetting process. There were several front men from prominent legal and political circles, but he was looking for the grease men not the show ponies. Before being revoked, he'd have had the answer in a phone call, but now, alone in a motel room with peeling wallpaper and urine stains on floor, he was striking out. He unpacked a new burner, walked down the street toward a McDonalds, and dialed El Centro one more time.

But before Vasquez could answer, something seized him. He ended the call. Standing on the shoulder of the divided highway, it didn't seem like a good idea to trust too much anymore. But he needed information that only people on the inside could get. Ms. Rachelle could easily find out, but she was likely being monitored too. As cars zoomed by, he jogged back to the motel and found the cell phone number for Austin Nicks, Ms. Rachelle's always-in-trouble nephew. He'd helped Austin on more occasions than either of them could count. Austin answered on the third ring and agreed to get a message to his aunt. Three days later the text message came from Austin's cell phone.

"Bob Gerhardt." The name was followed by an address in the Great Falls neighborhood.

Soon, the scope of his Remington 700 sniper rifle was trained at the door of the office building where Gerhardt's team was meeting inside. Royce took a bite of cold cheeseburger. A bag of beef jerky, roasted cashews, gummy bears, and a variety of junk food he'd grabbed from a rickety rack in a Mobil station sat next to him on the seat of a rental car. He was using a credit card meticulously linked to a false identity by a fixer he'd used in his border days. Even then, every time he swiped it, a surge of adrenaline made his heart pound such that he could feel it in his fingertips.

There was no way of knowing what the team was meeting about or how long the meeting would last, but as he watched people come and go from the building, Royce fingered the trigger on his rifle gently. The nomination process was nearly complete, and when it was, Gerhardt's team was likely going to stand down and blend into the woodwork. He couldn't be sure who, if any, of these people were responsible. But he was looking for proof. He wanted answers, not corpses.

The next day started at 4:30 a.m. at Bob Gerhardt's house, since he'd learned Gerhardt was ex-Navy, and therefore an early riser. Gerhardt woke promptly at five and ran ten miles around his Great Falls, Virginia neighborhood. After a military-short shower, he was in his car on the way to the office by seven. Through the sniper scope, Royce observed Gerhardt's every move. He was clinical in the precision of his movements—even the way he picked up the morning paper looked professional. When Gerhardt pulled out of his driveway in a black Mercedes S500, a pretty fancy car Royce thought, he followed at a safe distance. It felt good that his Quantico training was still with him.

Ten hours later he was still sitting in the same spot in the same seat in the same car in the same parking lot, surrounded by wrappers from day-old fast food and plastic cups filled with urine that had recently been iced tea. He'd become a machine for turning brownish liquids into yellowish ones. Just as the situation inside the car was becoming unsustainable, the revolving doors to the building swung open, and Bob Gerhardt walked out, followed closely by three other men. Royce scanned the foursome quickly with his scope, not knowing what he was really looking for. He was used to that by now in this investigation. He knew Gerhardt already—the kind of guy who wouldn't give an inch, even if tortured. So he scanned to the men behind him. From this distance, they all looked indistinguishable from the thousands of lawyers who were probably headed out of their offices on K Street and around the District about now.

Then Royce noticed that the man at the back was hanging his head and wasn't engaging with the others. The men in front were exchanging looks and banter, but this guy wasn't being a team player. Royce focused the scope on him, putting the crosshairs right between his eyes.

The man was in his forties, smartly dressed, and carrying an expensive bag overstuffed with binders. He didn't look like a hit man or even someone who could order a hit on a law professor with a secret. He looked more like an accountant finishing up a long day counting rolls of paper towels in a warehouse or balancing books for an audit. But the look on his face was that of someone who'd seen or heard something upsetting. It was a look Royce had seen more times during his career than he wanted to remember. He saw it on the faces of hundreds of people staring up at the Twin Towers as he ran out of the building carrying survivors; he saw it on the face of a mother who saw him handcuffing her only child and dragging him away forever.

Instinct said this was the weak link in Gerhardt's team. Royce nicknamed him Charlie Brown.

The men split off and headed toward their respective vehicles. Charlie Brown beeped open a BMW M3 and settled into the driver's seat. He sat there staring out the front window into the darkening evening. A minute and then two passed. Royce kept his foot on the brake and the car in gear, but as two minutes turned into five, it looked like he picked the right person to tail.

Charlie Brown finally pulled out of the parking lot and headed west on Route 50 toward Fairfax. Best guess said he was headed home, wherever that was—it was pushing seven o'clock, and he'd been sitting in a conference room all day. But a few miles outside of Arlington, Charlie Brown pulled into the empty church parking lot. Royce drove past to the next break in the road and turned into the parking lot of a Dunkin' Donuts. From there, he watched through the sniper scope as Charlie Brown exited his car and stared for a few minutes at the side of the Saint James Catholic Church.

The bright interior of the donut shop looked inviting. He thought twice, but knew he might be close to something, so chose the mission over comfort. When he looked back, Charlie Brown was gone. His M3 was still there, but otherwise the parking lot was empty. Royce watched the church, but eventually the grind of the past few weeks caught up to him. Two hours later he woke up, and the M3 was gone. Cursing, he drove back to the hotel.

In the morning, he headed back to Saint James, parked in the Dunkin' Donuts, and grabbed a dozen doughnuts as food insurance for an uncertain day. Inside the church he avoided the nave, because he felt like a trespasser. He limped down the aisles running along the side of the church to reach the rectory at the back. There he found Father David Case sitting at his desk preparing his sermon for the coming Sunday mass.

"Excuse me, Father."

"Please, come in," the priest said.

"Thank you. Sorry to interrupt your work. I'm Special Agent Johnson from the FBI." Royce flashed his badge quickly at the priest, even though it was long since nothing but a prop. The priest looked much calmer than most people when that badge flashed at them.

"Of course. Please, have a seat. How can I help you?"

"Last night at around seven-thirty you had a man visit the church. Medium height, fancy suit, reddish hair. This man is the subject of a federal investigation, and I was hoping you might be able to give me some information about him. Were you here last night at that time?"

"I was." The priest responded, as would a well-trained witness in a trial. He answered the question and nothing more.

"Did you meet with the man or was he in the church to pray?"

"I did meet him. I can't say whether he prayed before or after our meeting."

"Is this man a parishioner? Are you familiar with him?"

"He isn't."

"And are you familiar with him otherwise?"

"I'm not sure what you mean by 'familiar,' Agent Johnson. If you mean, do I know him, the answer is no. If you mean have I ever seen him before, the answer is that I have."

This was going nowhere. Time for a Hail-Mary pass.

"What did you discuss with him, Father?"

"You know I can't tell you that, Agent Johnson. I don't discuss private conversations I have with the faithful with anyone. It is a matter of clerical ethics and my own personal moral code. Our vow of confidentiality is one of our most sacred."

Royce murmured noncommittally.

"I'm afraid your badge does no work here, Agent. I'm sure you are aware of the clergy-penitent privilege." The priest was visibly irritated and looked at his watch as if to tell Royce it was time to go.

"Of course, I understand and respect that, Father. I know of the privilege between attorney and client or priest and penitent. But when a crime is about to committed or when someone's life is at stake, the privilege doesn't apply. Right? You can't tell me that you'd keep a secret that you knew would save someone's life."

"I understand my legal obligations, Agent. We covered this in divinity school too." His voice failed to hide his irritation. "I assure you that I do not currently know anything that could aide in any possible criminal investigation."

"Clerical privilege doesn't apply in cases involving child abuse, though, especially child sex abuse."

"And I'm sure you are aware that this exception applies only in cases involving abuse by a parent or guardian. And furthermore, I can assure you that I have no information about the abuse of anyone, let alone a child. In fact, I have not said more than fifty words to the man who was here last night, and none of his words or mine involved anything that I could tell you about a crime or danger to anyone."

The priest stood and walked around toward Royce with his hand extended.

"It is time for you to go, Agent Johnson. I'm sorry that I can't be more helpful to you or to your investigation. I wish you luck with it. God speed."

This called for another strategy. Rather than push and make an enemy, Royce shook his hand and walked out of the church.

Father Case opened the bottom drawer of his desk and pulled out a Redweld folder stuffed with sealed manila envelopes. He pulled out several of the envelopes and fingered them, as if he were trying to divine their contents. But the envelopes remained sealed and their contents unknown. Every few days a man in a suit whose name he did not know stopped into the church after working hours and delivered an envelope to the priest. In fact, he had delivered one last night, and obviously had been followed by the FBI agent who had just left.

When the man came the first time, some weeks ago, he introduced himself merely as Mr. F. and told the priest he had information that had to be safeguarded at all costs, and the Catholic church, *this* church was the safest place he could think of to hide it. He explained to the priest he had grown up in devout Catholic family in Boston, and he knew the priest would keep his confidences, no questions asked. He asked for the priest's cell phone number and told him that he would text the priest a blank message every day indicating that he was okay. If the priest did not get a text from him for five straight days, he was to deliver the entire package to *The New York Times*.

The priest stood, leaving the envelopes on his desk, and walked over to the credenza by the window of his small office. He poured himself a large glass of scotch and stared at the pile of envelopes. The secrets they contained were of interest to the FBI, and someday soon the text messages were going to stop. He was now certain of that. He wanted more than anything to tear one open. But Father Case's entire life was about denial of desires in the search for some deeper meaning and truth. He finished the scotch and put the folders back in his drawer.

CHAPTER 40

For ten days, Royce followed leads, ran down angles, and pushed everywhere he thought there might be a weakness in the shield around the people who had killed his brother. After one hundred man hours of nearly constant motion in an around Washington, he was no closer. All he'd succeeding in doing was stinking up his rental car and adding a few dozen points to his cholesterol levels. The truth seemed to be slipping further and further away into the dimming light of the past.

On the eleventh night, he was still in the car, parked on the street, gazing at the lit windows of Sean Flanagan's house. At this point he knew his name, routines, and everything about him that one could learn from publicly available information and from trailing him constantly. He knew Flanagan was back working on his regular law firm caseload now that the confirmation of Chief Justice Pham was through the senate and he had taken his seat on the court. He knew Flanagan no longer visited the priest and that he often sat at a desk in the first-floor library of his home staring at the walls until the wee hours of the morning.

It was 7 p.m., and NPR was running a story about the first Asian-American Supreme Court justice, and the likely impact his appointment would have on the big cases the court was about to hear, as well as the broader impact the rebalancing of the court would have on American life. Royce fumed, not because of the message, although he disliked it as well, but because of the messenger. A messenger from hell.

The lights were all off in the Flanagan house, save the first-floor library and the third-floor bathroom. After 10 p.m., a progression of lights had already turned off on the second floor, as the wife put her children down for the night. Royce knew that she often went to the third-floor master bathroom at this time and soaked for up to an hour.

Royce put his hand out to open the car door once, twice, three times, but drew it back each time. Then, heart racing, he left the car, walked in shadow over the lawn, and peeked in the open window of the library. The man of the house was sitting at his computer typing away, probably on a legal brief for one of his upcoming cases. Music played softly—a Bach overture on period instruments, Royce surmised—and he sipped intermittently from a glass of red wine.

At the back of the house, no one else was to be seen on the ground floor. A pair of heavy bi-fold glass doors was unlocked. Royce slid one back slowly, on whisper-quiet sliders, and walked in on tiptoe. Pulling his service weapon from the fanny pack, he held it by his side and walked slowly toward the library in the front of the house, scanning rooms as he went. It was not lost on him that he was in the process of committing multiple felonies.

At the doorway of the library, he pointed his pistol straight at Flanagan's chest and cleared his throat quietly. The lawyer looked up.

"I assume you're one of Bob's guys?" He closed the laptop, staring admiringly at the burglar. "Did you know that from this angle, the front of your gun looks like a perfect circle inside of a perfect square?" he said with eerie calm.

Royce raised a brow but kept looking down the sight.

"It almost looks fake."

"It's not."

The gun stayed perfectly steady.

"I'm a special agent with the Federal Bureau of Investigation. I'm *Alex Johnson's* brother." *No, I'm not*, Royce thought to himself, choking on the words he used to say with supreme confidence and pride. Both were gone.

Sean laughed a knowing laugh.

"What can I do for you? And, if you don't mind me asking, why'd you sneak in through the back door instead of announcing yourself with the bell like everyone else?"

"I'm not here to arrest you. I want answers."

"Answers about your brother's death." He looked genuinely sorry. "Friends at my firm went to law school with him, a few were his students, and they all spoke highly of his mind and his character."

"Spare me the bullshit, Counselor. I know you played a part. Pakistan. Marcus Jones. Ring any bells?" He jerked the pistol aggressively and took a step in Flanagan's direction.

"I don't know what you think you're going to accomplish here tonight, but you don't need to do anything risky. I'm already a dead man."

"I don't just shoot people I don't like. That's why I'm a good guy and you aren't."

"Oh, that is rich! You just broke in, you're pointing a gun, and you're the white hat in this scenario? I don't think so. I know that badge, that gun, they are all as legit as a three-dollar bill. You are—"

"Why don't you help me get the people responsible? If you come in and tell your story, we can protect you."

"Do you think the FBI is going to let you bring down the president and the chief justice? Did Washington call and tell you to back off, to wrap it up and move on to other things because there was no case? That was *me* telling you that. ME!" Flanagan almost stood up but reconsidered. Then, in a resigned voice, added, "You've got no chance, Agent Johnson. None."

Royce realized for the first time what he was up against. It wasn't just Gerhardt and his team of lawyer-killers. It was

Uncle Sam in his red-blooded entirety. Silence hung between them.

Flanagan broke it, "Now you want me to run into the FBI's arms begging for protection. Hilarious!"

"Okay I'll make it simple. How about doing the right thing?"

"The right thing is a death warrant for us both."

"Ask me if I give a shit. I want to know *why*."

"Pham is the last hope for this president to remake the Supreme Court in a way that will make America a fundamentally better place. How's that?"

"Really? Then what's the priest all about, Flanagan? You've been giving the priest evidence, haven't you?"

"I want to protect my family. I want some leverage, I guess. Look, I'm not going to testify against the president or anyone else. No. I'm not going to go in front of the assembled media and talk about how I destroyed innocent people to further a political agenda and my career. It's never going to happen."

"So where does that leave us?"

"It leaves me here at my desk working on an appeal in an asbestos case, and you walking out the door and into the darkness. Hopefully never to return or say a word to anyone."

"You wish. He raped my brother. He's still raping boys. I've seen it with my own—"

"I know what he did. I know who he is. What do you want me to say?"

"I want to know who pulled the trigger on Alex."

"I can't tell you that."

Royce cocked the trigger. Flanagan put his hands flat on the desk and closed his eyes. They both stayed motionless— one man with a gun, one without. Seconds ticked by. Royce let out a breath. He lowered the pistol, uncocked it, and put it away. He walked back along the dark hallway through the kitchen, and out into the chilly night air.

Several yards away from the house, the kitchen lights went

on. Royce paused. The back door opened. Sean Flanagan stood under an overhead light that hollowed his cheeks and eye sockets into a mask. He shaded his face from the light and peered out into the shadows. "You still here, Johnson?"

"Yeah."

"Ask Bob Gerhardt. He's the only one who knows." The door closed.

CHAPTER 41

March 2015
Arlington, Virginia

Bob Gerhardt was late. His team, Sean Flanagan included, was assembled in the twelfth-floor conference room waiting nervously for the man who was never late. The men fiddled with their binders, played *Threes!* on their phones, or paced around, staring out the windows trying to get a glimpse of the Washington Monument. Just when the boredom was turning to worry, the conference room door swung open, and in he strode with a phone pressed to his ear. An aide holding a briefcase in each hand trailed behind him. Gerhardt hung up and took his seat at the head of the conference table.

"Let's get started. I've just come from the White House."

A murmur went through the room, and everyone looked up from their phones.

"I've activated Chicago."

"Holy shit, Bob. Are you serious?" Jay Rudolph, athletic with a shaved head, walked over to the credenza on the far wall where he poured himself a glass of water. He downed it in a single gulp, then looked back at Gerhardt. "Fuck, Bob...fuck."

"Once we learned Songbird was going to sing, his fate was sealed."

"Wait, what does that mean, 'activated Chicago'?" Sean Flanagan asked sheepishly.

"Don't be a child, Sean, you know what it fucking means."
The other lawyer rolled his eyes.

"No, I don't. What are we talking about here, Bob?"
Flanagan was not playing dumb.

The looks on the faces in the room were not what Gerhardt
wanted to see. Doubt, concern, reservation, and even a bit of
mutiny were there in their eyes. No one said anything. They
looked at Gerhardt like he was their father; their abusive, al-
coholic father.

"I was with the president when she made the call. It was
not easy. She struggled. If it makes you feel better, I saw all
sides of this. We really have no choice."

Gerhardt thought a bit of historical perspective was needed
to seal the deal.

"Have I ever told you guys about Wei Rulin?"

Without waiting for everyone to say what he already
knew, Gerhardt went on. He loved being the smartest one in
every room.

"Wei was a general in the army of the Chinese Nationalists
during the war between China and Japan in the thirties. The
Chinese leader, Chiang Kai-shek, knew they were powerless
to stop the Japanese army, but they needed to buy time.
Chiang decides to deliberately breech the levees holding back
the Yellow River, knowing it would flood thousands of square
miles, bogging down the Japanese advance. Pretty great idea.
So, under orders from Chiang, General Wei secretly ordered
his men to dig holes in the levee. When the levee broke, a wall
of water as tall as a man rushed down the Yellow River valley,
wiping out everything it its path. The Chinese citizens down-
stream were taken completely by surprise; thousands were
drowned and washed away. But the standing water, which
flooded thousands of square miles, caused the real toll. Crops
were ruined and diseases flourished. Nearly a million people
were killed as a result of the decision, and millions more were
forced to become refugees. But, you know what, it worked.

The Japs were stalled too, and it saved China. A million lives saved the rest of the people. Saved the nation."

He finished and looked pleased with his story.

The silent critics were not silenced. They fidgeted and rubbed their eyes; they breathed heavily into their cheeks, puffing out breath.

Gerhardt felt the team, and therefore the mission, was at an inflection point.

"If you want out, there's the door!" he pointed emphatically at the exit. "Leave and there will be no hard feelings. I'll give you a top-notch recommendation."

No one got up to leave. Perhaps because no one thought it was a real option.

"Okay, good. We are all in this together. Agreed?"

A chorus of agreed echoed through the large conference room, some more honest than others.

"Outstanding. Huzzah!"

"Whatever you need, boss." Rudolph stood and stretched his legs.

"I've got a tape to play." He motioned to an aide, who set a briefcase on the table, and pulled out a small digital recorder. She pressed play. Gerhardt leaned back in his leather chair and looked up at the ceiling. The team heard a voice, but no one knew who it was. It was obviously a fragment of a longer conversation.

"Are you really going ahead with this?" the first voice said.

Then they heard another voice. Sean Flanagan recognized it as Alex Johnson.

"I have to, Roger."

"You know that your life will be over."

"You think they'll kill me?" The two men could be heard laughing.

"Funny. No, you'll survive."

"Oh, good!"

"I'm just saying that if you out a Supreme Court nominee,

your students, friends, colleagues, everyone will look and treat you differently. You'll be a celebrity for a while, but then you'll have to adjust to...well, something different."

"Sounds like a chance to start over. It actually sounds nice."

"If you are going ahead with this, you know I've got your back. If you want me to testify...I've interviewed enough victims to know what a real one looks like, and you, my friend, are a real one."

Then Alex Johnson's voice could be heard again.

"Trying to process all of this under the kind of duress I'm under is...well, it just sucks. I don't want to bring you down with all my mess."

The recording cut off. Gerhardt paused and looked around the room into the eyes of his team. Rudolph sat up in his chair and cleared his throat.

"I assume that is the other professor, what was his name? Evans?"

"Havens," Gerhardt said.

"Evans, Havens, whatever."

Sean Flanagan had heard enough. "Am I the only one here who thinks this is nuts?" It came out of his mouth with a lot less conviction than when it left his brain.

The conversations in the room stopped like a bomb had gone off, and everyone turned to look at him. Flanagan took stock of the faces staring holes through him.

"Finny, what are you thinking about?" Bob walked over toward him and loomed over the attorney.

"I just can't believe this is happening. I mean, we are talking about people's lives here. We are talking about...stuff... that is illegal and...immoral." It seemed to Flanagan that no one had even blinked, and he could feel the beads of sweat forming on his palms and in his armpits. He started to waver. "Look, there is no doubt that I support the president and Judge Pham, and I understand the stakes here. I'm a team player. But where do we draw the line? Is one or three or ten too many? Certainly not a million, like that Chinese guy. We wouldn't do that, would we?"

Bob Gerhardt made his way back around the large, oak table to the front of the room. He put his palms down on the table and hunched forward. He made eye contact with everyone in the room, then turned to Flanagan.

"Do you know how many people I've killed, *personally?* With these hands." He held them up like a butcher would show a roast to a customer over a counter.

"I don't, Bob, and I don't see how that is relevant." Gerhardt's question frightened Flanagan.

"In every case, the order came, directly or indirectly, from the president of the United States. The president made a call that a particular individual or group of individuals was a threat to the United States and tasked me with eliminating that threat."

"And?"

"Do you think I read all the intelligence reports or verified them in some way before I acted?"

"No, of course not."

"*Of course not.* I relied on the president. I relied on the chain of command. I relied on the system. I believed in the system, the American system. I am an instrument, Mr. Flanagan, just as you are. We are just tools of power."

"Are you saying we should never question orders?"

"I'm not a fool." Gerhardt rose and stood close to the table. "I would not follow an order I knew to be illegal or immoral. We all carry our moral codes around with us like clothes on our backs. But as soldiers, we cannot deploy ours willy-nilly. We have to ask instead whether the decisions are so out of bounds they cannot be justified by any defensible moral grounding."

"And this one?"

"You are kidding, right?"

"I'm not."

"What upsets you, Mr. Flanagan? That he is innocent? What did the Pakistanis and Afghans and Somalis and Yemenis that I killed do exactly? They threatened America, meaning they threatened harm against Americans. Well, that is what these professors are doing too. I don't care if they are Americans or not—we vowed to fight enemies, foreign *and* domestic. And I don't care that they are on American soil. I'd have killed the people I've killed anywhere they were."

"Fine. But those are different cases, Bob. I mean, the threat is much more direct. If some guy threatens to blow up the Mall of America, the risk is much higher than the threat from some professor maybe influencing the vote on a Supreme Court nominee who maybe changes the ruling on a case, which maybe reduces the chance of some policy maybe helping some people. I mean, this is apples and oranges."

"How do you know who presents the greater harm, Mr. Flanagan? Does the shepherd in Yemen who's been to a terrorist training camp and talks about coming to America and killing the infidels really present more of a threat than a guy who might be able to single handily cause the dismantling of a new social safety net for tens of millions of Americans?"

"Well..."

"Sacrificing a life or two is never easy, Finny, but on the other side of the ledger is the wellbeing of millions of Americans—it is about giving people education and decent housing and a retirement that isn't filled with anxiety; it is about lifting up the tens of millions in poverty and dramatically improving their lives. If you told me I could do that, but a few roadblocks would have to be removed, I'd move heaven and earth to do that. Wouldn't you?"

CHAPTER 42

July 2015
Washington, D.C.

Bob Gerhardt had dropped clean out of sight. His house was quiet, except for the multiple air-conditioning units spinning ceaselessly to keep up with the oppressive heat of another swampy D.C. summer. The guys at his gym hadn't seen him, the poker game he attended in the back of an Indian restaurant in Rosslyn went on without him, and the unmistakable S550, with a semper fi bumper sticker, was nowhere to be seen.

The only way to track him was through one of his team. Someone still close to Gerhardt. Royce picked Jay Rudolph. The man's bald head was unmistakable, as was his athletic physique accentuated by aggressively tailored suits, each one costing more than an FBI agent's mortgage. He was an easy tail.

They headed east on foot down K Street, Royce dawdling along, Rudolph carrying a lunch in a brown bag in his left hand, while holding a phone to his ear. At 17th Street he waited for traffic to clear, looked both ways, and crossed against the light. Royce waited with the other pedestrians, and watched Rudolph find an open spot on a bench in a park under a statute of David Farragut. When the light turned again, he followed into the park, and took a seat on a bench out of Rudolph's line of sight. A Washington Capitals hat was pulled down over his bald head, and he raised a copy of the *Post* just high enough to create a relaxed impression. Clichés existed for a reason—they worked.

Rudolph methodically ate what appeared to be a turkey on wheat bread while scanning his phone with his other hand. There were dozens of people doing exactly the same thing on benches throughout Farragut Park. Half an hour passed. Then, in a jump, Rudolph rose to leave. His phone slipped from his hand, crashing to the sidewalk. He froze, then reached down with his right hand to pick it up. When he did so, his suit jacket hoisted, revealing a holster and the handle of a pistol in his belt.

What's a lawyer doing carrying at work? Royce wondered. It changed the dynamic significantly. While Royce liked his chances in any encounter, even with a former SEAL like Rudolph, the last thing he needed was shootout. Time for Plan B.

The tail went on from a distance for several days, as he tried to find a safe way in. Every day, he pinged Jenny from a burner, but, according to their agreement, never heard back. As he meticulously cataloged Rudolph's every move, every meeting, and every activity, he wondered how much Jenny knew. Were they still at the family cabin in Deep Creek? Did they know he was involved in a shootout with the Secret Service on the streets of Pittsburgh? His knee was better but longing for family made him ache.

At precisely 8 p.m., Rudolph walked through the front doors of his gym and emerged again at 9:59 p.m., one minute short of closing time. The life Royce was recording in his Moleskin notebook was straight from BUD/S training: the day began at 5:30 a.m. with a run of between eight and ten miles, followed by a shower at an apartment he lived in alone; breakfast was eaten standing at his kitchen counter, usually oatmeal with blueberries; then Rudolph walked the fifteen blocks to his office on K Street. He took his lunch, always the same, in Farragut Park, then walked straight back to the office. He left work every day at 7:45 p.m., then walked to his gym, where he worked out until the place closed. Lights out by ten. Repeat.

Satisfied that he knew Rudolph's routine, it was time to strike. Back at the hotel, he flipped over the mattress and emptied the stash into a black duffel bag. He loaded his Mossberg ATI Tactical with six shells, checked the clip on his Smith & Wesson M&P45, then zipped them into the bag as well. The Captain's advice before any family trip, no matter how innocuous, was top of mind: "No plan survives contact with the enemy." It made no sense when they were on the ferry to the Magic Kingdom, but it did now. Prepare to be unprepared.

Rudolph entered the gym on time, as usual, but for the first time in ten days, Royce followed him in. Stopping at the front desk, he told the manager that he had just transferred to D.C. from San Francisco and was interested in joining. The manager offered him a tour. Over the next twenty minutes he saw Rudolph several times, working out with free weights and running on a treadmill.

Near the end of the tour, they went by the pool and Royce asked if he could take a few laps. The manager agreed and showed him to the men's locker room. Pointing at his black bag, the manager said, "You can store your gym bag in one of the open lockers. Members get lockers with their names on them, but we have ones available for guests. If you need a lock, you can buy or rent one at the front desk."

It was 8:30 p.m., and the manager noted that the gym would be closing at 10 p.m.

Before striding off, she said, "Have fun!"

She left him alone. The locker room was mostly empty—a few men were standing around in towels or drying their hair at the wall-to-wall mirror on the other side of the large room. Taking a seat on a bench, he pulled a laptop out of his bag.

He peeled off his shoes and socks, then pulled out his laptop and pretended to be working.

A few members came and went over the next thirty minutes. None lingered long enough to be curious about why this stranger wasn't moving. By 9 p.m., the locker room was empty. When he was completely alone, Royce perused all the lockers and located Rudolph's. He fished his burglar's tools out of his duffel. The lock—a standard Yale key lock—was open in seconds. He located the holster and piece in Rudolph's right shoe, under a neatly folded Armani suit. The weapon tucked neatly into Royce's waistband. He retreated to his spot on the other side of the locker room.

Around quarter to ten the door swung open and he heard someone undressing on the other side of three, freestanding rows of lockers. Walking cautiously away from the showers toward the door, and parallel to the rows, he peered around the banks of lockers to verify it was Rudolph. He then gently bolted the door to the outside and waited until he heard the shower.

Royce drew his M&P45, screwed a silencer into the barrel, and made sure the safety was on. His approach was muffled by the hissing spray of the shower and Rudolph singing a tune he didn't recognize. He raised the weapon as he stepped into the showers. Rudolph was facing the showerhead on the far wall, his bare ass, with a large tattoo of a tiger on his right cheek, presented an impressive sight. The steam rose all around him, and he hummed gently as he soaped his bald head. A metal trash can sat against the wall. Royce flipped it with his free hand and it clanged loudly. Rudolph spun around, wiping the soap from his eyes.

"What the fuck!" he screamed, stepping out from under the spray.

"Don't!" Royce raised the weapon, pointing it at where Rudolph's heart would be. "Not another step."

Rudolph knew the drill. He froze and cupped his hands

behind his head.

"You've got the wrong—"

"Shut it. I know exactly who you are: Jay Alden Rudolph, Princeton class of 1998, enlisted after 9/11, Navy SEAL, two tours in Afghanistan, Yale Law, Supreme Court clerk, big-time lawyer with a tiger tattoo on your butt. Blah, blah, dee-fucking blah."

"Look, this is awkward, let me at least come out and get a towel from my locker…"

Royce reached into his waistband with his left hand and pulled Rudolph's 9mm into view. He dangled it like bait.

"So you can use this on me? You might need another plan, Counselor." Royce tucked it back into his belt.

"What do you want? To kill me?"

"If I wanted you dead, I would have put a slug in you any number of times over the past few days. Maybe while you were masturbating the other night to porn on your computer—that would have been fun for the boys at the coroner's office."

"Fuck you, you sick prick. You have nothing on me. I'm going to walk out of here—" Rudolph took a half step.

Royce flipped off the safety and fired a round into the shower wall two inches to the right of Rudolph's left ear. The man fell to the ground on instinct.

"Crazy fucking…" he muttered as he rose back to his feet.

Royce strode toward him, weapon aimed at Rudolph's brow. After a few paces, the mist from the shower enveloped him. It felt surreal.

"Here's what's going to happen. You are going to give me your boss. I want Gerhardt on a silver fucking platter. Then you can get toweled off and go back to your miserable life. Okay?"

"First of all," Rudolph stalled, "why do you think Gerhardt is my boss or that I could *give him to you*, whatever that means? What exactly do you think I do? I'm a fucking lawyer, you psycho. I represent—"

At the sound of that arrogant, condescending tone, Royce kicked Rudolph into a pile on the shower floor. Pain shot up his knee but it was worth it. The .45 pointed itself at the moaning man's head, while the shower poured over his shoulders.

"Tell me! Where is Gerhardt?" The .45 reached out, inches from Rudolph's face.

The man stared back blankly, POW training kicking in.

"Do you really want to die here to protect that sick shit?"

He lowered his left knee into Rudolph's chest, letting two hundred plus pounds press into his sternum.

Rudolph couldn't speak, even if he wanted to. He squirmed under Royce's weight and glare. His right hand rose meekly, as the breath left him.

"Let me up," he gasped.

Royce stood, and stepped back. As Rudolph tried to rise, Royce surged forward, grabbing him by the throat and shoving the pistol into his mouth. He slammed him against the tile of the shower, and they both stood under the high-pressure water.

"Tell me where he is." The pistol shoved so far in his mouth, Rudolph started to gag.

"Fah 'ou," he mumbled around the steel of the .45.

The image of Alex flashed into Royce's mind. Dead in his living room, a pool of blood soaking him like marinade. He pulled the pistol out of Rudolph's mouth and slammed the butt into his teeth. Wood and steel blasted through the enamel causing teeth to spray in every direction. Blood poured down his chin, as Rudolph collapsed into the fetal position, water from the shower pushing the streaming blood and shattered teeth into a swirling circle around the floor drain.

The room was filled with steam, but the tip of the silencer was still inches from the man's face.

Rudolph spit blood and flesh and bits of teeth into the drain. He wiped his face with his arm and glared up at Royce.

"Sant Mackel," he spat.

Royce turned off the shower and backed out. It was a

shame he hadn't brought any duct tape in from the car, but there were a few plastic zip ties in the bottom of his duffel.

"Stay there," he ordered, and went to retrieve the duffel. Rudolph was in the same place still dribbling blood when he got back. He threw him a towel as a reward.

"Cooperate, Counselor, and you'll be rescued by morning." Rudolph grunted.

"Zip this around your wrist." He tossed a plastic tie over and waited while Rudolph complied. "Now pull this one through a slot in the drain. Fasten it to the bracelet." It took a few tries because his motor coordination was screwed up, but Rudolph made it.

Royce walked forward and put the .45 against the man's forehead.

"Relax. I'm just going to check your work." With his free hand, Royce pulled on the ties and tightened the wrist bracelet a notch.

Bang, bang, bang! Hammering on the change room door made them both jump.

"One word and you're dead." Royce closed the duffel and walked out with the .45 hidden behind it.

A key was already scraping in the door from outside.

"Coming!" Royce strode over, threw back the bolt and opened the door wide. The manager was standing there, more than a little disgruntled.

"This door is not supposed to be locked!"

"Sorry, force of habit. Did I delay you?"

"Well as a matter—"

"The pool is great. I need to come earlier tomorrow."

Smiling in spite of herself, "Yes, it's—"

He snapped off the lights. "Let's go home then."

"Please don't lock this again."

"Promise I won't."

They walked together to the exit. The parking lot outside was dark and lit with ghostly sodium lights. Royce waited like

232

a gentleman while she locked up. Too bad he hadn't had a chance to collect Rudolph's clothes and phone, but it was probably okay. A toothless man would have a hard time gumming through a plastic bracelet.

CHAPTER 43

The way to Saint Michael's was east on Route 50, across the Chesapeake Bay Bridge toward the Eastern Shore. It was a small enough place that there was only one grocery store. As sweat dripped from his armpits, Royce bet it wouldn't be too hard to spot a black Mercedes S500 in one of the driveways of the pretty, tended houses in the town or surroundings.

He spotted it at the end of a long drive belonging to a white, center-hall colonial right on the water, protected by a high wrought iron fence. Royce drove past without braking, until he found what he was looking for about half a mile away: a slim public access strip to the water. It even provided parking.

He pulled a waterproof bag from his duffel and loaded it with the Remington 700 sniper rifle, his Mossberg, the .45, as well as a Taser and duct tape. No plastic handcuffs left, damn it. *Prepare to be unprepared.*

At midnight, the surface of the inlet was glassy calm. He stripped to his Under Armour lycra long johns, connected the bag with a cord to his waist, and lowered it gently into the water. The air in the bag kept it afloat, although it dragged low in the water under all the weaponry weight. Holding his breath, he slid into the water beside it and started an easy breaststroke in the direction of Gerhardt's mansion.

All the houses had large docks with boats and watercraft secured on lifts and tie lines. When he'd swum about a quarter mile he stopped at a dock and climbed onto an outermost pier to pull out the sniper scope. Tracking the shoreline, he tried to identify the back of the house he'd seen from the road. Lucky guess, he was right next door.

There didn't seem to be cameras watching the water. Like the other mansions along the shoreline, Gerhardt's house had a large dock, which housed a boat with two powerful outboard engines and a pair of jet skis. The boats were secured by lifts that would have been bobbing on waves had the water not been so calm. No one walked along the shore, and it was impossible to make out anyone inside the house from this distance.

He put the scope away, made sure the bag was secured, and lowered back into the water. He swam on. Approaching Gerhardt's dock, he positioned himself so that the boats on their lifts were between him and the sight lines of the house and the backyard. Slowing his strokes, he kept lower in the water to reduce visibility. He inched forward under the dock, fishing the bag in close, and stretched down to find the point where he could put his feet on the bottom. When he felt mud squish between his toes, the adrenaline surged.

He waded farther under the dock to the point where he could kneel and remove the Remington from the bag. Still dry. He checked the sight and the mechanism. Leaving the relative safety of the dock, he moved to his right, hugging the shoreline, which was protected by tall marsh grass and some low-lying shrubs. Still dragging the bag, he army-crawled ashore, and took up a position on a low dune, among the grass. The house was on a gentle rise, and he had to look up to see the backyard.

A small breeze picked up as he found a ledge to secure his left elbow—then he raised the Remington's night scope. In the greenish glow of the sight, he saw two figures, one light skinned, the other dark, walking aimlessly in the large backyard. They came together near some lawn furniture arranged around a dormant fire pit. Then they walked away, small orange glows appearing intermittently about six feet off the ground.

This small security detail was proof that although Gerhardt holed up in his seaside crib after the threat was found on Royce's phone at the Double Eagle Pub, they had no idea how close he really was. Flanagan hadn't blabbed. The element of surprise was still on his side.

Royce fingered the trigger and imagined the shots that would take those men out. They were clearly pros, likely former SEALs. Both wore thick beards, fashionable with Middle East special ops. The Hechler & Koch MP5 submachine guns slung to their sides signaled that they'd spent time in hostile territory. Against these two, surprise was going to be essential.

Royce dropped the barrel of the rifle gently into the dune and looked up from the scope. Reaching once more into the bag, he put the .45 in his waistband. Six rounds clicked into the chamber of his Mossberg, and he swung it cross-wise over his shoulder. The duct tape went into his pocket and he crawled up to the hedge that separated the dunes from the yard. He waited until the closest of the men was within range.

The darker-skinned guard was headed right at him, although he didn't know it. The MP5 dangled at his side, bouncing gently off his hip like a metronome. His right hand moved a cigarette from his side to his mouth in a rhythmic pattern. When he was ten feet away, moonlight illuminated his face. He looked bored but seasoned, maybe by the mountains of Afghanistan. He was an inch or two taller and bigger than Royce by at least forty pounds, most of which was probably stateside barbeque and beer.

Royce slid the Taser out. When the SEAL got to the edge of the grass, he took aim and shot electrodes into the man's chest. His expression turned from surprise to anguish, as the electric shock coursed through his heart. With a strangled cry, his eyes disappeared and teeth flashed, arms contorting.

Royce wiggled the Taser, like he could send extra juice down its wires. Before the SEAL could catch his breath enough to shout, Royce dropped it, spun the Mossberg off his shoulder, leapt over the hedge, and flung the butt end at the man's face. The shuddering body went down like a load of butcher's meat.

Royce was on top of him in an instant, pinning his shoulders to the ground with his knees, as blood poured from the man's nose and collected in his beard. He gurgled and wriggled like a fish gasping for air. Royce flipped him onto his stomach to keep him from choking to death. Then he grabbed the man's hair and banged his head into the grass several times, the man's earpiece flinging loose and swinging in a circle out of time with his head.

He was out. Cold. Royce pulled out the duct tape, wrestled the man's limp arms behind his back, and secured them until the tape pinched into flesh. More duct tape went around the man's head three times, making sure to cover his mouth, still gurgling with foamy blood and saliva.

Royce dismounted and lay in the grass for a moment, looking up at the stars. Then he got to his knees and dragged the man by his feet, as slowly and quietly as possible. When he reached the hedge, he rolled him into the bushes. Then he crept up the hill, moving toward the tree line that separated Gerhardt's property from his neighbor to the east. Looking back, the SEAL was still lying against the bushes. He hadn't moved a muscle.

Halfway up the hill toward the house, Royce knelt behind the trunk of a large sassafras tree. Its single trunk split in half about four feet off the ground, providing a narrow v-shaped gap for him to plan the next attack. He rearmed the Taser and slung the Mossberg back over his shoulder. The other guard was circling the far side of the yard, headed back toward the porch.

This one was smaller, wirier. His posture was intense, and he chewed gum aggressively as he stepped purposefully across the flagstone patio. He spoke into his collar and used his left hand to press his earpiece further into his ear. With every step the look on his face turned toward killing mode.

The first man was easy. A few weeks strolling in Gerhardt's yard without any signs of action or even any idea of what they were up against had softened him. And he hadn't seen anything coming. But this guy was going to be a different game. Royce suspected he was suspicious since his partner, bound and gagged in the bushes, wasn't responding.

As he strode closer, the man reached down with his right hand and raised the MP5. He spit out his gum and grimaced angrily. Royce turned his shoulder against the trunk of the tree. He slowed his breath, keeping his mouth shut and using only his nose to move the night air in and out of his lungs. His pulse started to pound in his fingers. The SEAL reached the edge of the yard, scanning the trees with eyes. Royce held his breath, then when footsteps crunched the pine straw and passed right by, he exhaled quietly.

The SEAL took a few paces, then on sheer instinct turned and dropped to one knee, wheeling the MP5. Before he could squeeze off a shot, Royce kicked the weapon out his hand and crashed into him, both of them rolling down the hill. The Taser flew to the ground and bounced into the darkness. Both men were on their sides, weapons awkwardly pinned under them, their straps twisted tight from the falls.

Royce tried to free his shotgun, but before he could work it around to a firing position, the SEAL's fist landed heavily on his right eye socket. Comets of pain flew through his darkened vision. He could feel the man about to pounce, so he reached behind into his waistband. The .45 was gone, dislodged in the ruckus. Royce got to his knees, his good eye scanning quickly for the pistol. The barrel of the MP5 was rising up toward him. He planted his hands into the pine straw and swung his leg around in a half circle as fast as he could. His shin connected painfully with the SEAL's leg, knocking him to the ground. Royce jumped up and lunged. But the man was quick too. He avoided the blow, trying to bring his weapon back around to the front of his body.

Royce got to his knees, as did the SEAL. They were face to face. Royce lowered his shoulder and exploded downhill like a linebacker firing into a tackling dummy. He planted his shoulder into the man's chest, driving him to the ground with a thud. The man's ribs cracked, as Royce let his entire weight fall into him. Royce grabbed him by the scruff of his beard, pushed his head back, and pounded him with his right fist. He landed blow after blow until his knuckles ached.

But the SEAL wasn't done. Eyes full of fury, he kicked with his leg hard into Royce's groin, and thrust and wiggled his hips until he threw him to the side. He got to his knees, and reached back for his weapon. Royce swung his around first, raising it a foot from the SEAL's face before the MP5 was able to join the fight. He fixed on the SEAL's eyes, the muscles in his right arm tensed and ready to pull the trigger.

"Shhh...don't do anything stupid. Drop it...Don't! Let me see your hands."

The SEAL wrinkled his nose and brought his empty hands around to the front of his body, letting them fall into his lap. Blood trickled down from his left eye, which was rapidly swelling shut. He stared unblinking, as if to make an appointment for round two.

Royce stepped cautiously toward him, unsure what to do. *No plan survives contact with the enemy*, he heard the Captain say in his head.

"I'm not going to kill you," Royce reassured him.

"Well, I'm going to kill you, motherfucker," the SEAL spat.

Royce pumped the shotgun. The shell seated in the chamber, and he looked down the barrel into the man's stony stare.

"You'd better shoot me, 'cause—"

The Mossberg struck the side of his head, crushing it flat as it deformed under the blow. He toppled over, blood streaming from eye and ear.

Royce prodded his ass with the barrel of the shotgun. No movement. He reached down and flipped him onto his back.

The man's face was a pulp, foamy bubbles forming at his swelling lips. He was alive.

Royce set the shotgun in the pine straw and pulled the tape from his pocket. When the man's hands were secured, he taped over his mouth. Then pulled it off again. The man's nose was surely broken and taping his mouth shut might be a death sentence. And, at this point, even if the man woke up and managed a shout through his broken jaw, there would be no one to hear him scream. At least, not for long.

CHAPTER 44

"Granzow!" Gerhardt shouted into the night. "Granzow, where the fuck are you!" From his vantage in the shadows behind a large planter, Royce saw the big man step out into the center of the porch and raise a large flashlight, scanning the landscape in prison-yard sweeps. "Granzow!...Shit."

A small smile crossed Royce's lips. If there were any other security in the house, it wouldn't be Gerhardt on the porch.

The barrel of the Mossberg scraped along the brass planter making a *sequeeeee* sound. Gerhardt cocked his head and listened. Royce did it again. Annoyed, the man thumped down the steps in his sock feet, walked over to the planter, and saw the shotgun leveled at his chest. In a flash, Royce saw what he must be seeing: a bald guy, soaking wet from head to toe, with pine straw stuck to his long johns. What he didn't figure in was the look in his eye. It was the look that stopped Gerhardt in his tracks. He put his hands up halfway.

"If you're looking for Granzow, he's tied up down the hill. The other one's rolled up in the bushes."

Gerhardt grunted in surprise.

"If I were you, I'd be disappointed. They went down easy."

"I doubt that, Agent Johnson," he muttered.

"They're down, that's what matters. Now go sit in one of those lawn chairs."

Gerhardt did as he was told. Royce lowered his shotgun and raised the Taser. He aimed it at Gerhardt's face, then his torso. Squeezing the trigger filled him with euphoria, as he watched the electrodes sting the man's chest and the dance of torment began. When Gerhardt sagged, semi-conscious in the chair, Royce went to work with the duct tape.

By the time Gerhardt woke up, Royce was also sitting, shotgun resting on his legs, and a bottle of Fiji water, procured from Gerhardt's space-age refrigerator, rising and falling from his lips.

"I knew you were coming."

Royce had to hand it to him. The old warhorse had balls.

"The guys who found my phone gave you a jingle?"

"No. Sean Flanagan told me." Gerhardt smiled devilishly. "Before he died."

Words froze in Royce's throat.

"So, you didn't know." Gerhardt smiled the most evil smile Royce had seen in all his years looking into the eyes of assholes. "Mysterious causes. Last night. Days after a man who looks just like you was recorded on surveillance holding a gun on him at his house."

"You son of a bitch."

"Duty calls."

"Why'd you do it?"

"Do what?"

"Don't be coy with me, you prick!" Royce smacked the side of his head with the barrel of the shotgun.

Gerhardt grimaced, then refocused on Royce with a steely glare.

"I follow my chain of command. Unlike you. Where's all this going rogue going to get you?"

"Justice."

"Justice? For your brother? Are you fucking kidding me? Come on, Agent Johnson. I thought you were smarter than that. Your brother was a casualty of war. You need to think of it like that. And as for justice—"

"I'll never think of it like that, asshole. I follow the law."

"Ha! We are all *way* beyond the law, my friend."

Royce shook his head. "No, no, we're not."

"You have no badge, no right to be here. You've violated more laws than I can count. Get off your high horse. Please! You have your code and your sense of right and wrong. I've mine. Grow up, Agent Johnson. This isn't going to go down like you think. There will be no heroes."

"I don't want to be a hero. I just want—"

"What do we do now? Why are you here? Why am I taped to this fucking chair?!" Gerhardt convulsed against the restraint.

"I want a trade. Your life for somebody's else's."

Gerhardt narrowed his eyes. "Who?"

"Marcus Jones."

"The black kid we got in jail? Are you fucking serious?"

"Yes, him. The *black* kid, you prick. I want him freed. I can't get your pedophile off the Supreme Court, and it's too late to impeach that bitch in the Oval Office. But I can set an innocent man free."

"Why the hell do you care about him?" Gerhardt scanned the yard with his eyes.

"I wouldn't expect you to understand." Royce raised the gun. "Now tell me who did it."

Gerhardt shook his head in disbelief.

"You get to live, Bob. I go back to my life, as much as I can salvage of it. It's a good deal."

Gerhardt blinked. Once. Twice.

Royce pumped the shotgun. He aimed center mass.

"Granzow!" Gerhardt sputtered to life. "It was...Granzow."

"The flat head out there in the yard?"

"Yes, him."

Royce lowered the gun. "Prove it."

"There's footage of him entering your brother's house. It's your reasonable doubt."

"Show me." Royce cut the duct tape.

Gerhardt stood and squiggled to work out the kinks from being stuck in an iron chair for an hour. Royce kept the Mossberg ready, and followed him back into the kitchen. Instead of going to an office or study, Gerhardt led to a room off the kitchen that was supposed to be a pantry but had been made into a bare bones office. A laptop and printer were sitting on stacked cartons of canned goods and toilet paper. Gerhardt booted up the computer and spent a few minutes staring at the screen. Royce took note of every move to be sure he wasn't sending a distress call.

A video screen flickered up. A time stamp showed the day Alex died, 10:50 a.m. Grainy, dashcam footage showed the unmistakable wiry build and intense posture of Granzow come into frame, as a black man in a Rockefeller-green sweatshirt, stood on Alex's porch ringing the bell. He bore a passing resemblance to Marcus Jones in that outfit. But it wasn't Marcus. The man in the video was lying in the bushes outside. Onscreen, the man shoved his way inside, Granzow bounding in after him. Royce felt sick. Minutes later, the ex-SEAL in the sweatshirt exited the front door, paused briefly, then walked slowly down the sidewalk. He raised his right hand to his ear. The footage flickered to black.

Gerhardt picked a flash drive out of a drawer and stuck it into the laptop's USB port. "What will you do with this?"

"Make copies for Reverend Lincoln of Operation LIFT, my guys at the FBI, and the U.S. Attorney for the Northern District of Illinois."

"And where did you get it?"

Royce thought for a moment. "How about Sean Flanagan?"

"But...Flanagan is...was on my team." Gerhardt fingered the flash drive. "I think I'll take the Mossberg."

"He went rogue, Bob. It happens."

"I don't know if they'll buy it."

"They might, though." Royce eased the Mossberg around.

Gerhardt gulped. "Yeah, they might." He handed the flash

drive over. "Is this really how it ends?"

"Yeah, Bob, this is how it ends."

Royce started to back out toward the patio.

"One more thing." Gerhardt stopped him in his tracks. "I think this is yours," he said, holding out a clear plastic evidence bag sealed with red tape at the top. Royce reached out for it reluctantly, and when he held it in his hands, he saw that the seal was broken and that his iPhone was inside.

Royce was unsure whether it was an act of chivalry or one last insult. He pulled the phone out and flipped it over. He pressed the home key hoping to see Alex's face. But the phone was dead, the screen was shattered into thousands of glass shards. A distinct hammer mark perfectly centered. The phone fell to his side. He glared up at Gerhardt and moved his lips as if he were going to speak. Nothing came out.

What Royce didn't say was that once Father Case didn't hear from Sean for a few days, he was sure a dead-man's switch would activate. Team Gerhardt was going down.

A smile formed on Royce's face, and Gerhardt squinted back at him, his head cocking to one side. They held each other's stare, then Royce turned heel and headed out into the night.

CHAPTER 45

The priest checked his phone one last time on the night of the sixth day. He had battery and four bars. But there was no message from Mr. F., just as there had been none for the past five days. The priest had already broken his promise about sending the package. It should have already been in the mail. But he doubted that a day more would matter and wanted to be sure. He'd packaged up the envelopes, put an abundance of stamps on the package, and identified a reporter at the *Times* he thought would be eager to read and write about their contents. On the assigned day, he'd even gone to the post office and opened the door to the metal box of outgoing mail. But he thought he would give it one more day, just to be sure.

The next day, the priest put on his black coat over his black frock and walked out of the church. A light drizzle was falling, so he opened an umbrella and put the large package containing the envelopes under his coat. He turned south and started to walk the ten blocks to the Fairfax post office. The rain started to fall harder, and the priest raised the collar of his coat up against the wind. He lowered the umbrella and angled it into the wind, but it was futile. Rain swirled and pounded him from all sides. He cursed his decision to walk and started to worry that the package he was holding would end up damaged as the rain penetrated his thin overcoat.

Just then, he heard the polite beep of a car horn and noticed a car pulled over next to him. The driver rolled down his window.

"Kind of a heavy rain to be taking a walk in, Father," the man said.

The priest eyed him. He was a big man, dressed in a suit, and looked very fit, with a touch of grey at the temples. He was probably a lawyer or a lobbyist headed to work.

"Proper Scottish weather," the priest said in a fake accent. "I just wish I had me clubs," he went on.

The man and the priest shared a laugh.

"Where are you headed, Father?"

"Just down the road to the post office. I have a package to deliver and it is quite urgent. That's why I'm out in this weather."

The man snorted a laugh that made him rock back in his seat.

"That's quite a coincidence. I'm headed to the post office too."

"Oh, it is."

"I decide to make up for missing mass for the past few weeks, so I pull over to help a priest, and lo and behold, his errand is my errand. Let me take the package, Father. As penance for my sins and my lack of commitment, I'd be happy to deliver it for you."

The man moved to get out of the vehicle, but the priest shook his head no. He reached with his free hand to grasp the package, which he held under his armpit of the arm that was holding the umbrella.

"No thank you, my son. I don't want to inconvenience you. I have to be sure the package is delivered. I need to pay for it, get the insurance, and sign the appropriate return receipt documents. You know? It isn't just a matter of dropping this package off."

"Wow. Sounds important. If it is that important, you probably shouldn't be out in this weather with it. At least let me give you a lift. Help a poor sinner feel better about himself. What do you say?"

The priest nodded. "Sure. I'd appreciate it. As long as it is no trouble and you are going there anyway. I don't want to put you out at all."

"I'm certain. It would be my pleasure. Hop in."

The priest walked around to the passenger side. He closed the umbrella, shook it off, and climbed in. He took the package out from under his coat and rested it on his lap. It was safe and sound, and soon his promise would be fulfilled.

The man turned down the radio and asked the priest about how he became one. As the priest began his tale of how he'd gone to law school but discovered the Lord and went directly to the seminary after graduation, the man shifted the car into gear, checked his mirrors, and moved out into traffic. The sedan sped away into the rain.

CHAPTER 46

Royce gasped. He sat up with a jerk and nearly spilled the Big Gulp of sweet tea balanced between his knees. Raising the disembodied sniper scope, he tried to focus on the driver of the silver Toyota Camry. But he had only a second before it drove off. In that instant, he could make out a middle-aged man behind the wheel, but the priest's head prevented him from getting the look he needed to get. The rain didn't help either. It drew a watery veil over the Camry and its passengers. The driver could be Gerhardt or one of his assassins, but there was no way to be sure. Maybe it was a good Samaritan. Despite what he'd been through, Royce still believed they existed.

He had been waiting for days for just this moment—feeling like a pilot landing a 747 after an overnight flight—hours of boredom culminating in ten seconds of terror. For the past week, he'd followed the most boring man in Virginia, if not the United States. Father Case was a penitent man. His parishioners would have been proud at the ascetic life he led. The cleric rose early, drove a beat-up Chevy Aveo two-point-seven miles to his parish, where he worked all day, presumably taking lunch at the desk. At precisely seven every evening, except Sundays, he drove home, made a barebones dinner and spent the remainder of the night reading the Bible and typing at his laptop. What went on inside the parish was of little concern to Royce. Souls could be saved and the truth revealed, or not.

All he cared about were the secrets in the envelopes that were surely addressed to 620 Eighth Avenue, New York, NY 10018—the headquarters of the *New York Times*. Royce thought about breaking in and triggering the dead-man switch himself but couldn't be sure where the documents were stored. And he had no reason to think Gerhardt knew about the priest. No, better to let things play out as Flanagan had planned. Intervening when it wasn't necessary might just make things worse. Royce decided he'd just be insurance.

Surveilling the priest didn't exactly make exciting police work. The rental now had plastic bottles filled with pee stored in the back, and the passenger foot well doubled as a garbage can for fast-food wrappers and the bits of fat in beef jerky that got stuck in his teeth. Waiting for the end game, he'd dozed off dozens of times—the hectic past months were finally sending their bill. Thankfully, every time he woke up, his heart in his throat, the priest was right where he'd left him. And neither Gerhardt nor his men were anywhere to be seen.

In the boredom, Royce fretted that he'd missed the priest dropping the envelope in the mail. He'd seen the priest exit the parish with a package a couple of times, fingering it like a ticking time bomb. Each time, Royce's hand crept to the gear-shift and he thought about driving by and grabbing the package or even the priest. But then he'd relax and fall back in the seat. Every time, the priest turned back, reluctantly.

Then, when the priest finally took that first step toward justice for Alex, when he finally was on his way, Royce was convinced that the priest took a ride with the devil.

The rental steered into traffic, trying to keep at a safe distance. He was pretty sure he hadn't been spotted. Yet, Gerhardt seemed to know things that he couldn't possibly know. And the priest was his last card to play.

The Camry stopped at a traffic light; Royce was three cars behind. The Camry's tail lights flickered in the driving rain; the rental's wipers could barely keep up. The rain came in sheets. Royce glanced over at his Mossberg on the passenger seat, the tip of the muzzle peeking out from underneath the Penn State windbreaker. He reached over and petted it like a dog that had retrieved a ball. *Good boy.*

The light turned green, and the Camry inched ahead in the growing traffic, slowed by torrents of rain. Royce typed "Fairfax post office" into Google Maps with his right thumb as he drove—the closest one was five clicks ahead. The priest was headed there, he had no doubt. Royce let himself relax for a moment, hoping for the best. The outlines of two heads and shoulders were visible through the traffic and the rain. They didn't seem to be in conflict. Royce let his heart beat slow.

But a few minutes later, the Camry sped past the post office on Pickett Road. They were headed, the map told him, toward the Little River Parkway. Then, either east toward the Beltway or west toward Interstate 66. Out on the open road, they would be untraceable and the game would be over.

"Fuck!" Royce shouted, pounding the roof of his Buick with the palm of his hand. "Fuck, fuck, fuck!" He gripped the wheel with two hands and hit the accelerator.

Suddenly the Camry lurched right without signaling, into the entrance of a McDonalds that fronted the road of a large shopping center. Royce's stomach turned—his worst nightmare. He was on enemy ground with limited visibility, and now he'd lost the element of surprise.

Royce floored the accelerator and turned sharply to follow the Camry. But he swerved too early and was headed for a small hedge that provided a border between the parking lot and the road. Turning the wheel furiously, he overcompensated, causing the Buick to fishtail wildly. Muscle memory kicked in, gained from years of training under these conditions at Quantico. But not before the Big Gulp emptied into his lap and some lunch goers leapt backwards in fright as they raced toward their cars in the rain.

Back in control, he scanned the horizon for the Camry. It

was gone. *No, no, no,* he shouted in his head. *Where are you, you bastard!?* Royce drove in farther toward the mall, guessing they went right. He circled around past a workout place, a tattoo parlor, and a restaurant advertising an Indian buffet. The parking lot was mostly abandoned on account of the rain, so he didn't worry about cutting short corners. He swerved in and out of the lanes, but the Camry was nowhere to be found.

Then he spotted the distinctive taper of the its taillights, turning right past the Potbelly, headed out of the mall. Royce gunned it. But before he could make any progress, a woman darted in front of his car. She was making a run for it in the rain, hoping to get into the shelter of the Bed, Bath & Beyond as quickly as possible. She didn't see Royce and, with his mind on the priest, he didn't see her.

He slammed the brakes, but it was too late. The woman buckled and tumbled onto the front of his car. She landed with a thud, then did a one-eighty-degree barrel roll. Royce caught a glimpse of the scared animal in her eyes, a look he'd seen a thousand times before. But that didn't make it any easier to see. She fell to the pavement, out of sight on the side of the car. Royce jammed it into park and leapt out. Racing around to the front, he saw the woman getting to her feet, dazed and angry, but seemingly not too worse for the wear. It was enough.

Seconds later, he was back behind the wheel. Guilt washed over him, as he looked into the rearview mirror and saw the woman surrounded by people who'd rushed to help, all looking at him speed away.

Royce guessed Gerhardt, or his minion, was headed toward the Beltway—there would be more traffic and more choices that way, and it was in the direction of the house on the bay where they'd had their showdown days earlier. Yes, he'd retreat to home turf, where he knew the roads and had reinforcements.

Out on the Beltway, Royce weaved in and out of traffic,

leaning hard on the horn. The rain continued to pound, making every driver more cautious. The speedometer hit one hundred as he searched desperately for his prey. When traffic slowed near the intersection with Interstate 395, he swerved onto the shoulder, racing past stalled cars, their passengers wide-eyed as he blew past. Outside the passenger window, the Camry was nowhere to be found.

Several exits whipped by, each providing a nearly foolproof escape. He was betting the Camry had headed home, confident it had left Royce searching in vain back in Fairfax. Then, he saw them. Several cars ahead and in the far-right lane. The Camry cruised along, its driver relaxed and the priest sitting nervously beside him. The driver only had one hand on the wheel. He guessed the other held a weapon of some sort in the left ribs of the priest.

They hadn't seen Royce yet, so he'd regained the element of surprise. He slowed and tucked back into traffic from the left shoulder. He cautiously changed lanes, one at a time, using the turn signal and checking mirrors. For a moment, he looked like a commuter, navigating his shiny metal box on a daily grind. He eased in a few cars behind the Camry, and now was going along with traffic. Royce bided his time, taking the opportunity to make a plan.

It also gave him time to pick up the Mossberg, chamber a round, and put it across his lap. It wasn't an easy decision. Mentally, he clicked through the price of eliminating Gerhardt. When all was said and done, his excellent FBI record etcetera, etcetera, he figured five years behind prison bars. Maybe ten. *Is it worth it?*

Even now, he was probably looking at a year or more, without doing much more than he'd done. Hit-and-run, weapons charges, assault, false imprisonment, B&E. It was a hefty list. Unless he got his man, won over public opinion with justice, it was going to be...*well, best not think of that now...*

The traffic eased up, and the Camry accelerated into more open road. Royce had his chance. PIT training from the academy told him to pull up so that his front right wheel was about even with the back bumper of the Camry. Royce could hear his Quantico instructor barking commands when an arm reached out of the driver's window of the Camry revealing the menacing shape of an H&K MP5. A spray of glass shattered into Royce's face, 9mm rounds riddled the hood of the car. Royce instinctively jerked the wheel to the right. *CRAACK!* The rental slammed into the Camry's bumper. He slammed the brakes and dove into the passenger seat. The car behind squealed to a stop, and crashes sounded on three sides. Disoriented, Royce checked for blood on his shirt. He hadn't been hit, although he could feel bits of glass in his face. He caught his breath as the rain pelted the roof of the car.

Grabbing the Mossberg, he crawled out the passenger side. He popped his head up between the door and the frame of the car. The Mossberg led the way. The Camry turned sideways, its front end smashed into the Jersey barrier separating the lanes. All of its windows were shattered. Smoke billowed from the engine compartment. Royce stepped around the open door and raised the Mossberg. He couldn't see anyone through the rain, but decided to announce his presence with authority. He squeezed off a shot into the driver's door. The metal quickly looked like Swiss cheese. No movement. At the sound of the shot, drivers who had emerged to inspect the damage to their vehicles bolted back into their cars. Royce stood alone in the center of the Beltway, shotgun raised and ready. The rain was soaking, but Royce couldn't feel anything.

Moving forward cautiously, and he saw the priest slumped into a pillowy airbag. He wasn't moving. Blood dripped from his left ear. Royce stepped toward helping him, then thought better of it. He raised the Mossberg purposefully, sidestepping around the back of the Camry. The rear of the sedan was folded like an accordion from the impact of a Range Rover,

now on its side, wheels spinning aimlessly. Cries and whim-
pers came from inside. Royce had the urge to help, but he
fought it off. For Alex. He held the shotgun in his right hand
for a moment, using the other hand to wipe the rain from his
eyes. As he came around between the Camry and the Range
Rover, the driver of the Camry crawled away from the scene,
right leg dragging limp behind him. In his right hand, a package. *The* package.

Royce walked up behind him. The man wasn't making
much progress army crawling on the rain-drenched pavement
in a daze. Then, Royce was on him, using his right foot to pin
the man's leg to the road. The man let out a whelp. Royce
fired a round of buckshot into the ground beside him, and the
man went limp. Royce reached down and flipped him over. It
was Gerhardt. Blood was streaming from his face and nothing
was behind his eyes. Royce pumped the Mossberg and pointed
it center mass. He smiled, but Gerhardt was too stunned to
respond.

Reaching down, Royce uncurled Gerhardt's fingers. They
gripped like rigor mortis had set in. He picked up the package, wet with rain and streaks of blood, and tucked it into his
waist under his shirt. Then he surveyed the scene. Sirens
sounded in the distance and shouts started to echo around
him. "There he is!" a male voice shouted through the rain.
Royce looked back and saw the priest, still motionless in the
passenger side of the Camry.

Gerhardt still hadn't moved, eyes glassy and face distorted
in pain. Royce raised the Mossberg and readied to put the
butt into Gerhardt's nose. He took a half swing, and he saw
Gerhardt close his eyes with resignation. Royce stopped short.
He didn't feel pity exactly, but the weakness of his foe stole
the moment.

The shotgun slung back over his shoulder, Royce turned
back in the direction of travel. An open road was ahead of
him. He took off at a jog, but accelerated until his lungs

burned and his legs couldn't carry him any further. About a mile from the scene, he jumped over a guardrail and was gone. Another few months added to the prison-time tally in his head. He skidded down a muddy embankment, using his hands underneath as brakes and steering. At the bottom of the slope, he jumped up, made sure the package was still secure, and headed off perpendicular to the highway. He was quickly alone in the woods. After a few minutes, he found a fallen log within sight of a house in the distance. There was time to sit for a moment to catch his breath and savor the feeling of victory.

EPILOGUE

Sandra Jensen had been *The New York Times* Supreme Court reporter for just this side of six months. Stepping into the shoes of Adam Liptak was no easy task, just as it hadn't been for him when he replaced Linda Greenhouse. It was a marquee job at the Paper of Record, earning front-page real estate several times per year, for sure. The job was one she'd always dreamed of having since her days as an undergrad at Northwestern. Law school had been her choice, not because she wanted to be a lawyer, but because she wanted to be a legal reporter. Now, after years at papers in South Bend, Indianapolis, and Chicago, as well as writing for SCOTUSblog, she was at the pinnacle of her profession.

On this Wednesday morning, she was at her desk writing what critics would say was a puff piece about the first Asian-American Supreme Court justice. Sandra Jensen was not a doctrinaire Liberal, but she had a preference for diversity and left-leaning politics, like every other reporter she knew who wasn't writing for the *Christian Science Monitor* or the *Wall Street Journal*. And even they couldn't help but be proud America finally put an Asian-American on the High Court.

"Package for you, Ms. Jensen," the mail clerk shouted over the top of her cubicle.

"Thanks, Fred," she said nonchalantly, motioning to her inbox. "Put it there." She didn't look up from her typing.

"I...you might want to just take this one..." His voice made her jump.

She glanced up and saw an outreached hand holding a large manila envelope that looked like it had been dragged under a subway car. The sides were bent; one was torn. The entire thing was covered in dirt and what appeared like blood.

"I guess we should have someone go down and talk to the boys in the mail room," she joked, taking the envelope in her hands like someone who wished she were wearing surgical gloves.

She didn't need a letter opener. She merely grabbed a torn end and pulled. She reached in and took out a stack of papers three inches thick. Sandra Jensen turned off the monitor on her computer, and started reading.

At just that moment, two hundred and fifty miles southwest, a man walked into a police station in Fairfax, Virginia. He was carrying a copy of the *Washington Times* under his arm and holding a takeout cup in his hand. He walked over to the duty desk and put his paper on the table. He took a sip of his coffee, then put it down on the paper.

"May I help you?" the officer said.

"My name is Royce Johnson. I'm here to turn myself in." His voice was confident and full of relief.

"What have you done, Mr. Johnson?" the officer's tone was slightly jocular. The man looked like he'd never even jaywalked.

"Hit and run," he said matter of factly. This got the officer's attention.

"Is that right?"

"Three days ago. In front of the Potbelly in the Pickett Shopping Center. It was raining hard and I was in a hurry. I stopped briefly and she seemed okay. But I couldn't wait for the police. It was...Well, I just couldn't. I'm sorry, and I'm here to accept my punishment."

The officer came around the desk and took Royce by the arm.

"This way, sir." He led Royce into the processing room, where he would be printed and booked for leaving the scene of an accident. The officer looked over at him, as he led him down the hallway. The man was smiling.

ACKNOWLEDGMENTS

Elaine Ash provided invaluable editing and advice from start to finish. She was also a patient and kind mentor. This book would not exist without her help.

Thanks to my agent, Alex Hoyt, who believed in me and my story.

Many friends from the University of Chicago, especially Saul Levmore and Scott Eggener, were generous and supportive readers. Their encouragement was essential; their friendship is treasured.

M. Todd Henderson was the biggest baby born in Tennessee in 1970. A professor at the University of Chicago, he is mostly renowned as being the tallest law professor on Earth. He's also written dozens of books and articles on business law and regulation. Prior to becoming an academic, he worked as a designer of dams, a judicial clerk, a Supreme Court lawyer, and a management consultant. A graduate of Princeton and the University of Chicago, he lives in the Hyde Park neighborhood of Chicago with his wife and three children.

On the following pages are a few
more great titles from the
Down & Out Books publishing family.

For a complete list of books and to
sign up for our newsletter,
go to DownAndOutBooks.com.

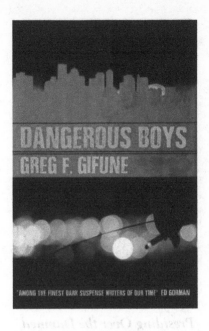

Dangerous Boys
Greg F. Gifune

Down & Out Books
978-1-946502-52-0

All they had was each other...and nothing to lose...

Part coming-of-age tale, part dark crime thriller, *Dangerous Boys* is the story of a group of young punks with nothing left to lose, fighting to find themselves, their futures, and a way out of the madness and darkness before it's too late.

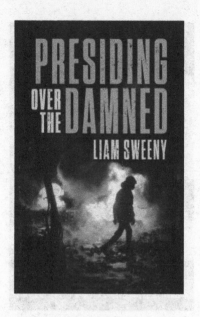

Presiding Over the Damned
A Jack LeClere Thriller
Liam Sweeny

Down & Out Books
August 2018
978-1-946502-93-3

An arson in New Rhodes reveals the body of an eight-year-old African American girl in the city's North Central District. Jack LeClere, the top homicide detective in New Rhodes, is paired with a new partner for the case, Clyde Burris, a former New Rhodes PD Internal Affairs detective.

In the heat of the ashes of an abandoned row-house, the search for a brutal killer awaits.

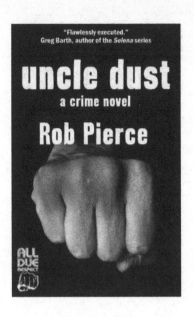

Uncle Dust
Rob Pierce

All Due Respect, an imprint of
Down & Out Books
April 2018
978-1-948235-21-1

Dustin loves to rob banks. Dustin loves to drink. Dustin loves his women. Dustin loves loyalty. He might even love his adopted nephew Jeremy. And, he sometimes gets a little too enthusiastic in his job doing collections for local bookies—so, sometimes, he loves to hurt people.

Told in the first person, *Uncle Dust* is a fascinating noir look inside the mind of a hard, yet very complicated criminal.

Hardway
Hector Acosta

Shotgun Honey, an imprint of
Down & Out Books
978-1-943402-51-9

Fifteen-year-old Spencer loves professional wrestling. It's the reason why he and his older brother Billy started their very own wrestling promotion in their Dallas apartment complex. It isn't long, however, before RBWL—The Royal Brooks Wrestling League—have a rival in Woodland Terrace. When a gym bag believed to hold Woodland Terrace's championship belt is stolen, the feud between teenagers and promotions escalates. Before long, Spencer will find the world of professional wrestling can be more real and dangerous than anything seen on television.

CPSIA information can be obtained
at www.ICGtesting.com
Printed in the USA
LVHW03s2338251018
594897LV00002B/196/P